A SPARK OF MAGIC

TARI RILEY

A Spark of Magic

Contact Info: www.authortaririley.com

Book Cover Design & Illustrations by Catarina Cruz
(Instagram: catarinabookdesigns)

Copy Edits by Gabby D'Aloia
(Instagram: gcdeditorial)

ISBNs

Paperback: 9789893564516

E-book: 9789893564509

First Edition: April 2024

To those drowning in darkness
Remember you are the light

The Playlist

Who Do You Think You Are | Kiana Ledé, Cautious Clay

Blue Hour | MOTHICA

Dance in the Dark| Au/Ra

Hanging On By A Thread | UNSECRET, SVRCINA

We Go Down Together| Dove Cameron, Khalid

Control | Halsey

Which Witch | Florence + The Machine

Is This What Love Is? | The Wasia Project

lovely | Billie Eilish, Khalid

Angel on Fire | Halsey

Chapter One

"I NEED YOUR HELP."

Isaac couldn't believe the words that left his mouth. A week ago, if someone were to tell him he would be asking Alice for help, he would have laughed. In which situation would he need a witch's help? None. His life was perfectly fine without any magic, and he didn't want anything to do with it. He was popular, part of the swimming team, and he was sure he would go to a prestigious university by the end of the school year. At least, that was him a week ago.

Today, he wasn't so sure.

"Let me guess," she closed her locker and turned to face him with an amused smile, "you need my help to improve your grades. What subjects?"

He laughed. Yes, he sucked at most subjects, but he would never study more than necessary. He didn't need to improve his grades; he just had to be sure he wouldn't fail any class. That, and his outstanding performance in the swimming team would get him far.

"That's not the case." He cleared his throat and glanced around the corridor, moving closer to her. Suddenly, he didn't know how to bring it up. "I need your help with *other* things."

"Such as…?"

"Such as… *magical* things."

Alice rolled her eyes, annoyed. "I don't sell drugs. If you want that, find someone who's always high. Not me."

She fixed the strap over her shoulder and turned around, leaving Isaac behind. He blinked slowly, trying to understand what had just happened. Yes, he expected Alice to reject his offer at first, but after mentioning magic, he at least expected her eyes to shine. Instead, he got the cold shoulder, and now she thought he was into drugs.

Great, he thought. *What now?*

He pondered for a while, glancing between both ends of the corridor, wondering if he should go to his car or after her. His urgency to solve this matter spoke louder. Isaac sighed and went after Alice, half-walking, half-running until he caught up to her.

"What do you know about merfolk?"

She glanced at him sideways for a while and shrugged. "The same as everyone else. They have a fishtail instead of legs and like to swim. They probably live in the ocean, I don't know. Merfolk are not of my interest."

"Why not?"

"Why do you care, Isaac? Did you bet with someone that you could annoy me for a certain amount of time before I lost my patience?"

He knew she was deflecting answering his question, probably to keep her identity hidden. Isaac knew Alice was a witch. Everyone knew. Even if she didn't walk around showcasing her abilities and doing magic tricks for everyone to see, she had done it in the past. That's what he heard, at least.

When it came to Alice, people liked to spread rumours, and her being a witch was one of them. How people came to that knowledge, he didn't know, but right now, Isaac wanted desperately to believe that one was true. He was betting his life on it.

He gulped and glanced at the corridor again. If he got caught speaking with her, he could kiss his hard-earned reputation goodbye. No one spoke with Alice. No one. He was starting to understand why. The rumours didn't help, but her personality was bad too.

Isaac took a few quick steps forward and stopped in front of her, causing her to almost trip on him. He caught the brief surprise in Alice's dark eyes and held her gaze for as long as possible. It could help assert his dominance over the situation if he wasn't so focused on how dark her eyes were. He couldn't distinguish where her irises started and her pupils ended. He was looking at a pool of darkness, disrupted by the occasional reflection of the fluorescent lights that reminded him of stars. He had never noticed she had such pretty eyes.

Truth be told, Isaac never lost much time staring at Alice. She moved like a shadow, and he rarely noticed her. Until recently, that was.

"Now we're doing a staring contest?" She crossed her arms over her chest. "I have somewhere to be. Don't make me waste my time, please."

"I know you're a witch, and in this case, you're the only person who can help me," he whispered, hoping his voice carried all the urgency he was feeling. "I need your help to deal with… a *situation.*"

Alice's expression grew sombre. Whether she was upset, disappointed, surprised, or all of the above, Isaac didn't know. However, he wanted to hide. Perhaps asking for her help while exposing her origin had been a bad idea.

Her eyes traced the space around his figure as if she was outlining him. Isaac gulped and fixed his posture, puffing out his chest to appear taller than he was. He wasn't short by any means, but the way Alice studied him was excruciating and it made him feel small.

She closed her eyes and took a deep breath. When she opened them again, she stared straight at him.

"You're a merfolk. How fun." It didn't sound fun coming from her, though.

His eyes widened and he took a step back, shocked. "How do you know?"

"I just do." She shrugged. "Besides, you asked for my help and mentioned merfolk. It could be a coincidence, but we both know you'd never ask me for help unless you didn't have any other option."

"Do witches read minds?"

"Are merfolk always annoying?"

"I don't know." Isaac rubbed the back of his neck in frustration and paced around. How had she been able to read him so quickly? Was that some sort of spell? How powerful was she? "Are you inside my mind right now?"

She rolled her eyes and shook her head. "I don't read minds. Witches can't read minds." She cleared her throat and fixed her posture. "What do you need my help with anyway?"

"I need you to help me not turn into a merfolk every time I come in contact with water." When she raised an eyebrow, he shook his head, ready to reassure her. "I can pay you. I can do what you want. I can make you popular, introduce you to Liam, pay you with money, anything. Just please, help me."

In all his playthroughs of how this conversation would go, in none of them did Isaac expect to sound this desperate. He expected to be calm and collected, make a joke to get her to smile or gain her trust. None of that was happening. Alice had him in the palm of her hand, and Isaac hated it.

"No." Her answer was so blunt that Isaac took a bit to process it. "Don't you ever attempt to ask me for such a thing *ever* again."

"But… but you can help me."

"I can't."

"You're a witch!"

"And you're refusing to accept your true origins."

"It could *ruin* my life!" he said, trying his best to keep his voice down. "Look, I'm part of the swimming team, and I haven't shown up for practice in a week. If I skip two more weeks, I'm out. I can't afford that. I have worked too hard for this, and I'm not willing to give up now."

"Were you expecting me to feel sorry for you?" She muttered something under her breath as she walked closer to him. "You're not asking me to help you. What you are asking me to do is to betray my values for you, which is something I won't do. I barely know you."

"Everyone knows me," he said, slightly offended. Then, he thought better of it and added, putting on his best charming smile, "As I said, I am willing to compromise."

She shook her head and moved past him. "I'm not interested!" she yelled, picking up her pace.

Isaac went after her. "Just help me out. Please."

"No."

This was why she didn't have any friends. She was too demanding and lacked basic understanding and compassion for other people. Alice might have pretty eyes, but her personality was the worst.

He reached for her hand, attempting to stop her. If she could hear him out and understand his situation, then he would probably convince her to help him. He had to try again. Just one more time. He could afford to beg for her help once more before his self-preservation senses kicked in.

As soon as his hand touched hers, Isaac was taken aback by how warm it was. When he blinked, he was in a room surrounded by shelves with books, strange vials and containers. The low light burning from the candles made it hard for him to make out more shapes but he spotted a large table at the centre and some flickering lights floating here and there. The scent of fresh flowers overwhelmed him, and he couldn't think properly.

Someone wrapped an arm around Isaac's neck and he blinked again, finding his blue sneakers against the school's grey flooring as Liam laughed.

"Thinking of skipping practice again?" his friend said.

Around them, more people chuckled and laughed. Isaac battled his friend for a while until Liam loosened his grip around Isaac's neck and let go of him. He fixed his clothes, his eyes darting everywhere looking for Alice's figure.

"Who are you looking for?" Liam asked, following Isaac's eyes. "Do I know them?"

"You don't," Isaac lied, but he wouldn't be caught explaining what had happened.

He ran a hand over his face, trying his best to register what had happened. One minute he was here, the next he was somewhere else, but when he returned, she was nowhere to be found. Had Liam seen him with Alice? If he had, he would have commented by now. That offered Isaac some peace of mind.

For a while, at least.

"You got stood up?" another one of his swimming team

colleagues asked, smirking. "You should have seen your face, dude."

Everyone laughed, giving Isaac blank stares, trying to emulate his expression from earlier. He laughed it off, trying to seem relaxed amongst his friends, but he was still freaked out. The worst part was that he couldn't tell them about this.

He couldn't tell anyone. If he did, his life as he knew it would be over.

"Let's get to practice," Isaac said and fixed the sports bag hanging from his shoulder. "I'm still sick, but I can watch. Does anyone need a ride?"

"Still sick?" Liam asked as his blue eyes scanned his features. "You look fine to me."

"Maybe he's *lovesick.*" More laughter. More awkward smiles from Isaac.

He rolled his eyes and kept walking, followed by his friends as they made him the victim of their jokes. He could deal with that. Soon enough, they would forget all about it.

Isaac, however, would not.

"Are you coming to my party this Friday?" Liam wrapped an arm around Isaac's shoulders. "Maybe you could invite this mysterious girl that has you like this."

"There is no girl," Isaac said. "There is no one."

He dared to glance over his shoulder to where he last had spotted Alice. If she was there, would he leave his friend group to try and ask her again? Isaac simply couldn't stop trying. He *needed* her help.

Isaac didn't find Alice at the end of the corridor. He sighed, rubbing the back of his neck. *Some other time, then.* He bumped his shoulder against Liam's, trying to focus on something that didn't turn his stomach upside down with desperation.

"You can count on me at the party," Isaac said, earning a huge grin from his best friend. "You know I never skip them."

"And that is the only way to properly live, my friend!" Liam laughed and everyone else agreed. "I have so many plans for it this time around. You're not going to be disappointed, I can assure you!"

They left the school building and walked to the parking lot. Isaac laughed at his friend's stupid jokes about the upcoming party, slowly returning to his usual self.

In the commotion of their excitement, Isaac didn't notice the shadow that followed him from a distance.

Chapter Two

ALICE WALKED TO HER aunt's flower shop with music as her only company. The sun painted the skies in hues of orange and purple, drowning the old buildings around her in a dim light. In the distance, a waxing moon peeked from behind the green mountains, its appearance slow and calculated.

She enjoyed her life in this quaint town. Alice didn't know much else; she had grown up here. She knew these streets like the palm of her hand, understood its customs and people.

That didn't mean they understood her.

As most businesses closed up shop for the day, some would remain open for a few more hours. The local tavern was one of them, with its wooden slacks decorated with fairy lights and small carvings of animals and flowers. The owner set up the outside tables for the evening, going to each of them to drop an ashtray before disappearing towards the inside of the establishment to grab something else. In the small corner restaurant, an employee wrote the menu on a charcoal board hanging on the wall. Alice wondered if anyone would stop by since they rarely got any customers. They blamed their location—they were *too* close to the flower shop—but they refused to move elsewhere. After all, the business on the other side of the flower shop, a coffee shop, thrived with customers.

The problem, Alice suspected, wasn't in her aunt's flower shop, but in the antiques store across from the restaurant. It was another place in town where magic hid in plain sight. As she crossed the town square, she glanced at its window shop, her eyes tracing the aura emanating from the objects on display. Some of them had a warm golden energy, while others carried something heavier and colder, their aura an icy silver. She shivered. This store never inspired a sense of trust or safety in Alice, and she avoided it as much as possible. However, everyone else—humans and magical beings alike—seemed to enjoy it and some even visited it often.

Alice stopped at the flower shop's entrance, saving her headphones in her backpack and checking her surroundings. Despite the busyness of the town square, very few people came to look for flowers this late in the evening. Still, one could never be too careful. If the wrong person stopped her, the damage could be astronomical.

She spotted the plaque with the word *open* hanging from inside and knocked. Alice's aunt wasn't at the counter nor was she doing inventory, which could only mean she was in the back room.

Alice knocked again, this time louder, and shielded her eyes to get a better focus on the inside of the shop. After noticing some light piercing through the back door, she turned on the door handle and stepped inside the premises.

The shop was smaller than its exterior made it out to be. Besides a wooden counter and a back wall covered in flowers of all different shades and sizes, everything else was space for vases and gardening tools.

"I'm here!" Alice dropped her school bag and took off her jacket, closing the door behind her. She turned the entrance plaque to show the word *closed* and locked the door.

"You're late!" her aunt screamed from the back room and a loud clang followed. "Damn it! You weren't there before."

On the furthest wall, Alice spotted flickering lights flying above the flowers, forming shapes like constellations. Most people would think of them as fireflies, but she knew very well they were not.

"Is everything alright?" Alice pushed the back door open, facing her aunt as she picked a couple of metal dishes from the floor, her dark curls falling from her headband.

"Everything's fine," she said, puffing some hair away from her face. "Just some housekeeping gone wrong. Where's Xavier?"

Alice looked over her shoulder, her eyes catching the golden hues of the sunset outside. After what happened today at school, she was looking forward to his company on the walk back home. It was rare for people to speak to Alice at school, let alone be so comfortable to bring up the fact that she was a witch. She didn't like that. She especially didn't like how easily that information was available despite her attempts to hide it.

"He has swimming practice today," Alice said.

Her aunt furrowed her brows, studying Alice carefully. "Since when?"

"Since today?" Alice gulped and grabbed a small peacock feather from a nearby counter, her fingers grazing over the smooth surface, admiring the shape and colours. "What are we doing today?"

"Do your parents know Xavier is not here with you?"

"Why does it matter, Vi?" she said, dropping the feather back in its place. "I'm here in one piece, no one followed me and I'm alright."

Victoria sighed, placing the dishes on the counter before fixing her headband and moving her hair away from her face.

"You know," she said as she wiped her hands on her apron, "I'll talk to your parents about this. This was not the deal they made with Xavier."

"You mean the deal *my* parents made with *his* parents?" Alice rolled her eyes. "Vi, I'm fine. Really. I don't need Xavier to be around all the time. It's not good for our friendship."

"Right." Her aunt didn't believe a word she had just said. She picked up the dishes again. "In this case, your safety is more important than your friendship, and a deal is a deal. Why are you late, though?"

Victoria gestured to a couple of gardening tools behind Alice, and she grabbed them, extending them to her aunt. There was no way she was going to tell her aunt about Isaac. Or their conversation. Especially not the latter.

"I took longer at school." Alice shrugged. "Next time I'll text."

"You know I don't have a cellphone."

"You should, though."

Her aunt narrowed her eyes on Alice, waiting for her to break and reveal whatever information she was withholding. When she didn't, Victoria glanced at one of the plants nearby, its flowers blooming back to life as a ball of light flew from one of its buds. Victoria gestured with her head to Alice, and the light stopped in front of her, revealing a tiny fairy with wings like a dragonfly, and a dress that reminded her of dandelions.

"That's new," she said, reaching the tip of her index finger towards the fairy's torso. She moved away, flying to sit on top of her finger instead. Alice narrowed her eyes, inspecting the fairy closely. "Is she new?"

"Yes," Victoria said. "She brought a letter. For you."

"A letter? For me?"

Alice's heart picked up pace. It was rare for her to receive any sort of correspondence. She didn't have any friends—Xavier didn't count—and she only exchanged texts with him and occasionally her parents. Letters were an even rarer occurrence since that wasn't a typical practice in this realm anymore.

For the past couple of months, Alice had been eager to receive one. She had been working hard to prepare her application for the University of Nadalan in Otherworld, hoping to get accepted in the Alchemy Major they offered. So far, she had only performed the theoretical tests, all under the scrutiny of Xavier, Victoria and a Council member, but she was hoping this letter would bring good news.

"Do you think it's from them?" Alice asked, following the fairy as she flew across the room, plopping herself on top of a small flower pot. "Do you think I got in?"

Victoria said nothing. She kept moving objects from one side of the back room to the other, occasionally stopping to curse under her breath and fix her headband. She shouldn't have gotten bangs. Hair as curly as hers would not deal well when forced to do anything it didn't want to.

"Where's the letter?" Alice said and moved her hands to

express her question to the small creature.

The fairy shoved her hand inside a flower bud, causing some pollen to fly nearby. She pulled the smallest envelope from inside; it fitted on the tip of Alice's finger. Carefully, the fairy placed it on the wooden table and threw light from her hands towards the envelope.

Alice took a deep breath, her eyes widening as the small envelope grew in size until it was big enough for her to grab it. It would always amaze her how this spell worked. Once she mastered it, she would make everything tiny in size and carry it in her backpack everywhere she went.

"I'm opening it!"

No answer. She picked the envelope up, its surface still warm from the spell. Her thumb traced the golden edges and the impeccable cursive handwriting on its front. Alice stopped.

She recognised this handwriting.

"Vi?" She searched for her aunt in the back room. "I don't think this is from them."

Alice pondered not opening it. If she didn't, then she wouldn't know what was inside. She was sure she would not be pleased with it. However, she had no other option. With her stomach churning in fear, she opened the envelope, pulled out the letter and read it.

Oh no, she thought as soon as she was done reading it. "Oh no."

"Is it from them or not?" Vi asked as she stepped inside the back room, placing a couple of pots on the counter. When her eyes met Alice, panic took over her. "Who is it from?"

Alice couldn't speak, couldn't move her feet. She extended the letter to her aunt and waited for it to be snatched away. Vi took the letter and mumbled the words under her breath as she paced around the room, growing more distressed by the minute.

"Gloria is coming to visit you," she said, a tone between bewilderment and something Alice assumed was fear. "This is not good."

"Not good at all."

Alice liked Aunt Gloria. As a kid, she liked her stories from the Otherworld, how she always seemed brave and smart and how she never took no for an answer. As she grew older, she realised that her aunt wasn't very nice. She didn't like her siblings and she made it known. Nothing was ever good enough for her standards, including Alice's education in the human realm. She only appeared to like Alice, but that was because she was a powerful witch and interested in studying Alchemy in the Otherworld.

Except, Alice wasn't a powerful witch. She couldn't summon magic or cast a spell. All she knew were the rules of magic, but practising them was out of her reach.

"She's probably aware of your application," Vi said, returning the letter to Alice. "She wants to see the progress of your magic."

"There's no progress," Alice said, pouting. "It's even worse than what it was."

The last time Aunt Gloria visited, Alice summoned light with her bare hands to show her skills to her aunt. She had received a big round of applause. She had been showered in compliments. Alice had never felt so worthy of magic.

Now, she didn't feel worthy of it. She was a shame to all witches.

"I'm sure until then, you'll be able to figure something out. She's only coming during the next New Moon, so until then, we'll keep practising. Alice," her aunt searched for her eyes as she rested a hand on Alice's shoulder, "I know it seems impossible now, but you'll be a master of your craft someday. You just have to work for it, okay?"

Alice was tired of listening to that. Everyone kept telling her that she should keep practising, that she should keep trying, that she would achieve greatness if she didn't stop. She had been doing it ever since she was six and for what? No matter how much theory she knew, she would never be able to summon magic.

Whenever she tried, she was back in that miserable place, a reminder of what she had done, of what she would never be, of who she was born to be. She was failing her magic and yet, she wasn't entirely human.

"Come here." Vi wrapped her arms around Alice, pulling her in for a hug. They stood there for a while as the fairies flew around the back room, gracing the flowers with their light and energy, sprouting them back to life, bringing colour to their petals.

Alice wished she could have that too. She wanted something to bring back colour to her life, to bring back her purpose to the surface. *Someday,* her aunt said. How many somedays did Alice have before she could feel like herself again?

Chapter Three

ISAAC WANTED TO JOIN in on the fun in the pool. Everything in his body screamed at him to jump in the water and swim, to give in to the warmth bubbling up inside him. It was within reach. If he got up from this bench, walked to the edge of the pool and ran his fingers through the water, if he jumped inside—

"Still not feeling better?" his swimming coach asked, dropping a clipboard and a towel next to Isaac.

Isaac blinked, returning to his senses. He didn't like this feeling. As much as he wanted to give in and do what he had always done, he knew how stupid that would be. He couldn't even fathom what would happen if his teammates saw him as he was now. He could get expelled from the swimming team and that was not an option. Isaac had always wanted to be a competitive swimmer, but now, that dream floated away, and Isaac wasn't sure if he was ever going to grasp it again before it was too late.

Maybe he had taken all of this for granted.

"Not really." Isaac shook his head, faking out a cough. "I have to skip today's practice too. I came to watch, at least."

Isaac hated to lie because he hated when people lied to him.

And here he was, surrounded by people he held in great esteem, lying over and over again between his gritted teeth, expecting everyone to believe his terrible acting skills. At least, he had come to watch practice. Last week, he hadn't dared to show his face.

"Watching is not the same as doing. You, better than anyone, should know that." His coach narrowed his eyes on Isaac, and Isaac gulped. He couldn't force Isaac to go and get changed, but his intense stare still put Isaac on edge. "You should get checked out. If you skip practice again, I'm afraid it will be hard for you to participate in the next couple of competitions. Every day you're not swimming is a day you're losing muscle memory."

Isaac nodded and lowered his head, focusing on his hands. He knew that. If he could, he wouldn't be sitting here. He would be in the water, laughing and joking with his friends, swimming to his heart's desire.

Coach blew a whistle, its sound carrying through the mostly empty area of the local pool. The screaming and laughter in the pool died down, and everyone swam to the edge, resting their arms and elbows on the white stone around it.

"Good afternoon. Have you warmed up yet?"

"Yes!" they all said in unison.

"Good." Coach nodded, satisfied. "We have a special visitor today. *Again.*"

"Who is it?" Liam asked as he fixed his swimming cap and the goggles on top of it.

"Someone who is considering joining our swimming team."

"This late in the game?" Liam scoffed and smirked at his teammates. "If it's a girl, she's only here to watch us swim."

Laughter bubbled in the pool and Coach blew his whistle again. "It's not a girl, and we have a closed-practice policy, boys. Now will you please behave?"

"We'll try, Coach," Liam said, saluting him. "Who is this dude, then? Do we know him?"

"I'm not sure. He doesn't go to your school, I don't think." Coach shrugged and turned to the door on the side of the pool, gesturing to someone on the other side. "Xavier, come on in."

The doors flew open, revealing someone who Isaac assumed was Xavier. Tall and muscular, he was probably in his last year of high school, much like Isaac. He wasn't built like most of the swimmers Isaac knew on the team, though. His shoulders were too wide, his arms too thick under his black shirt. He reminded Isaac of the rugby players he saw around the school corridors with their imposing nature and captivating aura. They always made him feel on edge.

"This is Xavier," Coach said, his voice deprived of excitement. "He'll be watching your practice today to decide if he'll join our team or not. It's *never* too late to join our team."

"Yeah, but it's rather late to join the competitions," Liam said, eyeing Xavier. "You should just leave. You'd be wasting your time."

"Well, that's up for me to decide, isn't it?" Xavier said, earning a wave of gasps and small chuckles from the rest of the crowd. He turned to Coach. "Where can I sit?"

"You can sit next to Isaac. He'll explain to you how these practices work."

"Isaac is on babysitter duty today," Liam said. "Better behave or Isaac will call you out on it."

"Cut it, Liam." Isaac glared at his friend. "He has every right to be here. Stop being an ass."

Besides, Isaac could use the distraction.

Liam rolled his eyes but did as he was told and didn't say anything else to Xavier. That didn't stop him from glaring at him as he walked towards the bench.

"Hey." Xavier waved and joined Isaac, dropping his bag on the floor. Isaac cringed. "You're Isaac?"

"Yes," he said, staring at the bag on the floor. He wanted to pick it up, afraid it would get wet. If it was already wet and Isaac touched it, he could have a problem. He decided against it. "I assume you're Xavier."

"Call me Xavi." He crossed his arms, looking out at the area around them. In the pool, Coach gestured to his teammates, who listened intently to his every word. "So… you're not swimming. Injury?"

"Sickness." Isaac bit his lip. Here he was, lying again. "It would be best if I didn't step into the pool. I want to fully recover."

Xavier nodded, ruffling his grey hair.

"Nice hair," Isaac said. "It might get ruined in the pool,

though. Chlorine is known to not deal well with bleached hair."

"It's fine." Xavier shrugged and offered Isaac a smile. "I can always dye it again. Besides, aren't we supposed to wear swimming caps?"

"Sure." Isaac cleared his throat, hearing the swooshing of water as his teammates swam across the pool. "They're doing breaststrokes now. It'll go on for a few minutes."

"You don't have to describe everything to me, you know." Xavier mindlessly gestured to the pool, keeping his eyes on Isaac. "I may not swim often, but I know how it generally works. If I have questions, I'll ask you."

Isaac nodded and went silent for a while. Truth was, he wouldn't mind the distraction that explaining their practice to Xavier provided, but he also wasn't in the mood to tell someone else all the things he could be doing if he didn't have a tail. Which he did.

And he still didn't know of a way to get rid of it.

As the practice went on and Coach got more distracted in correcting everyone's butterfly strokes, Isaac went on his phone and resumed his search in incognito mode. He had searched everything: from keywords to full sentences, to questions. All he got was what he already knew about merfolk. There was nothing about how one could get rid of a merfolk tail because, according to everything he found, magic wasn't a thing.

For a very long time, magic wasn't a thing for Isaac, either. That didn't apply anymore.

"What's bothering you?" Xavier asked, scooting closer to Isaac. Isaac hid his phone screen. "Texting someone important?"

"No," he said, slightly annoyed. "And even if I was, it would be none of your business."

"Of course not. I was just trying to make conversation." Xavier shrugged, not taking his eyes from the pool. "If it wasn't about texting someone important, what was it, then?"

"None of your business," he said and saved his phone in the pocket of his jeans.

"Fair enough." Xavier pursed his lips, narrowing his eyes on Isaac. "I do want to know what kind of business you have with Alice, though."

"Alice?" Isaac scoffed. "I barely know Alice."

"But you spoke to her earlier. What did you speak to her about?"

Isaac gulped, the hair on the back of his neck and arms rising as a tingling sensation took over his body. He stretched his neck as fear built inside of him. Whereas before Xavier's tone had been playful, now it was coated in ice enveloped by a darkness Isaac wanted to stay away from.

"I asked her some stuff. I needed her help." Isaac narrowed his eyes on Xavier, trying to get a read on him. "Is she your girlfriend? Because if she is, just know I wasn't hitting on her. I would never hit on her. In fact, if I didn't need her help, I would have never spoken to her. You've heard the rumours, right? About her."

"I have." Xavier sounded bored. "And I'm not her boyfriend."

"Then why do you care? Are you interested in her?"

Xavier bit the inside of his cheek and focused back on the pool. "There are some people I *care* about. Alice is one of them."

That didn't make any sense to Isaac. Why would anyone care about Alice? She never seemed to care about anyone but herself. Asking for her help earlier only proved that. If the rumours were true, why wouldn't she help him? He wasn't asking to become immortal; he was asking her to help him get rid of his stupid tail so he could return to his normal life and be his normal self again.

"Were you asking her for tutoring lessons?" Xavier would not let this die, would he? "Maybe you were complimenting her. Or you were making fun of her. Were you—"

"I was asking her about merfolk," Isaac eventually said, his voice a screamed whisper. He leaned closer to Xavier, glancing at his distracted teammates. He sighed in relief. "Please don't tell anyone."

"That you're interested in mythology or that you asked Alice about it?" Xavier raised an eyebrow, suppressing a smile.

"Both." Xavier chuckled and Isaac glared at him. "This isn't funny."

"No, it's extremely amusing." Xavier relaxed, returning to his playful self. "Alice won't help you with mythology. But if you're so interested in that, why don't you find some books in the library? I assume you know where the library is?"

"Very funny." Isaac might not be the studious type, but he knew where the library was. He was almost sure it was before the cafeteria and after the auditorium, but he'd check on his way out of school tomorrow, just to be safe. "Why do you think Alice won't help me?"

"She said no to you already, hasn't she?"

"Yes, but—"

"If she said no, then respect her word," Xavier said, staring intently at Isaac. "The library might be your best bet to get the information you need."

"I'll look there, then." Isaac blinked, unable to look away from Xavier's dark eyes. Something within him shifted and he nodded. "I'll look in the library for information. I won't bother Alice with this issue anymore."

"Good." Xavier stood and grabbed his bag, tossing it over his shoulder. He looked down at Isaac and smiled. "I don't think swimming is for me, after all. See you around, Isaac."

Isaac blinked as he watched Xavier walk away, unsure of what their conversation had been about. The haziness in his mind subsided and he focused on the swimming practice across from him, knowing what his next step to get answers would be.

Tomorrow, Isaac would go to the library.

Chapter Four

ALICE'S AFTERNOON COULD BE better. After her boring morning in classes, she went to the library where she spent the rest of her afternoon organising her study notes. This was part of her routine, but today, everything appeared harder. Concepts were more complicated, words had no meaning and her tasks seemed to have no end. In between regular school, a New Moon Ritual to prepare—one she had never performed before—and an unwanted visit from Aunt Gloria, Alice had her hands full. She wasn't sure how she would survive it all.

She stood from her chair and walked to some of the bookshelves nearby. Alice loved this place. The library was two stories high, its walls covered in wooden shelves carved with flowers and other nature motifs. Whenever she was too tired to study, she would get lost in the maze of bookshelves on the lower floor, her fingers tracing the shapes of the wood, her lips mumbling the book titles. It was a pastime that garnered her a couple of odd looks, but she was used to it.

At school, no one spoke to her. At lunchtime, no one sat with her. Even at the library, she learned it was best to sit at the furthest corner to not disturb other students. She wasn't disappointed by this, though. The fewer people she had to hang out with, the fewer people she had to hide her magic from. Hiding magic was a costly game, one she did not want to pay with her life.

She slowed down when she spotted a couple of mythology books, her fingers tracing their spines. This section was better organised now after she volunteered last summer to properly catalogue these books. For some reason, no one looked after them, maybe because of what they entailed. Some people saw magic as a disease, but its knowledge could act as a cure for their ignorance. Still, as much as Alice hoped to use her powers out in the open for everyone to see, she knew it wasn't possible. Not here, at least.

Beyond the shelves, the other students whispered and giggled, their voices louder than usual. Alice looked through the shelves, unable to spot the source of their amusement. Instead, she focused on the books on the highest shelves, spotting the title she was looking for.

The Moon: Mythology and Superstitions sat in the middle of other books, its gilded spine shining in the low library light making it hard to miss and ignore. She had read this book more times than she could count, but she loved its hand-drawn illustrations and moon cycle diagrams. Reading it before she had to perform a New Moon Ritual always soothed her soul, even though she knew most of its contents by heart.

This time, she wouldn't be performing the New Moon Ritual in the comfort of her aunt's flower shop. Since this ritual was more intricate than the previous ones, Alice would need more space to work with, and the forest was the chosen destination. She wasn't pleased with the idea and even suggested doing it someplace else, but this was tradition, and if she wanted to get accepted into the University of Nadalan, then she had to get it done. All she could do was hope that it all would go well. She couldn't afford to make any more mistakes.

She reached for the book on the top shelf, getting on her tippy toes to try and grab it. Her fingers grazed the middle of the spine, but she wasn't tall enough to pull it out. Alice stepped away, moving the small flying hairs away from her face as she inspected the bookshelf. If she placed a foot on the lower shelf, maybe she could gain enough momentum and grab the book.

Or she could destroy school property and ruin good books with her shoes.

Let's go again. Alice leaned her entire body on the bookshelf and bit her lip as she reached for the top of the book, her fingers only touching the embossed letters. *Just a bit more.* She spread her fingers wide, pushing her arm even further into the top of the book, closing her eyes.

"Hold on."

Alice opened her eyes in time as someone walked closer to her, their quick steps muffled by the library carpet. She startled and moved away from the bookshelf, her hand going for her pocket jacket. Except, she wasn't wearing her jacket. If something bad happened to her, she would have no way to contact Xavier. As much as she hated the idea of him following her around wherever she went, this was the one time she hoped he had done just that.

"Here." Alice kept her distance as the stranger extended the book towards her. "It was this one, right? If not, I can get you the right one. Or another one."

"It's this one." She snatched the book away, hugging it closer to her chest. When she lifted her eyes to thank the stranger, the words died on her lips. A tall guy with light brown skin stared at her, a polite smile on his lips. His eyes widened and his lips parted in surprise as he stared at Alice, something that she couldn't help but mirror on her own expression. It was not every day that she found Isaac in the library.

"Oh," she said after recovering her senses, unable to hide her disappointment. "It's you again."

Isaac chuckled, rubbing the back of his neck, glancing around. It had been a couple of days since she last saw him, but her heart jumped in her chest just as fast as that first time. Everything in her body asked her to run away, to get back to her table, leave the library and go home.

Just like last time, Alice found herself glued to the ground, tracing the soft lines of his aura twirling in the air around him like smoke. His aura wasn't one of a human. The hues of gold indicated to her that he had a magicstream. If he were human, his aura would twirl in a shade of dull grey mixed with whatever emotion he was feeling at the moment.

"Thanks for the book," Alice said, turning to leave.

"Wait!" Isaac reached for her arm and she spun, causing him to stop too close to her. She took a step back, noticing the dark circles under his bright green eyes, the lack of focus in them.

"Have you been sleeping?" she blurted out, unable to stop herself.

Isaac blinked, confused. Alice knew this was an odd question, but she didn't like what she was seeing in him.

"I guess?"

"You guess?" She raised an eyebrow. "You don't know how to rate your sleeping experience?"

"You ask really weird questions," he said, then thought better of it. "I didn't mean it like that."

"How did you mean it, then?"

Alice knew what most people thought of her. Her reputation preceded her, and throughout all these years, she could never escape it. If people believed she could curse them with just one look, then so be it. After seven years, she couldn't care less.

She was almost out of this place, anyway.

"Usually, most people ask *how are you* instead of, you know, *have you been sleeping*." He pursed his lips, keeping his eyes trained on her. "But I have been sleeping how I always have. And I'm doing well."

"Good to know." There was no reason for Isaac to be telling her the truth, and it was a good thing she wasn't in the mood to push this subject any further. "What do you want?"

Isaac nodded slowly, his body present but his mind elsewhere. He blinked as if returning to his senses. "Right." He furrowed his brows, scanning his surroundings. "I was wondering if you could help me. Maybe you could tell me which books I should read about merfolk."

"And what do I get in return? For helping you?"

She didn't like this. Isaac was a merfolk and he was clearly pushing down his magic, which was a terrible decision on his part. It was also terrible that he was counting on her to help him. There was also the possibility that he was a liar and that this was all simply an act for him to get closer to her and wait for the right moment to attack.

"Liam is throwing a party this Friday," Isaac said, shrugging. "You could come. It's fun. Maybe you'll like it."

He looked away as his throat worked. Isaac kept his head high as he read the titles, his lips parted as his fingers grazed the spines, his brows more furrowed with each passing book.

Alice watched in amusement as he pulled books out, glanced at their covers and put them back almost immediately. She should leave. She already had the book she wanted. She didn't need to stay here with Isaac. She didn't *have* to help him. She shouldn't. She should remain a shadow, a shapeless void inside everyone's mind.

She took one step towards him. Then another. When she was next to him, she reached for one of the books on the shelf, her hand brushing against his. Her eyes widened and she apologised to him, gulping away the heat spreading on her chest and cheeks.

"This one is good for merfolk mythology," she said, extending the book to him. She analysed the bookshelf and picked another one, struggling to open it while she held the other book close to her chest. "This one is nice, too. Try to pick up on the patterns described in this folklore. It's not the stories that matter, it's what's beyond them."

Alice dropped that book on top of the previous one. She picked out a few more but put them back on the shelf, unsure they would be helpful to Isaac in any way. Most of the books here were either extremely vague or too imaginative.

"Start with those two," she said. "After you're done with them, I can give you some better recommendations."

"Thanks." Isaac smiled at her, his eyes jumping between the books in his hands and Alice. "I appreciate this. I'll try to read them until the party. Maybe we could talk about them there?"

Alice nodded, taking a few steps back. "Sure. I'll see if I can go."

Isaac stared at her, his smile never fading. Alice noticed how one corner of his mouth was higher than the other. Before she could stop herself, she returned his smile, the gesture foreign to her face.

"See you around, Alice."

She waved at him and turned around, glancing back over her shoulder. This time, instead of worrying if she was being followed, Alice spotted Isaac turning the books in his hands, confusion settling between his brows the longer he stared at them.

For his sake, Alice hoped Isaac would give those books a chance. Before she could get disappointed by his choices, she returned to her desk and buried her nose in the old book, relaxing at the familiar pages spread in front of her.

From the corner of her eye, she spotted Isaac at the front desk with the books. As if sensing her gaze on him, he looked over his shoulder in her direction and offered her a thumbs-up and a happy smile. Alice lowered her eyes and focused on the moon diagram in front of her, occasionally glancing his way. For the rest of her study session, all Alice could think about was whether helping Isaac had been the right choice or if this was just another disaster waiting to happen.

Chapter Five

THE POUNDING ON ISAAC'S head was becoming unbearable, and he was almost certain it was because of the books he was reading. Their letters were too small, their pages tainted from old age, the illustrations hand drawn. This was so different from the books he used for most of his classes. If Isaac had to guess, he would say these books were older than him. Not that it mattered.

If he wanted new information, he'd have to read these, and then ask Alice for help. *Again.*

He wasn't sure why he was so nervous about this. For most of his tests and evaluations at school, Isaac only winged it. Yes, sometimes he reviewed the content, but most of the time he just hoped he wouldn't fail without studying. It wasn't an infallible plan, but he was a strong believer that one should not waste time if what they're doing is not worth it.

Studying was not worth it. He was the best swimmer in his school, the best swimmer in the entire district, and he placed second two years in a row in his category at nationals. This year, he was set to reach that first place, and for a while, his plan was working. Isaac was set to succeed this year and get a scholarship to a good university.

That was until his legs decided to give way to a tail every time he stepped inside a pool.

This changed everything. It put his entire life on hold. Everything he worked for, everything he didn't work for, was threatening to change his life forever and for the worse. All that stood between Isaac and his old life was reading a couple of old and boring books, getting in Alice's good graces and asking her for a solution to his problem.

Isaac massaged his temples, closing his eyes. This headache was not getting better, but he wasn't going to give up. He took a few more sips of his energy drink, flipped through a couple more pages, and got to reading and taking notes. For the first time in his life, Isaac was taking notes. If anyone saw him now, they wouldn't recognise him. Liam would probably laugh and find it ridiculous that Isaac was reading books to impress a girl. As much as he hated to admit it to himself, he needed to impress Alice to get her to help him.

With her, he couldn't just smile or compliment her, or pretend to be madly in love. No, that wouldn't work for Alice. He wasn't even sure if *this* would even work. For all he knew, Alice did as she pleased. She never had to do group projects, she could skip PE and no teacher ever batted an eye at that. Isaac found it unfair that he was constantly reprimanded for his terrible grades, but because Alice was the top student in their class, she seemed to have special treatment.

A knock on his bedroom door caused Isaac to jump in his chair. His heartbeat pulsed strongly through his entire body and he took a deep breath to try and steady it.

"Isaac?" his father said. "Can you come to the living room? I need to talk to you."

"One second!"

Isaac grabbed all his books and shoved them in his backpack, emptying his desk of anything that could raise any questions from his father. This situation was already embarrassing enough, but to tell his father about it? That would only make it more awful. For the time being, and for as long as he could, Isaac would keep this from him.

After exiting his room, Isaac climbed down the stairs to join his father in the living room.

“I’m here,” he said, crashing onto the couch. “What is it?”

His father continued to pace around the living room, hands behind his back. He stopped in front of the fireplace, turning to Isaac. “Your swimming coach just called me.”

Oh. Isaac gulped, unable to meet his father’s gaze. He knew he eventually would get caught, but he didn’t expect it to be now.

“What did he say?” Isaac asked, focusing on his cuticles.

“Well, he said you didn’t go to practice this week. Or last week.” His father raised an eyebrow at him. “Will you explain to me why?”

“It’s complicated.”

“Then uncomplicate it for me.” He sat next to Isaac. “What is it, son?”

Isaac took a deep breath, keeping his hands on his lap, chewing on his lower lip. He couldn’t simply tell his father the truth; he wouldn’t believe him. Besides, the fewer people that knew, the better. So far, only Alice knew, and he intended to keep it that way for as long as possible.

“I…” Isaac closed his eyes. “I haven’t been feeling well lately.”

There. He said it. Not a total lie, but not the entire truth, either.

“Your coach mentioned you’ve been sick. Or *pretending* to be sick.” His father grabbed Isaac’s chin, turning it to have a better look at his face. Isaac kept his gaze on the fireplace. “Have you been sleeping?”

“Yes.” He moved his father's hand away. “I just have a very bad headache, and it hasn’t gotten better.”

“I can tell…”

His father stared at him, almost a mirror image of Isaac. When he was younger, he didn’t see the similarities between them, but now, when he looked at the photos of his father around his age, he could see them. They had the same round face, the same freckles over the nose and cheeks. Sometimes, Isaac wondered if the only thing he had inherited from his mother were her green eyes.

“If you don’t want to swim anymore and want to leave the team, I hope you know you can let me know.” His father rubbed Isaac’s shoulder, giving him a comforting smile. “I don’t want you to lie to me, Isaac. It's never pleasant when I receive phone calls from your school."

"I know." Isaac nodded, his heart sinking in his chest. He couldn't tell his father what was going on. He wouldn't understand. "I have a lot on my plate right now. I promise that if I skip swimming practice again, I'll let you know."

"Fine." His father stood from his spot on the couch, pointing an accusatory finger at Isaac. "But you're grounded. You're not going to Liam's party tomorrow."

"Dad!" Isaac got up from the couch in an instant. "You can't do that!"

"I can. You have been skipping swimming practices without my knowledge, your grades are miserable—did you know you might fail four subjects this semester alone?—and that means that you're losing focus on what you said was important to you. We made a deal, remember?"

"I know," he said, avoiding his father's big brown eyes. "But I agreed to meet with someone at the party, and I can't leave her hanging. It's *very* important that I meet with her."

"*Her*?" His father crossed his arms, narrowing his eyes on Isaac. "You've been skipping swimming practice and neglecting your grades because of a girl?"

"No." Isaac shook his head. "It's just that I agreed to meet with this girl at the party."

"For what?"

"I plan to exchange some notes with her about some of the books I'm reading."

Isaac was losing track of the lies he was telling. He knew this would come to bite him in the ass sooner or later. Still, this wasn't technically a lie. Isaac had agreed to meet with Alice at the party for them to talk about the books she recommended to him. Not only that, but Isaac didn't want to leave Alice alone. He knew she could handle herself, but he was afraid of what might happen if he did. Liam had a tendency to be a pretty bad party host for a variety of reasons.

"You seriously expect me to believe that you, Isaac Kallan, want to meet with a girl at a party to exchange study notes with her?" His father chuckled. "It's okay to say you want to meet with this girl because you like her. But you should let her know that you're not going. If she likes you, then she'll meet you some other day."

The problem was that Alice didn't like him and she would not want to meet him any other day. This was his only chance to meet with her and his final attempt to ask her for help. If he didn't show up, then nothing would change. Isaac wouldn't be able to go back to his life before all of this happened. That couldn't be.

"Can't we reach a compromise?" Isaac asked. "What if I—"

"A no is a no, Isaac." His father held Isaac's gaze, his voice stern. "You need to understand that your actions have consequences. How about you spend this time you're not at the party studying? Text the girl and ask her to meet you some other day."

"I don't have her number!" Isaac stood from the couch and shook his head in anger. "You know what? You don't get it. You never do."

"Isaac!" his father called from the living room, but he ignored it. "Isaac, please."

Isaac slammed his bedroom door and collapsed on his bed, grabbing one of his pillows and squeezing it close to him.

Everything in his life was going haywire. He had nothing to hold onto. First, it was his school grades, then the swimming team and now his social life. What was Isaac left with?

He threw the pillow across the room, and it thumbed against the wall, falling on the ground. Isaac stood there, staring at his ceiling. He closed his eyes, trying to fight the migraine away, trying to wake up from this nightmare.

It was impossible. This wasn't a nightmare he could wake up from. This wasn't a migraine he could simply sleep through. No. This was his life, and his life had high stakes at the moment.

And to get what he wanted, to get what he needed, Isaac would have to break some rules along the way.

Chapter Six

ALICE SET THE TABLE for four people instead of three. After her witchcraft lesson, her aunt insisted on joining Alice and her parents for dinner, and there wasn't much Alice could do about it.

Every other day, she wouldn't have minded her aunt's presence at their dinner table. Today, however, Alice had a very big question to ask her parents, and she would have felt better if only the three of them were at home. As much as she trusted Victoria to keep a secret, she knew her aunt would possibly push her to speak about it sooner than she'd like or was comfortable with.

The three adults chatted happily in the kitchen as Alice remained on the living room couch, staring at the news on the TV. Her cat jumped to the coffee table, staring at her intently for a while before plopping down to lick its body, blocking the TV from Alice's view.

"Really, Whiskers?" she said, shaking her head. "You have the entire living room. Why there?"

Whiskers didn't care. He continued with his beauty regimen and Alice slid to the other end of the couch to have a better view of the TV. The news wasn't that interesting, but it offered a nice distraction from her wild thoughts.

Alice had gone over this scenario several times in her head, and in all of them, her parents had the same answer. *No*. It would be hard for them to say yes to her request, considering what she was asking them. She would be out in the open, exposed to everyone, and one step closer to impending doom.

"Dinner's ready!" her mother announced as she walked into the room, placing a large tray in the centre of the dining table. "Alice, darling, would you mind grabbing the beverages from the fridge? Your father is occupied with the salad."

"Sure." Alice stood from the couch, and Whiskers jumped gracefully from the coffee table. She glared at him, watching as he swayed his tail in the air, walking towards his box of toys.

Alice entered the kitchen to find her aunt and father whispering to each other while exchanging grand hand gestures. She tried to remain unnoticed as she walked to the fridge, her steps light as she kept most of her weight on the tip of her toes.

"I think we should tell her, Victor," her aunt said, extending her older brother a worried look. "She'll know something's wrong."

"Gloria will know nothing of this," he said as he seasoned the salad, his round glasses resting on the tip of his nose. "Whatever is going on with Alice is none of our sister's business."

"I know that, but you know she's pretty insistent on wanting Alice to go live with her in Nadalan."

Her father dropped the salt container, causing both Alice and Victoria to startle. He took a deep breath as he gripped the kitchen counter, his knuckles white. Alice took this as her cue to open the fridge and grab the juice carton and the wine bottle.

"Alice is safe *here*," her father said between gritted teeth.

"She won't be here forever, Victor." Victoria rubbed his shoulder, offering him a consoling smile. "She wants to study *in* Nadalan. Alice passed all her preliminary theory exams. I know you don't want this, but…" Her aunt's words trailed off when she spotted Alice near the fridge.

Before her aunt could mention Alice's presence, she left the kitchen.

"Here they are," Alice said, almost spilling both beverages on the table when she dropped them.

She had always known her parents had reservations about her going to study Alchemy in Nadalan, but she didn't know it was this serious. Besides, after what had happened here, shouldn't they want her to go there? A place where everyone had magical abilities and where she wouldn't have to hide hers?

Nadalan was perfect compared to whatever she had to go through here. Not using her magic was awful in every sense of the word.

"Thank you, sweetheart." Her mother smiled at Alice and pointed to her plate. "Give me your plate so I can serve you. Are you hungry?"

"A decent amount." Alice sat on her chair, catching her aunt and father leaving the kitchen through the corner of her eye. "Does it have extra cheese?"

"Yes. I made it how you like it."

Alice clapped on her seat, *too* excited given the circumstances. She tried to relax, but she was keenly aware of Victoria's eyes on her. After grabbing her plate from her mother, she dove right in to avoid meeting her aunt's gaze.

Dinner went as usual. Her parents and her aunt spoke of their last Coven meeting, complaining about something or someone. Alice wasn't required to attend Coven meetings, but that would change once she turned eighteen. She was only required to go whenever the Assembly gathered all the magical beings in the area to do the yearly census, to share new rules or laws, or whenever a trial was in session, which was rare. It wasn't her favourite event, but she got to dress up, so that made up for it. As she chewed her food, she couldn't help but wonder if she had ever seen Isaac at any of the Assembly events. It didn't matter, anyway. Alice rarely focused on the people attending.

"Have you told them Gloria is visiting?" Alice's father asked his sister, pushing his glasses back. "They should know."

Victoria chuckled. "I don't think I'll say anything. Last time I did, it was a nightmare."

"Yes, but people should be aware of her visit," her mother said. "She's a member of the Council."

"I'm not going to make this town bend to my sister's will, Ingrid."

"It wouldn't be that, Victoria. But you know how your sister is. People should be, at least, aware of her visit. She might not be visiting as a member of the Council, but she's visiting nonetheless."

Alice sighed, shoving some food into her mouth. Her mother's cooking never failed. This was delicious. She would take some leftovers for her lunch tomorrow at school.

"Do you have any idea why she might be visiting now?" her father asked, taking a sip of his wine.

Victoria glanced at Alice and everyone's gaze fell on her. She gulped, swallowing more than what her throat could handle.

"I think she's coming to assess Alice's progress. By now, she's probably aware of her application and her preliminary results, so she wants to see if everything is going according to plan."

"It makes sense." Her mother nodded, smiling at her. "How is your progress going? Your aunt told me you had exceptional results in your preliminary theory exams. Congratulations, darling."

"Thanks." Alice reached for her mother's hand and squeezed it lightly. "It's going well. It's better than what we were expecting… Right?"

Her eyes trailed back to Victoria. Her aunt took a deep breath and glanced around the table with pursed lips. She took a sip of her wine and frowned. When she lowered the glass, she focused on Alice's parents.

"Alice can't summon," she said, not beating around the bush. "She can do everything else, but when it comes to using her magic, she has a very hard time doing it on command."

Alice lowered her eyes, the weight of her predicament falling over her shoulders. Her aunt wasn't being completely honest with her parents. Alice couldn't summon magic in any way. It was as if she wasn't a witch at all. This was bad, and she wanted to fix it, but she couldn't figure out how or why this was happening. As a child, she used to be able to summon magic. Her magic even manifested earlier than everybody else's and she used to be pretty good at it. And then, after that infamous day, she couldn't do it anymore.

"That is a problem," her father said, his voice grave. "If Gloria finds out…"

"She will ask questions," Victoria added, taking another sip of wine. "And if we give her the answers…"

"She will be very upset," her mother concluded, wiping her mouth on a napkin. "I think you should continue your work with Alice, anyway. I remember when I was a student, it took me a very long time to be able to summon on command." She smiled at Alice, reassuring her with kind eyes. "You'll figure it out if you keep trying. I trust your aunt to guide you through this."

"I trust her too," Alice said, smiling shyly at her aunt. She merely kept her gaze on Alice, chewing slowly. "Thanks for your help."

"Anytime, kiddo." She winked but didn't smile. After staring at Alice for a while, she added, "Speaking of *you*, didn't you want to ask your parents something?"

"You have a question for us?" her father asked and her parents leaned closer as if to hear her better. "What is it?"

The air escaped Alice's lungs. She glared at her aunt who simply shrugged, grabbing her wine glass. This was the last time she shared something with Victoria that she could use as ammunition against Alice later. She had grown too used to her aunt always having her back.

"Yes, I do," Alice said, her voice hoarse. She drank some juice, her heart jumping in her chest as the food in her stomach threatened to come out.

"What is it, darling?" her mother asked.

"It's," Alice cleared her throat, "It's a request. Kind of."

"Kind of?"

"Yes." Alice nodded. She closed her eyes, unable to say the words while staring at her parents. "I was invited to a party this Friday, and I was wondering if I could go."

The silence stretched for a while. Alice focused on her heartbeat, pursing her lips as tightly as she could. As soon as she opened her eyes, her parents shook their heads at her.

"No."

"Absolutely not, Alice," her father said.

"Why not?" she asked, her voice higher than she intended. "I've never been to one and as Vi said, I'm doing mostly well on my witchcraft curriculum."

"And yet you still can't summon magic at will," her mother

said.

"More of a reason for me to go!"

"No." Her father shook his head, keeping his eyes on Alice. "Remember how it all started last time? Do you remember, Alice?"

"I was ten, Dad," she said. "I know how to hide and control my magic better now." *Mostly because I don't even know how to use it.*

"She's right," Victoria said, siding with Alice. "Besides, going to a party sounds like fun. It could do Alice some good to hang out with other kids her age."

"Whose side are you on, Vi?" Her father narrowed his eyes on his sister. "Alice is—"

"Alice is almost eighteen, Victor. This might be the last chance she'll get at experiencing something normal. Wasn't that the reason why you two moved here? So Alice could have a human upbringing, away from the dangers and disappointments of Otherworld?"

"And yet, those same dangers and disappointments followed us here." Her father ran a hand through his face. "We're not safe anywhere, Victoria. When will you understand that?"

Her mother sighed, pondering Victoria's words. Maybe it wasn't so bad she had her aunt here. She knew Alice well enough to know she had zero argument skills with her parents. Having her support meant the world to her.

"I suppose Alice could go to the party." Alice's eyes widened and her mother raised a finger, warning her with a look. "But only if Xavier goes with you."

"Can't I really go by myself?" Alice pouted at her parents. "You know that I'm responsible."

"It's not you I'm worried about, darling. It's everybody else. You either go with Xavier or you stay home. End of discussion," Alice's mother said, her tone final.

"What if Xavier doesn't want to go?" Alice asked. "What if he already has plans?"

"Xavier's job is to protect you from harm," her father said, holding her gaze. "If you want to go to that party, he has to go with you. Your mother and I are not budging on this."

Alice wasn't pleased about this, but it was better than not being able to go. It was a compromise, one between her ideal scenario and the worst possibility ever.

"I guess I'll call Xavi after dinner," she said, giving her parents a small smile. "Thank you."

"You should thank your aunt too," her mother said, gesturing to Victoria.

Alice smiled at her aunt. "Thanks, Vi."

"No problem." This time, the wink had a smile attached to it. "But you'll be doing the flower shop's inventory for next week starting tomorrow."

"That's fair." Alice couldn't argue with that, but that didn't mean she was pleased about it.

The atmosphere lightened as they shared dessert. The TV played in the background, but everyone's attention was on Whiskers as he attempted to cause mayhem around the living room. When he failed, he meowed in disappointment which made everyone around the table laugh.

After dinner, Alice helped her father clean the kitchen while her mother and aunt caught up in the living room. Once she was done with her task, Alice kissed her aunt goodbye and disappeared into her bedroom, collapsing on her bed. She grabbed her phone from her bedside table, its harsh light greeting her features, causing her to blink.

She considered texting Xavier with the details of her predicament, but this was a conversation better suited to have in person. Alice wanted to discuss more than just going to the party with him, so she decided to call him. He picked up almost immediately.

"Did something happen?" he asked in a low voice.

"I need to talk to you," she said. When he coughed, Alice raised an eyebrow. "Is everything alright?"

"For the most part." Xavier took a deep breath. "Give me five minutes and I'll be there. I'll climb through the balcony."

"Still not using the front door?"

"I don't think your parents would like to see the state I'm in," he said. "See you soon."

Alice hung up the call and placed her phone on her bedside table, opening her bedroom door. She went to the bathroom to brush her teeth and comb her hair. When she returned, Whiskers had plopped himself on her bed, his amber eyes following her every move.

"You know," she said to her cat as she closed her bedroom door, "I'm receiving a visitor you're not very fond of. Are you sure you want to stay?"

Whiskers didn't move. Alice sighed and sat next to him, running a hand through his orange fur and tail as he started to purr, a sound that made her smile. Her cat's moment of relaxation was interrupted by a knock on her balcony window.

She got up from her bed at the same time as her cat and went to open it, allowing Xavier to step inside. As soon as he did, Whiskers hissed, showing all his teeth to their guest who paid him no mind.

Xavier ran a hand through his grey hair as he sat by Alice's desk, taking quick breaths as if he had been running. His cheeks were a lovely crimson shade, and despite his best attempt at hiding his knuckles from her, Alice spotted the raw, red bruises in them.

"Do I want to know?" She sat back at the edge of her bed, gesturing to his hands. "Do you want some ointment? I think I have—"

"It's all good," he said, but Alice didn't believe him. "Why did you call me here, anyway?"

She narrowed her eyes on Xavier, unable to ignore how on edge he was. He kept shifting his sitting position, kept glancing at the balcony window behind him, kept closing his hands into fists before spreading his fingers wide in frustration. Truth was, she knew nothing of what he did when she wasn't around. Xavier might know everything about her life, but when it came to his, he refused to let her in. It was frustrating, but after dealing with him for six years, she knew it was useless to try and push him to reveal what was bothering him.

"Isaac invited me to go to a party at Liam's house," she said, rolling her shoulders back. "My parents only let me go if you go with me. Do you have plans for this Friday night?"

"I don't," he said. Xavier caught a glimpse of his knuckles and grimaced. "Why do you want to go, anyway? Are you sure it's a good idea?"

"I want to keep an eye on him." Alice sighed and walked to her vanity. She opened one of the top drawers. "The other day he asked me about merfolk, and I can see a golden aura around him… I think he might be a merfolk."

Alice pushed some of the small tins aside, all labelled with her handwriting, until she found a dark green tube labelled *healing ointment*. She grabbed it and walked towards Xavier, all under Whiskers' attentive gaze. His tail cut the air with furious movements, but he appeared comfortable curled near one of the pillows.

"So, he bothered you again?" Xavier asked, watching as Alice opened the tube on her desk and stretched a hand to him.

"I wouldn't say he bothered me. We just crossed paths at the library and he invited me to the party. Give me your hand."

Reluctantly, Xavier placed his hand on top of Alice's. She squeezed some of the ointment on her fingers and carefully spread it over Xavier's bruised knuckles. Under her fingers, his light skin grew warmer as the wounds shifted from bright red to a dull purple until they eventually faded from view.

"You think he's merfolk?" Xavier asked as he extended the other hand to Alice, following her every move. "I mean, his scent was off. His heartbeat was different too. Not human. I don't trust him."

"When did you meet him?" she asked.

"Swimming practice." At Alice's confusion, Xavier chuckled. "Did you really think I was going to join the swimming team? Instead of finding an answer, I only left with more questions."

She let go of his other hand and raised an eyebrow at him. "So does that mean we're going?"

"What part of *I don't trust him* did you not understand? We don't know him. And we don't know Liam that well either."

Alice sighed and after returning the ointment tube to the drawer in her vanity, sat back at the edge of her bed. She wasn't sure of how to convince Xavier that going was the right choice. She couldn't outright tell him that Isaac had asked her for help, but she couldn't ignore what she had seen at the library. She couldn't help but worry the worst.

Isaac could be putting himself and others in danger.

"I think he hasn't been using his magic," she said. "He's presenting signs of that. Alarming signs. And if he doesn't use his magic for much longer, you know what could happen and how dangerous that could be. I'm not asking you to go with me to this party to mingle and make friends. We'd go to keep an eye on Isaac and for me to answer his questions."

"What questions?"

"I recommended him some books on merfolk." She shrugged. "He said he would read them until the party, and that's why he invited me."

"So he's luring you into a house that isn't his own under the pretence of asking you about merfolk? Alice, do you even hear yourself? This could very well be a trap."

"I know that." She met his brown eyes and smirked. "But I also know that you're not one to resist a good mystery. Don't you want to find out if Isaac is a merfolk? Because I do."

Xavier rolled his eyes, pinching the bridge of his nose. "You know, when you called me, I thought your parents were going to scold me for being absent the past few days. Your aunt did that. But I'd prefer your parents scolding to whatever this is."

"And why have you been absent?" she couldn't help but ask. Xavier avoided her gaze as he met his knuckles, spreading his fingers wide. "So you're not going to tell me?"

"When the time is right, I will." He stood from the chair and smiled apologetically at her. "Thanks for the ointment."

"And the party?"

Xavier pursed his lips, running a hand through his hair. "I guess we'll go to that party, yes."

"Thank you," she said, trying not to sound too excited.

Alice opened her balcony door for him, and the cold winter breeze greeted her skin, causing her to stumble backwards. Xavier stepped outside, rubbing the back of his neck as he turned around to face her.

"I'm sorry for the past few days," he said. "I know you don't mind being alone, but I'm breaking my promise to you. It won't happen anymore."

"You're allowed to have a life away from me." Alice wanted to say more, to tell him that she wished he didn't keep her at arm's length, but kept quiet. "Goodnight, Xavi."

"Goodnight, Alice."

She closed the balcony door and watched Xavier as he sat at the balcony's edge and jumped to the ground with a silent thud.

He landed on the dry leaves below and rolled on his side, gracefully standing and wiping the dirt off his clothes before disappearing in the darkness. Alice drew the curtains shut and lay on her bed next to Whiskers, who whined at her proximity. She smiled at the ceiling, both excited and terrified of what she would find at the party, but ready for what it would bring nonetheless.

Chapter Seven

ISAAC'S HEAD WAS GOING to explode. At least, it sure felt like it.

He had spent most of his evening lying in bed, waiting for his father to fall asleep and for his headache to disappear. The medication wasn't working, and he couldn't say he was feeling any better. If anything, he was feeling worse. It felt like someone was banging a hammer right in his brain, the rhythm erratic and all-consuming, making it hard for him to focus on anything other than the throbbing sensation in his head.

He placed the back of his hand against his forehead, feeling it warmer than usual. There was a chance he was getting a fever, which didn't please him in the slightest. The air around him felt colder than usual, and he wanted to stay curled up in bed and skip Liam's party altogether.

Under normal circumstances, he would have stayed home to try and feel better, but that was not an option tonight. If he was getting sick, he could only hope it wasn't contagious. The last thing he wanted—besides not being able to hide the fact he was a merfolk—was to get half of his friends sick because of his behaviour. Isaac was rarely this reckless, but he couldn't help it. He *had* to find a solution.

Isaac *had* to speak with Alice tonight. He couldn't continue to delay this any longer.

After gathering all the strength left in his body, Isaac got out of his bed and walked to his wardrobe. He grabbed a large printed T-shirt and a new pair of dark blue cargo shorts and got changed. He knew it would be cold, so he grabbed a grey hoodie with his school's logo on it, the one he took to all his swimming events. It smelled of chlorine and fun, but he felt guilty wearing it. Was he even a part of the team anymore? Could he even return to the team? He hoped so. That was all he had at the moment.

Isaac took a deep breath and collected the rest of his belongings, shoving them in his pockets. Wallet. Phone. House keys. Then, he put on his sneakers and carefully walked to his bedroom door, peeking through it to the corridor.

The door to his father's bedroom was closed. Isaac sustained his breath, focusing on the sounds nearby. He couldn't hear the TV downstairs, but his father's light snoring seemed so close that Isaac feared he was sleeping downstairs. There was something else, too, something he had never noticed before. A light buzz pulsing all around him, coming from nowhere and everywhere. Even when he tried not to focus on it, he couldn't ignore it in its entirety. *This* was different.

He took a deep breath, exited his bedroom on his tippy toes, and closed the door behind him. His heart jumped in his chest as the door clicked louder than he anticipated. His eyes jumped to his father's room, and he waited to hear movement on the other side. Nothing. That was good. It was better to leave undetected than to be discovered on his way out.

After walking down the stairs as quietly as he could, he reached the main floor of his house. With one final scan of the living room and kitchen, Isaac exited through the back door.

Almost there, he thought as he put his hood on and went around the house hunched over near the building. If his father stared out the window, he wouldn't see Isaac. And if he did, it would be too late. Isaac could deal with his father later.

What he needed to do now was to get to Liam's party.

Isaac knew it would be risky to take his car, so he walked instead. He kept his hands in the pockets of his hoodie, his fingers grazing his phone. Although the night wasn't as cold as Isaac expected, he couldn't help but shiver at the breeze greeting his calves. He should have brought some pants instead. If he wasn't trying to keep a low profile, he would have gone home and changed, but tonight, he had to suck it up and deal with the consequences of his poor choices.

The journey to Liam's house didn't take long. They didn't live that far from each other, but nowadays, they barely saw one another except at swimming practice. At school, they didn't have many subjects in common, and the ones they had didn't require them to interact that much, which was a bummer. Isaac liked it when he shared classes with Liam. His friend was such a jokester, and he never failed to make him laugh. Classes with his best friend were never dull, but most teachers didn't appreciate it. Not that Isaac blamed them; Liam could be inconvenient and obnoxious. But he was charming and rich, so that made up for it.

Liam lived in one of the richest parts of their small town. His house was located in a street where houses were empty during most of the year, with the exception of summer. Because of his lack of neighbours, Liam was the designated party host in their group of friends, and Isaac couldn't complain. His father would never allow him to throw a party in their house, and merely thinking about it brought a shiver down Isaac's spine. He preferred to be a guest than a host. It was less worrisome and far more entertaining.

He tried to walk faster as soon as he heard the music blasting in the distance, but his legs seemed like jelly with each step, threatening to collapse on themselves at any moment. His skin was itchy and warm under his hoodie, and his heart jumped in his chest, making him dizzy. Isaac tripped on his feet as he stared at the dark sky, his lungs heavy. He stopped to catch his breath, leaning on a tree nearby, his hands gripping his knees. *What the hell is wrong with me?* A bead of sweat fell on his hand, and Isaac wiped his forehead, frowning at how clammy his skin was.

His eyes widened when the skin on the back of his hand tingled and pearlescent scales grew on it. *No.* Isaac wiped the sweat on his hoodie, taking a relieved breath when the scales receded and disappeared. *This is not good. Not good at all.* Usually, sweat wasn't enough to make scales grow. He needed to submerge his hand in water for this to happen. Were his symptoms getting worse? That couldn't be it. Could it?

He kept walking, careful as he stepped on the grey pavement, his breathing shallow and heavy. It didn't help that every sound around him seemed louder than usual. The worst was the music coming from Liam's property. Isaac was sure it would rip his skull or blow out his ears.

Isaac considered giving up, going back home, not meeting with Alice tonight and finding her at school some other day. It would be better, wouldn't it? He could barely stand, could barely breathe, could barely hear himself think over the chaos of noise around him.

And yet, his wobbly legs guided him to Liam's property. Before stepping inside, he ran a hand through his hair again, keeping his hands shoved in the pockets of his hoodie. He couldn't afford to expose himself here, in front of all these people. If anything, tonight wasn't about being social or chatting with friends. Tonight, Isaac had a mission: find Alice, exchange ideas with her and go back home.

What did I want to ask her in the first place? As much as he churned the ideas in his head, Isaac couldn't focus on a single thought. Nothing made sense. His mind was a mess.

"You've made it!" Liam said, bringing Isaac back to reality. Somehow, he had made it to the top of the stairs.

His best friend walked over to him and wrapped an arm around his shoulders, guiding him from the entrance to the packed living room.

"So, now that you're here, can you help me with Hannah? I think I am *this* close to getting her to agree to go on a date with me, but she has a new friend who doesn't leave her side, and I can't seem to find a moment to get her alone."

People waved at Isaac with bright smiles that he tried his best to reciprocate. He ignored handshakes and side hugs, his words slurred and delayed whenever he tried to speak. His tongue wasn't his own. It was as if his body had free will, and Isaac was merely here to enjoy the ride. He didn't like this ride. He didn't like this at all.

"Isaac!" Liam gripped Isaac's shoulder, screaming over the loud music. "Did you hear anything I just said?"

No matter where Isaac looked, he couldn't focus on anything. His vision was blurry, reminding him of looking through a kaleidoscope. He could make out shapes that repeated in endless patterns but couldn't locate their start or end. He closed his eyes, hoping this would stop. When he opened them again, not everything was right, but it was better. When he turned to Liam, it was as if they were both underwater.

"What were you saying?" Isaac asked, his throat dry. He stumbled again and leaned on Liam, who prevented him from falling. "I'm not feeling very well."

"You don't look so good." Liam stared at him until his features broke into a huge grin. "You know what would help with that?"

"What?"

"Booze!" Liam laughed, patting Isaac's shoulder and guiding him to the kitchen. "Come on. Let's get you something to drink."

"I don't think—"

Isaac stopped in his tracks, leaning on a wall nearby. His entire body seemed heavier than what he was used to. Walking was harder. Even speaking was a nightmare.

"Oh, come on, Isaac. You can sit outside while you enjoy a nice beer."

"What I need is water," he said, fanning himself. Was it too hot in here? Maybe he should go for a swim. Those always helped him.

You can't, he remembered. *If you do, they'll see. They'll see what you have become. They'll see who you are now. And they will laugh. They will laugh and point at you. And then you'll be just like Alice. Alone and miserable and rude.*

"You're acting weird, dude," his friend said, shaking his head in frustration. He squeezed Isaac's shoulder more than necessary, his angry gaze on him. "Beer also has water, but if you want to be lame, go get yourself some water. It's in the kitchen, next to the fridge. I'll be outside." He pointed a finger at him. "I will need you to distract Hannah's friend so I can convince her to go on a date with me. *Don't* let me down."

Isaac nodded, keeping his back against the wall as Liam walked away into the crowd. People danced and chatted around him, all oblivious to his predicament. He looked for Alice in them, trying to spot the girl he had grown used to looking for wherever he went, to no avail. Even if she was here, he wouldn't recognise her. His best bet was to wait for her to find him.

Maybe she's not coming. The thought came crashing down on him, the last slice to break him into small pieces. What if coming here had been a mistake? Alice hadn't confirmed she would come to the party, but he wanted to believe she would. *I have to find her.*

But first, Isaac had to regain his strength. He had to be able to see and hear clearly again. He walked to the end of the stairs near the entrance, almost tripping on his feet as he sat down on one of the steps. He would stay here for a bit, and then, he would look for Alice. She was easy to spot. Long black hair, probably alone, and a grim look on her face. He smiled at the thought and closed his eyes.

Alice would come to the party. There was no other way around it. Isaac had to believe that. He hadn't put this much on the line for his appearance at this party to be for nothing.

Chapter Eight

ALICE WAS ALREADY REGRETTING her shoe choice for the evening. She should have brought sneakers as her mother suggested, but the small black heels called her name. Besides, they went well with her short emerald-green dress, an outfit choice that had earned her a couple of stares from Xavier on their way to the party.

Despite Isaac's invitation, he had not shared his phone number or Liam's home address with her. Alice knew Liam lived in the richest part of town, but that was about it. Finding his house wasn't as bothersome as Alice thought it would be, and they didn't have to rely on Xavier's abilities as much as she initially expected.

"It's over there," Xavier said, pointing to a house in the distance. "Are you sure you want to do this?"

Alice lifted her eyes from the concrete under her feet and stared ahead. The house was the only one with people outside. From the windows on the upper floor, despite the closed curtains, Alice could make out the silhouettes of people, a pattern that repeated on the lower floor, where the crowd appeared bigger. She couldn't remember the last time she had been in such a chaotic place, but it was too late to back up now. Her hands curled into fists at her side and she held her chin high.

"I'm sure," she said, nodding to herself. "Remember, we're here to speak with Isaac. That's our goal."

Xavier remained by her side, his hands shoved in the pockets of his leather jacket. He had styled his silver hair back and added some small hoop earrings to his ears. From the two, he had an easier time blending in. Even if his grey hair made him stand out, it never drew people away. If anything, it was a magnet of curiosity, one that was safe to inquire about, as opposed to whatever Alice had going on. She had always envied him in that aspect. Xavier didn't even have to try to be accepted. Alice, however, had to work every day to undo her past mistakes, and that still wasn't enough for people to trust her.

As soon as Alice stepped inside Liam's house, her heart caught in her throat, its rhythm matching the music playing from the speakers. She tried to take a deep breath, but the mix of alcohol, sweat and something sweet and intoxicating in the air brought tears to her eyes and did nothing to make her feel relaxed. In what Alice assumed was the living room, furniture had been moved to stand against the walls. In the centre of the room, too many people attempted to dance, tripping over one another while laughing at their clumsiness.

Here, so much could go wrong in a heartbeat.

"Are you sure you're going to be fine?" Xavier asked over the loud music, resting a hand on her shoulder. He scanned the crowd around them, his eyes shifting from dark brown to gold. "There are a lot of people around here."

"Anyone we should be aware of?" she asked, looking for some familiar faces around the crowd.

She spotted Hannah with her curly brown hair in one of the corners of the living room speaking with Liam. Their flirtatious smiles and proximity told Alice that they were sharing a moment not worthy of interruption. She recognised some more of her classmates, all of whom offered her a strange look as they glanced at her outfit. When they found her shy smile, they moved in the opposite direction, not giving her a chance to say hi. Alice had hoped that coming here would be different, that people wouldn't look at her like they did at school. If anything, it was worse.

People whispered. They giggled. They pointed discreetly at her. The music was so loud she couldn't make out what they were saying, and because of the flickering and low lights, she couldn't read their lips.

One thing was for sure: no matter how many years had passed, no matter how much she had tried to correct her life and change its course, what had happened seven years ago wouldn't be forgotten. Alice was the urban legend of this town, but they had it all wrong. Sadly, disproving the rumours would only prove their point, and she wasn't going to risk it.

She couldn't afford to put herself or her family at risk ever again.

Her eyes shifted to a girl near Hannah, whose entire focus was on Alice. Her hair was in a ponytail, one hand clutching the centrepiece of her necklace, the other holding a cup. She grinned at Alice before taking a sip of her beverage, never breaking eye contact. Something about her was awfully familiar, and Alice couldn't ignore the cold taking over her, the pulsing of her heart that urged her to flee.

Xavier squeezed her shoulder and she looked back at him. "If you don't move, people will only stare for longer."

"I know." Alice glanced back at the spot where she had seen the girl only to find it empty. "Do you think this will ever stop?"

"No." His tone was final. "So you might as well make do with it. Let's go."

He gently pushed Alice forward, keeping his hand on her shoulder. As they crossed the dining room, a wave of silence fell around them, their presence absorbing all life around. Next to the dinner table, someone dropped a small ball that bounced and rolled closer to Alice, but no one dared to move, no one dared to speak. They were anticipating her next move, waiting for her to do something out of the ordinary. When she moved past them, they collectively sighed and returned to their beer pong game, bursting into laughter and loud exchanges.

Once they were outside, Alice looked at the dark sky, locating a slice of moon in it. She smiled. It was comforting to know that, no matter where she went, she'd always have the moon there to keep her company. They were so close to the New Moon; Alice was giddy about the ritual this time around. If her latest witchcraft practices and lessons were any indication of her success, then maybe Alice would be able to celebrate yet another accomplishment soon. She could do it—even if she still struggled to summon her magic—but it took longer than it should for a witch with her abilities.

"This is nice," Xavier said once they stepped outside. "He has a nice backyard."

As soon as Alice lowered her eyes, her entire body stiffened. The backyard was larger than her own, with a barbecue area and a porch that stretched around the back of the house with stairs at the centre that led to a pool area. People jumped and swam around as an upbeat song played, sometimes leaving the water only to jump right in again, causing large splashes to reach the bystanders, earning some giggles and annoyed gasps from them.

Alice couldn't move. Her eyes were glued to the pool, its water shifting as people moved inside of it. She imagined its waves crashing against her and pulling her in, lulling her to a terrible sleep that she would never be able to wake up from. A place where she couldn't see, she couldn't hear, she couldn't *breathe*. Alice reached towards her heart, noticing the fast heartbeat under her palm. She focused on that as she closed her eyes, trying to calm her shallow breathing.

"I'm going to try to find something to drink," she said, stepping back and bumping against Xavier. She turned and tried to smile at him. "Why don't you look for Isaac? If you find him, text me."

"I'm staying with you, remember?" He studied Alice carefully, narrowing his eyes on her. "We can leave if you want. There's no reason for us to be here. You weren't even properly invited."

"So far, Liam hasn't told me I was trespassing." She shrugged. "I'll be back. I don't need you to follow me."

"I'm not—"

Before she could hear anything else, Alice stormed into the house and turned right on the first door, entering the kitchen she had spotted earlier. She leaned against the wall, its coolness grounding her. She focused on her heartbeat again, taking deep breaths to relax herself. Once she could hear herself think, she opened her eyes.

The kitchen was different from the rest of this house. Most of the counters were covered in empty pizza boxes, the remaining slices on a greasy paper plate on the kitchen table. Alice grimaced, trying to ignore the strong smell of beer around this place. The only nice thing about this room was the quietness.

She rubbed a hand across her face, regretting it right away. Alice was sure her mascara was smeared all over her eyes, and maybe even her lipstick was smudged too. As much as she wasn't one to focus too much on her appearance, she wanted to look her best tonight. If she was an intruder at this party, then she wanted to be one with style.

"You're here."

Alice lifted her eyes at the familiar voice. Isaac leaned against the counter near the sink, his eyes slightly shut as he glanced her way.

"I thought you wouldn't come," he said, his lips curling into a smile.

"I considered it." She sighed and glanced at the cabinets around the kitchen until she spotted one with clean glasses. "Enjoying yourself?"

Alice grabbed a glass from the cabinet and walked to the sink to fill it with water. Isaac took a step back, increasing the distance between them as his eyes traced her figure. His lips parted to speak, but he didn't say anything. Alice raised an eyebrow at him, taking a sip of her water.

"You look nice," he eventually said, his voice slurred. "Very pretty. Green is a great colour on you."

Was he drunk?

"Thanks?" She glanced at him sideways.

Isaac *looked* different. His hair was shinier than usual as if it was covered in water. His large shirt was wet around his neck and armpits. Around his forehead, small drops of sweat dripped down, causing him to wipe them away with one of the hoodie sleeves wrapped around his waist.

"Are you okay?" she asked.

Alice took one step closer to him, focusing her senses on the space around him, trying to locate his aura. It was there, like last time, but it was more distant. The gold wasn't as bright, fading to a murky brown.

"I'm thirsty," he said, pulling the collar of his shirt away from his neck, trying to cool himself down. "I'm—"

Without thinking twice, Alice grabbed the hand on his collar, her eyes widening. His knuckles were white, covered in small pearlescent scales that reflected the light. His skin was clammy too, with a bluish undertone taking over in blotches that stretched across his arms, growing and connecting the more she stared at them, replacing the warmth of his brown skin.

"When was the last time you swam, Isaac?" she asked, holding the tip of his fingers to get a better look at his scales. This wasn't good. The scales were showing up on dry skin. "Isaac?"

He stared at her with that empty expression she recognised from the library, eyes foggy and lips parted. She reached to pinch his nose, but he didn't flinch. When she threatened to punch him, he didn't move. Isaac blinked, then closed his eyes.

"Can you keep holding my hand?" he whispered as if it was hard to speak. "It feels nice."

Alice pursed her lips, unsure if she had heard Isaac's words correctly. She had just attempted to punch him, and he was focused on the fact she was holding his hand? Something was definitely wrong with him, and Alice didn't like it at all.

"Isaac?" She tapped his cheek, noticing the blueish hue tingeing the skin on his collarbone, spreading upwards to his neck and cheeks. "Isaac, can you hear me?"

His hand slipped from her grasp and he collapsed on the floor. His limbs bent in odd shapes that appeared too painful to anyone who had normal bones, but Alice knew Isaac wasn't human.

Then she saw it. His elbows were covered in the same scales as his knuckles. His ears changed shape, becoming pointier than what they were. In between his parted lips, she spotted his teeth becoming sharper.

Isaac was turning into a merfolk right before her eyes.

Alice dropped her cup in the kitchen sink and clumsily searched her pocket for her phone and called Xavier. "Kitchen. Now," was all she said to him before she hung up. She glanced over her shoulder to make sure no one was coming into the kitchen, her heart ringing in her ears, making it hard for her to think. She wanted to get out of this party, but this wasn't the way she wanted to leave. Not like this. Not with Isaac going through a blackout.

"What is—"

"Close the door," she said to Xavier as soon as he stepped into the kitchen, quickly locating Isaac. His eyes widened in horror. "Xavi, close the door!"

He did as he was told, then lowered himself next to Alice. "What's happening to him?"

"He hasn't been using his magic." She touched his forehead, then his cheeks, then placed two fingers on his neck. She held her breath and closed her eyes, searching for a pulse. Alice sighed. "He's alive, but it's clear his magic is taking over his body. Do you see the scales?"

"Yes. You think he's entering a magical blackout?"

"He's not *entering*, Xavi. He *is* in a magical blackout." She faced him, unsure of how to say it. "If he doesn't get a life potion right now, he'll become a merfolk, and he won't be able to change back. We need to get him out of here. We *need* to take him to my aunt's flower shop."

"How?" he asked. "We're surrounded by people who know who he is, and who clearly despise us being here. If we simply walk out of here with him—"

The kitchen's door swung open. "How many times do I have to…"

Alice didn't think Liam could get any paler. His blue eyes jumped between Isaac's body, Alice crouched next to him, then met Xavier with confusion.

"What did you do to him?" he asked, his voice shaking in fear. Liam clenched his jaw, his eyes filled with an anger Alice had grown numb to. "What did you do to Isaac?"

"We didn't do anything." She checked Isaac's pulse again, its rhythm weaker than before. She whispered to Xavier, "We need to get him out of here."

"Hell no." Liam shook his head, taking one small step towards them. "You're not leaving this party. I'm not letting you sacrifice my friend to whatever freaky thing you wicked people do."

One thing was spreading gossip about magic, another was witnessing in plain sight. Liam was human, his aura a fading silver, and most humans should never experience or see magic in their lifetimes. This was bad. Not as bad as what was happening to Isaac, but bad enough that if Liam decided to scream or yell or do something nefarious towards either of them, things could end badly. Why was it that every time Alice tried to do something different, she only ended up messing something up?

Xavier sighed and shook his head, muttering something under his breath she didn't understand. He stood to his full height and walked towards Liam, towering over him. Liam gulped loudly and took a step back, trying his best to stand his ground with his chest puffed out.

"Liam, is it?" Xavier said as if he didn't know his name. He clutched his shoulder, causing Liam to grimace. "Here's what you're going to do. You're going to forget everything you saw in this kitchen and once you step outside, you're going to tell everyone to go to the backyard and that the last one to jump into the pool is a loser or something similar. Are we clear?"

Liam kept his focus on Xavier, his eyes hazy. His lips parted in confusion as he took a step back, blinking slowly. When the focus returned to his gaze, Liam nodded to himself.

Xavier let go of Liam's shoulder who stepped outside of the kitchen and yelled, "The last one in the pool has to clean the entire house!"

"We don't have much time," Xavier said. He grabbed Isaac's arms and pulled him so he was now sitting. "Help me get him on my back. Then, we'll go to the flower shop. Are you calling your aunt?"

"I don't have to," Alice said. "I'm going to prepare him a life potion."

He stared at her, his lips pursed. "Alice, you know—"

"Yes, I know the risks. Still, the last thing I want is to live with the guilt of refusing to help someone because of some code of conduct. Xavi," she pleaded, "please ignore the rules for once in your life. *Please.*"

She held Xavier's gaze, not budging. Yes, she didn't like this either, but she wasn't going to leave Isaac lying on someone's kitchen floor while his body slowly morphed into something else. She couldn't do it.

"Fine," he said. "But I'll stay with you until he wakes up. For all we know, he could be an enemy."

Alice quickly helped Xavier get Isaac onto his back. She peeked out of the kitchen, finding their path clear. The people who remained were too drunk or passed out to remember this in the morning. If they did, they'd probably consider this a shared hallucination. They would forget about it after a day or two.

She crossed the dining room and living room at a fast pace, Xavier closely behind. Her heels clicked on the floor, drawing unwanted attention, but she didn't stop for anyone. None of them did.

Alice slipped out of the house, followed by Xavier, and closed the entrance door behind them. After they were at a safe distance from the house, they slowed down their steps. Alice fanned herself and smiled, satisfied with their escape.

"Do you think anyone noticed?" she asked, glancing at Xavier.

A soft pink greeted his cheeks as he carried Isaac, but he didn't seem bothered by the effort. His eyes flashed golden and he shook his head. "The path is clear. Good job getting us out of there."

"Good job with Liam." She winked at him, but Xavier kept his focus on the path.

They increased their pace again, walking towards the flower shop, sticking to the hidden paths and less busy streets. Despite their efforts, Alice couldn't ignore the coldness enveloping her, nor the hairs sticking up on the back of her neck. Someone was watching from the shadows.

It shouldn't surprise her, though. *They* were always watching. The question that haunted her now was who were they watching and why?

* * *

"Are you almost done?" Xavier whispered between his teeth, breathing heavily.

Alice focused on the lock in front of her, turning and pushing two small thin metal pieces inside to try and unlock it. "Almost there," she said, feeling it shift under her fingers. She bit her lower lip and pushed one of the pieces further and heard a soft *click* followed by the door opening inwards. "Done. Come on. We can't stay here for long."

She moved aside to allow Xavier to step inside as he carried Isaac on his back, oblivious to what was happening. Throughout their journey here, he had opened his eyes, mumbled a couple of words, but that was it. She couldn't get much more out of him.

"Drop him on the couch in the back room." She closed the flower shop door, locked it, and drew the curtains shut. "I'll look for the vials while you set up the potion book."

"Your aunt wouldn't like that."

"My aunt isn't here," Alice said, losing her patience. She held up her hair and twisted it into a bun. "Just grab the book and open it on the table."

Xavier grumbled, but Alice ignored him. She entered the back room and went to some of the back shelves where she grabbed most of the glass equipment she would need. After carefully dropping it on the table, she went back to a cabinet and opened it, pulling out a few flasks with ingredients such as fish scales, shaved dragon teeth and Nadalan algae.

"Are you sure you can do this?" Xavier asked, sitting Isaac on the couch. "You know you'll have to cast a spell, right? We should call Victoria, Alice. Or someone who can—"

"I can do it," she said, not giving too much thought to Xavier's concern. If she did, then all of this would be lost. Alice couldn't afford to lose the small hope she had. "We don't need to call anyone. I can do this."

She was betting everything on the small chance that she would be successful at preparing this potion and casting this spell.

The commotion in the flower shop woke most of the fairies, whose lights dangled throughout the room, moving closer to the table and Alice. As soon as they spotted Isaac, they flew towards him, stopping in front of his mouth and nostrils, moving to his ears and peeking into them.

"He's not dead," Xavier said as he signed to the ones staring at him before sitting on one of the benches. "He's just heavily unconscious."

The fairies exchanged some hand gestures to communicate with one another, and two flew towards Alice while the others remained near Isaac. One flew to Xavier but he shooed her away as if she was a mosquito.

"Why are they so annoying?" he asked no one in particular.

"They're just doing their job," Alice said, adding a few drops of salt water with a pipette to her flask. "You're lucky they're fond of you."

"I *am* charming. Everyone likes me."

Alice chuckled, grabbing the next ingredient. "Not everyone. Whiskers hates you."

"That's because he's a cat." Xavier took a deep breath. "Are you almost done?"

"Just three more ingredients."

Alice grabbed a knife and cut the Nadalan algae into small strips, shoving them inside the flask. As soon as they touched the liquid, they dissolved, giving it a dark blue hue. Finally, she added a pinch of fish scales and then some shaved dragon teeth. The liquid bubbled, but it didn't spill. She waited until most of its foam disappeared to mix it with a metal spoon, the warmth of the mixture greeting her fingers as she grabbed the flask. Alice cursed under her breath, but she didn't stop. Once the liquid started to turn into a slimy consistency, she knew it was ready.

"I've got it."

She dropped the spoon and walked towards Isaac. All the fairies moved away from him, giving Alice all the space she needed to work. Some flew towards Xavier, but this time, he allowed them to sit on his broad shoulders and crossed arms, reminding Alice of a Christmas tree.

"This is going to taste bad," she said to Isaac, opening his mouth. "But it's for your own good."

She brought the flask to his lips, allowing the potion to spill into his mouth. She grimaced, shaking her head at the smell. Life potions were the worst to prepare because they never smelled good. This one smelled like rotten fish. It probably tasted like it too. Good thing she would never have to ingest it.

Once all the potion was gone from the flask, she closed Isaac's mouth and dropped the container on the table, walking to the book. She moved the hairs from her face to the back of her ears and searched for the page with the spell.

For magic to work, in most cases, two steps were required. The first was to prepare a potion for the desired effect. The other was to cast a spell to activate it. Some spells didn't require potions, but they always required some sort of tangible material to summon the magic.

Her fingers traced the cursive letters on the page, her lips mouthing the words. She went over it several times until the enchantment was engraved into the back of her eyelids.

"I'm going to cast it now," she said, turning to Xavier. "I won't be able to know if it works right away. Because of his state, we'll have to wait a few hours."

"And if it doesn't work?"

Alice gulped. Her eyes turned to Isaac, her heart shrinking in her chest. She knew that was the most likely scenario. And yet, here she was attempting to save someone's life.

How ridiculous and pitiful of her to try and play the hero.

She took a deep breath and grabbed one of Isaac's hands, his skin cold to her touch. She placed her left index and middle finger where Isaac's hand and wrist connected. She felt a shimmering current under her fingertips, something faint and cold. Alice focused on it, attempting to pull it to the surface.

"His skin is turning blue, Alice."

She lifted her eyes to look at Isaac and nodded. "It's supposed to happen," she said. "And please, be quiet. I don't want my odds of ruining this to be higher than they have to be."

From the corner of her eye, she saw Xavier raise his arms in defence, specks of light flying away from him.

Alice focused back on the current, now something that reminded her of dripping honey; its golden colour and sweetness intoxicating. *Magic.* She continued to pull it to the surface, allowing it to come in waves, pushing away from her only to come crashing again after a while.

She searched for something else too, something warmer, something rich and mellow. When a metal tang reached her tongue, she knew she had found it.

Her right hand curled Isaac's fingers into a fist as she whispered the words. She focused on the two currents moving under her fingers, one a wave on a rocky shore, the other a wave on a lake's surface. She stood there, waiting until they matched their rhythms, until they were equal.

"It's done," she said, opening her eyes and his fist. "Now, we wait."

She let go of his wrist and dropped his hand on his side. She noticed the shimmering gold under his skin, the blue fading in plain sight as the warmth returned to his complexion. *I hope it works.*

Alice collapsed on the couch next to Isaac, trying her best to control the quivering of her lips, the darkness dampening her vision.

"You did all you could, Alice," Xavier said, his voice soft. "There's nothing more you could have done."

She chuckled. "Is that supposed to comfort me?"

He didn't answer. Xavier knew that his words were a lie. She could have done more. She could have taken Isaac home and asked her parents for help. She could have asked her aunt to come here. All of them knew more about magic than she did. All of them knew how to summon magic properly, and Alice didn't. And yet, she chose not to call any of them, and she didn't know exactly why.

"You can go," she said, not looking at Xavier.

"I'm staying."

"I'm in a flower shop surrounded by fairies, Xavi. You can go."

"You're also sitting next to a merfolk we know nothing about. And *if* you saved his life, then I have to question him. A lot about his story doesn't add up."

"Will you ever drop your sense of duty?" Alice pinched the bridge of her nose, closing her eyes. Her lids were so heavy, she couldn't open them again. She relaxed on the couch, leaning her head on one of the pillows. Nearby, something rustled. A soft fabric grazed her legs, warming her body. She searched for it and pulled it towards her neck, snuggling closer to it.

"Never," said a familiar voice. She didn't know if it was close or not. It sounded so far away. "Rest well, Alice."

She adjusted herself on the couch, moving closer to the source of warmth next to her. Her hand brushed against something. Isaac's hand. *It feels nice*, he had said to her when she held his hand at Liam's party. Slowly, she wrapped her fingers around his hand, keeping their hands together in between their bodies on the couch. When his grip shifted to hold her hand better, she smiled.

Alice drifted into a sleep for a while, only to be woken up by Isaac's scream.

Chapter Nine

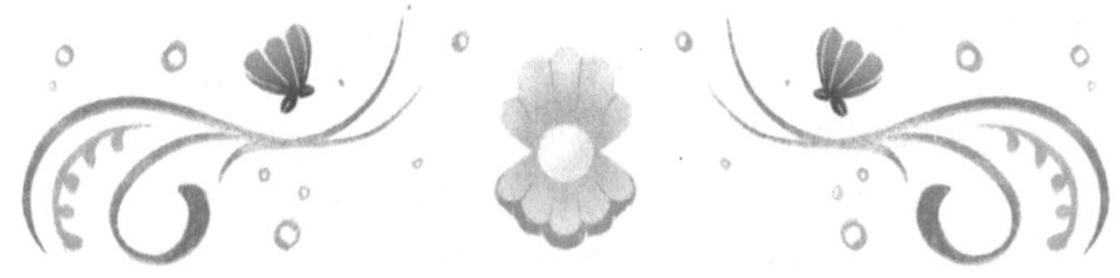

A SMALL, SHINY, HUMANOID figure stood in front of Isaac's nose, looking at him curiously. He yelled, trying to crawl away from it, only screaming more when the creature flew away from him, disappearing in the distance. The back of his head hit something soft, and he blinked, taking in his surroundings.

Around him, he spotted tall shelves with books, containers, and other objects that Isaac assumed were gardening utensils. The low ceiling had a couple of cracks here and there, and a long table took over the space where books, vials and other containers tumbled over, disorganised.

"Where am I?" he whispered, the words strange in his mouth.

Something about this place was familiar. Isaac had never been here, but he had seen it before. *Where?* He couldn't pinpoint it. It hadn't been a picture or a video, but he could have sworn he had seen it.

"He's awake," a male voice said from his left. With the low lights, he couldn't make out who had spoken, but it wasn't the first time he heard it.

When the weight shifted next to Isaac, he recoiled in the

opposite direction, turning to Alice as she stood from the couch.

"Welcome back," she said, a soft smile on her lips. "How are you feeling?"

Isaac blinked, more confused than ever. He cleared his throat, regretting right after. "I need water," he said, his voice hoarse.

"I'll go get it," the male voice spoke again. "Don't lose him out of your sight."

"I won't!" Alice screamed, rolling her eyes. She focused back on Isaac. "Besides water, do you need anything else? How are you feeling?"

"I'm fine, I guess." He focused on his body for a while, furrowing his eyebrows. His head no longer throbbed in pain. His surroundings no longer swirled as he tried to focus on them. As Isaac took a deep breath, his chest didn't hurt anymore. "What happened?"

"Here you go." He accepted the glass of water from Xavier and chugged it all in one go, feeling much better right after. "Do you need more?"

He shook his head, returning the glass to Xavier. "I'm good now. Thanks."

Isaac adjusted himself better on the couch, keenly aware that Alice hadn't stopped staring at him since she got up. For some reason, he couldn't meet her gaze. He was scared he wouldn't be able to look away.

"You had a magical blackout," she said, keeping her arms crossed over her chest. "Since you probably haven't been using your magic, you fainted at Liam's party because of it. We brought you to my aunt's flower shop, and I gave you a life potion."

"You should be grateful to Alice." Xavier narrowed his eyes on Isaac. "If it weren't for her, you'd be a fish by now."

"A fish?" Isaac's eyes widened. "You mean I would— You saw my tail?"

"Not your tail." Alice shook her head. "But we saw your scales. Your ears changed shape too."

Isaac traced both of his ears with his fingers, relaxing when he didn't find anything abnormal about them. He glanced at his hands and elbows, resting his palm over his heart as he leaned back on the couch.

"Why haven't you been using your magic?" Xavier asked, moving closer to Alice. His shadow stretched on the wall behind him and Isaac gulped, the hairs on the back of his neck standing up. "You know how dangerous that is, right?"

"I don't know anything," he said. "The tail only appeared two weeks ago. Did you tell him about our conversation?"

He turned to Alice, enraged. He thought that she, better than anyone else, would understand his need to hide a secret. To hide *this* secret. "Next time, I might as well confirm everyone's suspicions that you're a witch. That's what you're asking for, right?"

"Do that and you're a dead man," Xavier said, his tone cool and sharp, cutting the air like a knife. Isaac didn't miss the anger in his eyes, either. This wasn't something Xavier was saying to frighten him. He was saying it because he meant it.

Isaac didn't care anyway.

"And how exactly are you planning to kill me?" He stood from the couch, walking towards Xavier. "Knife to the throat? Bullet to the heart?"

Before Isaac could react, Xavier's hand was around his neck and his back struck a wall. Plant vases fell from nearby shelves causing a few specks of light to fly from them like fireworks. Instead of fading as Isaac expected, the light travelled across the room, disappearing somewhere behind Xavier's large body.

"Enough playing, Fishboy." Isaac tried to breathe, but he couldn't. "Who the hell are you and why are you here?"

"I… don't… know," Isaac said, attempting to speak. He was kicking his feet to hit Xavier while he tried to uncurl the fingers around his throat. Xavier didn't waver. He was solid as a rock.

"Was it Ariah?" Xavier said in between greeted teeth as he slammed Isaac against the wall again. "Did she send you after Alice?"

"Let him go, Xavi," Alice demanded. "It's clear he doesn't know what we're talking about."

"Do you really believe his story?" Xavier said, clenching his jaw. Isaac's vision darkened around the edges. "He could be a spy."

"Or he could be someone whose magic is only manifesting

now. Let him go before he faints again. Please."

Xavier pondered while Isaac struggled, his arms losing their strength and falling back to his side. When he let go of Isaac, he fell on the floor like a heavy potato sack, curling over his stomach as he coughed, taking deep breaths. His lungs were on fire.

"You better explain yourself," Xavier said, pacing around the room, hands behind his back.

Isaac rubbed his neck and crawled back to the couch, his attention jumping between Alice and Xavier. How she remained so calm after Xavier almost choked him to death was beyond him.

"I don't know what happened. Two weeks ago, I was swimming at the local pool and then it happened. I freaked out. From that point onward, every time I came in contact with water, I got scales on my body and every time my legs got wet, I'd have a tail instead. I started skipping swimming practice after that, and I asked Alice for help."

"Based on what knowledge?" Xavier asked. "How did you know she could help you?"

"Well, for starters, there were the rumours." He dared a look at Alice as she flinched, focusing on her feet. "And then, I came across her in the library when I went to look for books on merfolk, so I asked her for some recommendations. I read all the books you recommended, by the way. I was hoping we could have discussed them at the party."

He expected Alice to smile at that, but she didn't.

"Did you grow up in the area?" she asked, still not meeting his eyes.

He shook his head, a heavy weight settling in his heart. "I moved here when I was twelve."

Alice and Xavier exchanged a knowing look, and he nodded. "Do you know if anyone in your family has similar abilities?"

Isaac let out a bitter laugh. "*No.* It's only me and my father. And he hates any recreational activity that has to do with water. The closest we ever get to it is whenever we go fishing. And we haven't done that since..."

"Since...?"

Isaac gulped, his voice a whisper. "Since my mom died."

He kept his head down, trying his best to fight his emotions.

Isaac didn't like to talk about his mother, let alone talk about her under these circumstances. She was his best friend, the person who taught him how to swim, the person who instilled in him a love for the ocean and waves. After she passed away, everything changed.

"It could be your mother," Alice said, her voice more factual than anything else. "She might be the reason why you're like this now."

"How so?"

Alice sighed and leaned against the table. "Magic is hereditary. If your father is human, there's a chance you inherited this from her. Since merfolks aren't native to this area, moving here might have delayed you coming to sense your magic, but you would always come to sense it."

"Couldn't it have waited a bit longer? Maybe while I was in college? Or an old man?"

She shook her head. "Under normal circumstances, you could have delayed it until you turned eighteen, but that would be it. Some people don't follow that rule, though. I came to sense magic when I was six and Xavier when he was eight, right?"

"Yes." He nodded. "I was eight when I turned for the first time. Not a fun time."

Isaac's eyes jumped between Alice and Xavier before focusing on him. "So, you have magic too?"

"Yes," Xavier said as he straightened his back, puffing out his chest. "I'm a shapeshifter."

"What does that mean?"

"I turn into a wolf."

"Ah." Isaac nodded. "So you're a werewolf?"

"No," Xavier said, almost in a growl. "I'm a shapeshifter."

"That's a common misconception he can't stand," Alice pointed out, giving Isaac a warning look. "He's a shapeshifter and I'm a witch. But that you already knew." She let out a nervous laugh. "I would ask how, but I have my suspicions."

The tone in her voice let Isaac know he should not pursue the topics at hand any further. He waited for any of them to say anything else, but Xavier continued to pace around the room while Alice tried to make sense of the mess that was on the table.

"So… what happens now?" Isaac asked.

"Well," Alice said, not turning away from her task, "since we can't ask your mother for help, we'll figure out your lineage in some other way."

"Can't you just do a spell or something to fix my problem?"

She shrugged, picking up a couple of flasks. "Spells are temporary. We need to figure out what lineage you belong to and then find a way to solve your problem."

"So you'll help me?" Isaac didn't expect to sound as hopeful as he did. If it wasn't for Xavier's dead stare, he would have attempted to hug Alice.

"After you read some books. I won't be figuring this out for you."

She dropped something on the table, wiped her hands on her dress, and disappeared to the back of the room, the shadows swallowing her. Isaac shifted on the couch, trying to find a comfortable position in which he could block Xavier from his view, but that was impossible.

"You're making me uncomfortable," he said, glaring at Xavier.

Xavier smiled. "Good. That means you won't make anything stupid."

"Like what?"

"I don't know. You tell me."

Unbelievable. This guy was unbelievable. First, he was nice to him when he was at swimming practice, then he tried to kill him, and now he was acting as if he was some sort of wanted criminal.

"Who's Ariah?"

Xavier stiffened. "No one you should concern yourself about," he said, rubbing the back of his neck and messing up his hair.

"Just so you know," Isaac said, raising his arms in defence, "I have no idea who she is."

Xavier nodded, studying Isaac for a bit longer. When Alice returned from the back of the room, he focused on her, raising an eyebrow.

"Won't your aunt notice those books are missing?" he asked, glancing at the thick books Alice carried in her arms.

"I can say I took them to do some further reading." She

gestured with her head to the table. "Can someone move these things? I need to put the books down."

Xavier swiftly moved all the flasks and vials out of the way, wiping the table with a piece of cloth. Alice dropped the books and took a deep breath, undoing her hair bun and redoing it. A couple of hairs escaped the elastic, so she put them behind her ears.

"Do I have to read all that?" Isaac asked, noticing a pile of one, two— he stopped counting after reaching four books. "That's a lot."

"It is." She glanced at him sideways. "For someone like you, that is."

It was unclear whether Alice was trying to offend Isaac, but if she was, then she had failed. He wasn't offended. Not at all.

"You probably couldn't do half of what I do," he said, leaning back on the couch. "I'm a great swimmer, okay? I don't need to read."

"Good, then." Alice closed one of the books, glancing at Xavier. He smiled at her. "Then that means that my job here is done. You can go back to your swimming team since being a great swimmer means you have all the answers to your problems."

"I didn't mean it like that." He rolled his eyes. "Do you take everything personally?"

She didn't answer. Alice dropped a thick book on Isaac's lap, her expression devoid of emotion. He bit his lower lip to prevent a yell from escaping. This book was thick *and* heavy.

"Read that," she said. "It's about merfolk lineage and how to identify it."

"Do I have to read it all?"

She grabbed another book from the table, glanced at some pages inside, and closed it, a cloud of dust escaping it.

"How old are these books?" Isaac asked.

"Older than all of our ages combined." She let the second book drop on top of the other one, and Isaac scrambled to prevent them from falling. "That one talks about merfolk abilities."

"Abilities?"

"It relates to how you can wield your magic," she clarified, picking one more book up. She pursed her lips, scanning the pages.

"What does that mean exactly?" Isaac turned to Xavier, hoping he could add some clarification.

He sighed. "Different magical orders have different ways to connect with magic. What you can do is different from what Alice and I can do. Besides that, different merfolk lineages have different abilities."

"Such as…?"

Alice dropped one more book on Isaac's lap. This time, he yelped. "That's your job to find out. You're the one interested, not us."

"Oh, I'm very interested," Xavier said, an amused smile taking over his features.

"Can you *stop* dropping books on my lap like that?" Isaac grabbed all the books and stood up. "It's kind of mean of you."

"Mean?" she said. "How about despicable? I'm sure that's what you heard about me, right? How despicable and cruel I am?"

He gulped, looking away from her. Alice placed one more book on top of the ones Isaac was carrying, wiping her hands on the side of her dress again, tarnishing its deep green with a muddy grey.

"Once you finish reading those books, come find me at the library so we can discuss your findings." She pointed an accusatory finger at him. "And no word about this to anyone. Not even your father. Not even your friends. Xavier and I are the *only* people you can discuss magic with until I say otherwise. Am I clear?"

"Yes." Isaac nodded. "I won't tell anyone."

"Good." She took a deep breath. "Xavier will take you home."

"I must stay with you at all times," Xavier said to Alice and pointed with his thumb at Isaac. "I'm *not* taking him home."

"You are taking him home." Alice crossed her arms. "He has centuries worth of grimoires with him, not to mention he almost died four hours ago. I don't trust him to be alone. He's not like us."

Isaac gulped. What did Alice mean by that? Had Isaac

almost died?

"Well, you can't go home alone, either," Xavier said, walking closer to her.

"I'll wait for you here." She glanced around the space, pursing her lips. "I don't want my aunt to suspect we were here, so there's a lot of cleaning to be done. Meet me back here. Then, you'll walk me home. Sounds better?"

Xavier bit the inside of his cheek, glancing between Isaac and Alice. He pinched the bridge of his nose and sighed. "Fine," he said. "But you can't leave this place without me. Are we clear?"

Alice nodded and Xavier looked at Isaac.

"Don't leave anything behind," he said, making his way to the door. "I'm sure you won't be returning here anytime soon."

"I'm not sure I'd like to return."

"Good." Xavier opened the door and gestured to Isaac to follow him. Before he exited, he glanced at Alice one more time. "I'll lock the doors. Call me if you need anything."

Alice didn't reply, already busy working on getting the room in better shape. Xavier closed the back door and the two left the flower shop, diving into the night's darkness.

Chapter Ten

IT HAD BEEN A week since Alice last spoke with Isaac. Despite seeing him at school, he never said a word to her. Sometimes, when no one was around, he would offer her a small smile or a shy hand wave, but when his lips parted for him to speak, no sound came out.

Alice had mixed feelings about it. As much as she was relieved she didn't have to interact with Isaac anymore, she was upset he hadn't even bothered to return her books. Those were heirlooms, grimoires that passed through several generations of witches and other magical beings within her family. Couldn't he, at least, acknowledge how important those books were to her? He might not like to read or study, but he could have some sort of consciousness. Still, this was exclusively her fault. She had chosen to trust the wrong people *again*, so she would have to deal with the consequences of her actions.

Hopefully, Xavier wouldn't give her too much of a hard time about it.

Not having to interact with Isaac meant she could focus entirely on the New Moon Ritual she would have to perform in a couple of days. In her spot at the library, Alice spent her afternoon reading her notes and other witches' retellings of their Rituals. They weren't always the same, but all had a similar pattern they followed that could be split into three phases: Ascension, Culmination and Descent. The Ascension and Descent were described similarly amongst the testimonials, but the Culmination differed among witches.

She would only know what her Culmination was after she went through it. That was *if* she went through it. So far, she had been unsuccessful with every New Moon Ritual she had performed. This time, she hoped it was different. Not only was she doing it in the forest, but after what had happened at the flower shop with Isaac, and considering her slight progress with light summoning, maybe her magical abilities had finally reawakened.

Alice knew her parents weren't pleased about her desire to leave this realm, but staying here hindered her magic. She didn't want to keep it hidden; she wanted to feel proud using it. She didn't want to be outcasted for it; she wanted to be celebrated for it. While she kept living here, she would have to hide her abilities and keep people at a distance.

Students around Alice started to whisper and giggle amongst themselves, shifting their focus from their notebooks and coloured pens to the library entrance. At first, she tried to ignore it, but eventually, her curiosity got the best of her.

Isaac walked through the different corridors of bookshelves, clearly lost. He glanced at every table and every face around him, looking for someone. He was looking for her, Alice realised when his eyes found her and relief washed over his face. His steps became quick and certain, his posture one of confidence. All around her, people shifted their attention from Isaac to Alice. Their whispers didn't subside, and their glares and stares towards Alice burned her skull causing her to lower her eyes to her book. She hated the attention.

Alice preferred the shadows.

"Mind if I joined you?" Isaac asked, grabbing the chair across from hers. She slowly looked up, not hiding her displeasure.

"Here to return the books I lent you?" she asked. "If you didn't intend on reading them, you could've said so."

"I read them all. I'm sorry for being such a slow reader. I'm not used to it, you know."

"It's not hard to believe that." She gestured to the chair across from her. "Have a seat. People are staring."

Isaac nodded and sat across from Alice. It surprised her that he didn't mind being seen with her here. These people would talk about their encounter, but maybe they would think it was a prank of sorts. After all, Isaac wasn't the kind of guy who went to the library just because. They'd make up stories about this and laugh behind her back while calling her names. She was already imagining it. It made her sick.

He opened his backpack and pulled out the stack of books she had lent him, and Alice sighed in relief. They were all in good condition and she noticed some colourful sticky notes coming from some of the pages. For someone who didn't know how to study, he did have a pretty good method for gathering information. Whether that information stayed in his brain was a different story.

"So, I have some questions. For instance," he opened one of the books and skimmed through the pages until he stopped, "in here, it says that I can identify my lineage through—"

People around them urged Isaac to hush, startling him. He looked around and then leaned closer to Alice, worried.

"Did I do something wrong?"

She nodded and whispered, "We're at a library. We're supposed to keep quiet and not talk. If we must talk, then we have to whisper, okay?"

Whether Isaac had heard what she had just said, Alice couldn't tell. He kept staring at her lips, parting his as if inviting her to kiss him. Then, he met her eyes, completely entranced by them. Isaac didn't look at her with disgust or fear. There was curiosity and care in the way he studied her features, as if he were admiring it.

She didn't like it. Alice didn't like how it made her heart jump faster in her chest, how it made her cheeks warmer.

"Stop staring," she whispered, and Isaac blinked slowly.

Alice returned to her studies as Isaac dealt with whatever thoughts were running through his mind. Even though witches couldn't read minds, they could see people's emotions in their auras, and she could tell he was embarrassed.

The golden smoke had returned in full force, twirling around Isaac with an excitement that hadn't been there when she found him at the party. In between its twirls, another lighter layer spun in the opposite direction, its shade spreading from blue and yellow to some hints of violet. Some witches' life work was tied to analysing these colours and tying them to emotions. The same colour could have different meanings, like yellow for instance. In some cases, it could represent happiness while in others it could be embarrassment. It was a hard field of study, and Alice had never bothered to dive deep into it.

Isaac cleared his throat and Alice focused her attention back on him, his aura fading from view.

"So, as I was saying," he whispered, "it says here I can identify my lineage through the colour of the scales on my tail."

"And have you done that already?" He shook his head and Alice narrowed her eyes at him. "Why not? Aren't you aware of the consequences of not using your magic? Isaac—"

"It's not that!" His eyes met hers as he pointed at the book. "My scales are not here."

"What do you mean they're not here?"

"Every active lineage here isn't an exact match to mine." He turned the book towards Alice. "Like, these are white but have golden hues, which aren't like mine. And these are what they call light white, which is a much more translucent shade than mine. It's not here."

"Maybe you're not seeing it correctly." As she glanced at the different illustrations on the page, she knew there was only one way to get this over with. "Are you free this evening?"

Isaac looked at her, confused, but merely nodded. "I was supposed to have practice, but our coach is sick and I still have a tail, so I'm free."

"Good." She closed the book, stood from her chair, and saved her belongings in her bag. "Meet me tonight by the local pool building entrance."

"Why?"

"Do you want to know your lineage or not?"

She pulled the books she had given Isaac close to her and carefully saved them inside her bag. They would be returned to their rightful home today.

"Of course I want to. But don't I need to swim for that?"

"How else am I supposed to see your scales?" she asked.

"You'll see my scales?" He stood from his chair, panicking. "You— How—"

Alice put her bag over her shoulder, grimacing at the weight. She wouldn't be able to study for the rest of her afternoon, and all this attention from strangers was making her uncomfortable.

"Bring your swimming gear," she said, trying to reassure him. "Leave the rest up to me."

"You have a tendency to ask me weird things, you know."

"You can refuse to accept what I'm offering you. It's your life, I'm not telling you how to live it. I'm simply presenting you with an opportunity that is good for you. You get to swim and we get to figure out what your lineage is once and for all. You don't want to keep your magic buried within you for too long again. You have to let it out every once in a while."

"Or else?" He raised an eyebrow at her.

He hadn't read any books on magic theory, had he? If he had, then it was clear to Alice that the information hadn't stayed in his brain. This would be a long and exhausting evening, but she wasn't one to give up that easily.

"Magic is like a second bloodstream. Do you know what happens when human veins get clogged because the blood is not circulating?" She focused on him. "In the worst-case scenario, it can lead to death. And you've been close to it, Isaac. I don't want you to go there again. I *especially* don't want to have to bring you back."

She sighed and fixed the bag strap on her shoulder, watching as he put the pieces together. Alice wanted him to be scared. Not using one's magic was dangerous and he had experienced first-hand the side effects of it.

For someone Alice didn't know that well, she sure cared a lot about him, and she didn't love that about herself. Hopefully, this wouldn't last much longer. They didn't have much in common besides being magical beings.

But even then, they belonged to entirely different orders.

Chapter Eleven

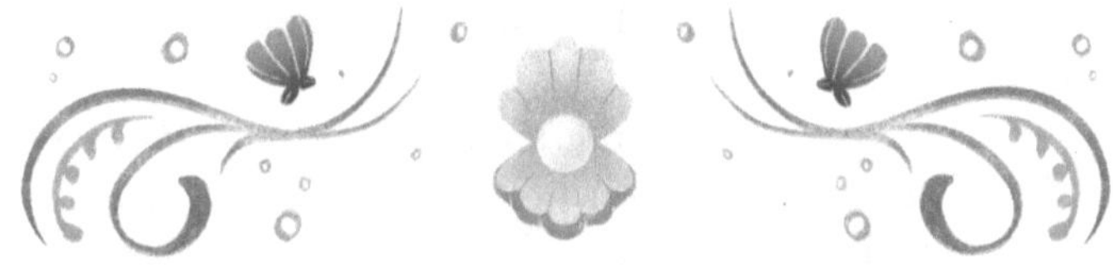

WHEN ISAAC GOT TO the local pool building, he found it drowning in darkness. As he peeked through the glass double doors, the safety lights on the walls painted the space in a faint green, preventing him from making out any details inside beyond a few steps. He glanced at his watch, fixing his swimming gear bag on his shoulder. Although the evening wasn't particularly cold, whenever a soft breeze brushed his skin, he couldn't help but shiver.

Alice arrived right on time. Isaac spotted her walking from the main street at a slow pace, keeping her eyes on the trees and streetlights nearby, a kind smile on her lips. Even though it was late and most people were asleep by now, Alice was comfortable in the darkness around her, fully awake, a certain glow emanating from her. She was probably in her element tonight.

Isaac couldn't help but smile at that thought.

"You're here early," she said as she climbed the stairs towards him, not smiling.

"Well," he shoved his hands in the pockets of his pants, "I drove here. I also didn't want to be late. I know you're punctual, so I wanted to be here when you arrived."

"That's smart." She nodded and saved her headphones inside her backpack. She stepped closer to the entrance door and narrowed her eyes, glancing inside. "Did you see anyone walk by?"

"No." He shook his head. "Most people don't come this way at night and, if I'm correct, the last practice session ended three hours ago."

"Good." She lowered herself, inspecting the door lock. "I think sneaking in will be easy."

Isaac panicked.

"Sneaking in?" He gulped. "I thought this was merely a meeting point! You can't be serious."

"*Oh*, I am." She smiled at him, delighted. "Step back for a bit. I need space to work. Make yourself useful and be on the lookout."

"Shouldn't your shapeshifter friend be on the lookout instead?" Isaac mumbled under his breath.

He crossed his arms, disappointed. Alice was always giving him orders, and he was growing sick of it. What made her think she could boss him around?

"Xavier's not coming." She opened her backpack, picking up two small thin pieces of metal. "He doesn't know I'm here."

"Why not?"

Alice stared at Isaac as if the answer to his question was obvious. When he didn't answer, she turned to the door. "He'd talk me out of it. He most likely would tell my parents about it, which I want to avoid at all costs."

"Are your parents against you leaving the house at night alone?"

"No." She rolled her shoulders back and stretched her neck, focusing on the door lock opening. "They simply don't want me to hang out with anyone. Let alone someone they don't know."

"Is that why you don't have many friends?"

That was a dumb question and Isaac knew it. The reason why Alice didn't have any friends wasn't because of her parents. It was because no one wanted to be friends with her. Isaac used to include himself in that group of people, but now, he didn't mind the time he spent with her. Despite Alice constantly pushing him away, he was almost certain she was starting to warm up to him.

"Try focusing on the sounds around us." She pushed the two thin pieces into the door lock, her movements precise and confident. Was this her first time breaking into a place? Isaac was afraid to know.

"Why the sounds? How about the streets I can see?"

"Merfolk have a heightened sense of hearing. Only underwater can you see in the dark. You'll locate people faster if you focus on the sounds around us."

"Fine."

He didn't focus on the sounds, not for long, at least. Whenever he tried to, the *click-clack* of Alice's lockpicking overwhelmed his senses. It was too loud, too raspy against his ears.

Isaac stared at the road across from them, spotting the tall trees that shielded the road from the wilderness of the forest. This town was so different from where he had grown up as a kid. Here, no matter where he glanced, the forest prevented his escape—it blocked out everything beyond it. He missed the freedom of being near the sea. One short car ride in the backseat of his father's car and he was near the beach, ready for a swim.

Here, everything constrained him into one location, suffocated him beyond understanding. The trees never relented their growth, never stopped being imposing, except for that *one* spot in the forest where nothing grew. Isaac had been there once during a bonfire party Liam threw near the lake. He marvelled at the large opening to the sky, displaying the stars as bright dots in the distance. He knew the rumours associated with such place—rumours of its creation—but in there, he could *breathe.*

Isaac heard it first, in the rustling of leaves from one of the bushes across from him. His heart jumped in his chest as he narrowed his eyes on the shaking low branches, trying to spot what was beyond them.

"Alice?" he called, his voice coated with worry, too loud for his taste. "I think someone's here."

In one swift movement, she was next to him, scanning their surroundings. He pointed to the location across from them, glancing at her. Much like him, she narrowed her eyes there and as she was about to take a step forward, he held her wrist, earning a glare from her.

"What do you think you're doing?" he said. "Are you planning on heading there alone? Seriously?"

"Well, yes," she whispered. "It could be a threat."

"Exactly! Do you even watch horror movies? Do you know what happens to the characters that go after the threat? Do you, Alice?"

The rustling increased and Isaac's eyes shot to its location. He refused to let go of Alice.

"Are you afraid I might die or are you afraid you might have to stay here alone?" she asked, her voice coated with amusement.

"Is it weird if I say both?"

"No," she replied. He dared a glance at her, catching a brief smile on her face before it faded.

Isaac followed her line of sight, finding an animal standing in the middle of the street. Isaac's first thought was that it was a huge cat, but it was too big for that. Its ears had small black tufts, its beige fur covered in small dark spots that spread through its torso and legs. In the low light of the streets, its eyes glowed in an unnatural manner, the colour shifting from a green to a momentary golden. If Isaac had blinked, he would have missed it.

"That's a lynx," Alice said, keeping her eyes locked on the creature. "Just ignore it. It's nothing to worry about."

Alice let loose from Isaac's grip and returned to work on getting the door unlocked. Isaac focused on the lynx. Its eyes buried into him, entrancing him in such a way that Isaac found himself unable to move, even if everything in his body wanted him to run.

"Will you take much longer?" He shifted his swimming gear bag to stand in front of his body when the lynx stepped closer. "The lynx is *still* there."

"It will go away eventually," she said. "And I'm almost… Done!"

Isaac sighed and turned around to find Alice pushing the door open, gesturing to him to follow her inside. Once he was in the building, he looked over his shoulder to find the lynx returning to the woods, disappearing in between the low vegetation. Even though Isaac should feel relieved, his heart remained on edge and his senses had never been more alert.

"Try not to touch many things," Alice said, waking Isaac from his thoughts. "Now, go get changed. I'll meet you at the pool."

After closing the door behind her, Alice saved her belongings in her backpack, and put it over her shoulder, raising an eyebrow when she noticed Isaac hadn't moved.

"Is there a problem?" She looked over her shoulder. "The lynx is gone. And even if it wasn't, I doubt it'd join us in the building, so relax. Where's the pool? Is it that way?"

Alice was distracted reading the information signs that she missed Isaac taking a step towards her.

"Actually," he said, "there is a problem."

"What is it?" She crossed her arms, looking sideways at him.

"I don't like when you boss me around."

"I'm not bossing you around."

Isaac walked towards Alice, stopping when he was close enough to see her features clearly. It wasn't just the darkness of her eyes that was breathtaking. It was the way her mouth always curved downwards even when relaxed, as if she had a permanent frown on her face. Isaac wanted to wipe it away, replace it with a smile that was just as endearing on her as any frown. He noticed a small scar on her left eyebrow that made it look slightly uneven near the bridge of her nose. What was the story behind that?

"Maybe…" She bit her lip, staring at his mouth briefly. She cleared her throat and took a step back, avoiding his gaze. "Maybe, I'm not thinking enough about my choice of words. How about you get changed while I make my way to the pool? Does that sound better, *Isaac*?"

"Much better." He smiled at her before walking to the changing rooms and pointed in the opposite direction. "I'll see you at the pool. It's that way."

It didn't take long for Isaac to get changed. Whether it was the excitement to get back into the water or his fear of being alone while trespassing, he couldn't tell, but in a matter of minutes, he was in the pool area. Alice sat at one of the benches the furthest away from the pool, gripping a book so tightly, her knuckles were practically white.

She didn't lift her eyes when Isaac approached, focusing on

the water's surface as if she were in a trance. He placed his bag next to her with his towel on top and glanced at the book in her hands. It was about merfolk, specifically, the different lineages. Eventually, she blinked and turned to look at him, her eyes tracing his naked torso before finding his smile.

Even under the dimmed light, Isaac didn't miss the pink shade blotting her cheeks as she buried her nose into the book pages.

"Whenever you feel ready," she said. "We can stay for as long as you'd like."

Isaac stretched and warmed up. He paced around the pool for a while, his hands behind his back, a bittersweet smile on his lips. All his life, he had loved swimming. When he lived with his parents in a small coastal town, nothing delighted him more than going to the beach and following the waves, allowing them to carry his small body to the shore, to the comfort of his mother's embrace. He always trusted the sea and he always believed their lives were somehow connected.

After his mother passed away, he moved away with his father to this town, and he was disappointed by the lack of sea. He could still swim, so he kept doing it, but it wasn't quite the same. The beach was freeing. Within a pool, he always had constraints. Ever since moving here, he learned to love swimming against the clock. If he couldn't be free in the water, then he would thrive in its constraints.

Tonight, the pool wasn't as inviting as usual. Whenever he glanced at his reflection on the water's surface, he remembered the day it all changed. He was glad everything happened when he was alone at the pool and no one saw the strange shape he turned into. Isaac didn't want this. His life was going well a couple of weeks ago. Why couldn't it have stayed that way?

He glanced across the pool to where Alice was focused on the book. Although she had told him they could stay here all night, he wasn't willing to stay here forever.

Isaac briefly touched the water with the tip of his fingers, and a wave of warmth took over his body. He dipped his entire hand, and where the water touched his skin, small pearlescent scales appeared, reflecting the low light in the pool area.

When he removed his hand from the water, the scales shrunk

until they were barely visible. Isaac glanced at his legs. Once they were underwater, they would be replaced with a tail. The more he delayed this, the harder it would be. Isaac couldn't avoid this forever—it would only delay his return to his ordinary life.

He jumped into the pool, allowing the water to tame his body. He was *home*. The urgency in his heart subsided as he took his first deep breath underwater, opening his eyes. The world was different here. It was secluded, hidden, safer. It was quiet, too.

Instead of returning to the surface, Isaac reached the bottom of the pool and swam for a while, never slowing down. Oh, how he had missed this. He wasn't sure if Alice could hear him laughing underwater, but he missed this happiness that burst through his chest, that prevented his legs from keeping still. *Tail*, he corrected himself. Now, he had a tail, and swimming had never been easier. The water ran smoothly over his body, and his movements were no longer slowed down by friction. It was easy.

When he decided he had gotten enough of a swim for the time being, Isaac returned to the surface. He sat by the edge of the pool closest to Alice, focusing on the scales of his tail that matched the ones on his elbows and knuckles. Isaac wasn't sure how long he had until they disappeared, so he called Alice's name softly.

"What is it?" she asked, turning to look at him.

Isaac lifted his tail and turned to rest it on the pool's edge. Alice's eyes widened.

She closed the book and placed it on the bench, walking towards him. He wished he could photograph the amazement and delight in her expression. Although he felt like someone who was anything but normal, she wasn't scared or repelled by him. If having a tail meant she would look at Isaac with such wonder and amazement, then he wouldn't be so upset by his circumstances anymore.

"It's pretty," she said, smiling at him. "How do you feel?"

When she smiled this genuinely, he was at a loss for words.

"Surprisingly okay with everything." Isaac cleared his throat, focusing on the shimmering scales. "What colour do you think they are?"

Alice leaned closer. "I'm not entirely sure. I'll go get the book."

When she returned, Alice flipped through several pages, her eyes skimming the contents on it. She gulped and took cautious steps closer to Isaac, keeping a safe distance from the pool's edge. After balancing the book on one hand, Alice lowered herself next to Isaac's tail and placed an open hand above it. Although she wasn't touching his tail, a wave of warmth spread through it, at first soft, then unbearably hot. He flinched and Alice's eyes shot at him in concern before she lowered her hand, defeated.

"I thought I could summon some light." She stood and avoided looking at Isaac, her cheeks flushed in embarrassment. "I'll go grab a flashlight, hold on."

"You can summon light?"

"In theory." She opened her bag and rummaged through its contents as the book rested under her arm. "I'm lacking in many departments, and light summoning happens to be one of them."

"What else can you do? Besides summoning light."

She pulled a flashlight from her bag and joined Isaac again, shining the light on his tail. This wasn't as pretty as having her light up his scales with her bare hands, but the effect was just as nice. His scales reflected the light in a satin-like way, shifting in hues of white and a shimmering blue, but never losing their opaqueness.

"They're so pretty," Alice whispered to herself. "I'm a bit jealous."

He laughed and she glanced at him, trying to hide her smile. She was allowed to smile and compliment his scales. Knowing they were pretty and lovely to Alice made it easier for Isaac to accept them, to accept himself.

"What lineage am I from?" he asked.

"Right." Alice nodded to herself and opened the book again, her eyes jumping between the page and his illuminated scales. She pursed her lips. "I think you're right. Your scales are not an exact match to any of these."

"What does that mean?"

"I don't know." She closed the book, deep in thought. "These are all the active merfolk lineages currently living in the Human Realm. If your scales are not here, it's either because you are from Otherworld or it is believed that your lineage is no longer active here. And both options would be unlikely since there are records of every crossing to and from this realm. They would know about you and your lineage. Something doesn't add up."

Alice turned off the flashlight while her eyes remained on Isaac's tail, her expression grim. As much as he wanted to know what else she was thinking, he was too afraid to ask. This was the one time in his life Isaac didn't want to be wrong about something. After all, not knowing his lineage complicated things. How was Alice supposed to help him if they couldn't identify it? This was a matter that could not be solved by reading books and gathering information that way.

"We have to ask someone about it," he said. "My father—"

"We're not getting anyone else involved." Alice shook her head. "We'll figure it out. I'll look at other books and try to find your lineage in older versions. I'm sure we have those around."

"And when you don't find anything?" She glared at him, but that didn't stop Isaac from speaking his mind. "There's a chance that might happen. Maybe Xavier knows."

"Xavier doesn't care."

"He seemed pretty interested in knowing who I was." Isaac grimaced at the thought. That night at the flower shop wasn't his fondest memory of Xavier, and part of him wanted to forget it had happened.

"He only cares about you because he thinks you were hired to kill me." Alice's eyes met his, but he didn't know how to follow that up. Did Xavier really think he was trying to kill Alice? Why? "We should get going. We've done what we wanted to do. There's no need to stay any longer."

"I'll swim for a bit longer," he said, already diving back into the water.

"Ten minutes and then I'm leaving."

He smiled and dove to the bottom of the pool, making a few laps under the surface, trying to go faster with each stroke. Isaac wasn't sure how long he would stay without swimming again, so he would make these ten minutes worth it.

His peace was interrupted first by a small vibration in his ears and then by a loud splash above him. When he looked up, Alice's body was sinking to the bottom as her arms stretched up, trying to cling onto something Isaac couldn't see. Panic seeped into her features and her mouth opened in a silent scream.

Chapter Twelve

ALICE WAS TEN WHEN it happened.

Even before her abilities manifested, she was already considered an outsider. Alice never understood why; she was no different from the others. Granted, she had a fascination with insects and spent the majority of her free time roaming at the forest's edge, but lots of people did that. She wasn't unique, just different.

Being different always scared others, always pushed them away. Not Ariah, though.

Ariah was a friend.

Much like Alice, she loved the moon. The two used to spend their evenings in Alice's backyard, staring at the starry sky, admiring it. Their conversations were rarely about school or whatever gossip seemed to fill their classmates' heads. They spoke of nature, of animals and their beauty, of flowers and their charm, of their surroundings and its mystery.

For the first time since Alice's abilities manifested, she was comfortable. She could hide it like her parents, and she could have friends. She could be normal. She didn't have to be different.

"We should go and have a picnic by the lake," Ariah suggested, her golden-brown curls stuck in a bun above her head as she clutched her necklace's pendant. "It could be fun. I heard the moon is pretty from there."

"It is," Alice confirmed with a firm nod. "I could take us there. We wouldn't have to walk far."

Alice had been in the forest enough times that she no longer got scared or lost within its tall trees and low vegetation. She knew which paths to take, which animals to avoid. She'd be able to take them to and from the lake safely. A picnic under a full moon was a wonderful idea, and it filled Alice's soul with excitement. Ariah seemed just as thrilled as they planned their outing together for the remainder of the afternoon, sharing ideas in between giggles and wide eyes, writing them down in Ariah's small notebook so they wouldn't forget any of it. Alice couldn't help but think how lucky she was that she had found a friend like Ariah.

Life could not get any better than this.

It could only get worse.

Since the full moon was happening in a few days, they decided to go on the day the moon's brightness was higher. Alice could barely contain her excitement about it. Her parents, however, weren't as happy. They were worried, concerned about Alice and Ariah's safety. The forest wasn't a dangerous place for a witch, but it was a dubious spot for two ten-year-olds to explore alone in the afternoon and evening. Although they lived in a peaceful and quiet small town, danger lingered in every unturned corner.

"She might not want to hang out with me anymore if I say no now," Alice had said to her parents after hearing their arguments as to why she shouldn't go. "But if things get bad, I can protect Ariah. I can summon light, remember? And I mastered fire a couple of days ago. We'll be safe. I promise."

Following their plan, Alice spent the morning of the picnic preparing homemade cookies with her mother's help, who guided Alice through each step of the recipes with care and delight. Since they would meet at her home in the late afternoon before heading out, Alice spent the rest of her time trying to decide what to wear.

When entering a forest, no matter the circumstances, a witch should always wear her best outfit or ceremonial clothing. Forests were sacred to witches, places where offerings were made, where sacrifices and important rituals were performed. Alice never glimpsed at them through a lens of marvelousness and wild nature. To her, a forest was a pillar to her life, an invitation to what she could become.

They headed to the forest earlier than expected. Before leaving her home, Alice's parents hugged her tightly, kissing her forehead softly.

"Have fun!" they said, but she couldn't ignore the worry in their eyes or

the shakiness in their voice.

"I'll be fine," Alice reassured them, slightly offended they didn't trust her to protect herself and Ariah. "We'll be back before you know it."

As soon as Alice left her home, the warm breeze kissed her skin, wrapping around her like a heavy blanket. After a few steps, the back of her dress stuck to her skin as a layer of sheen greeted Ariah's sharp cheekbones and forehead. Still, none of them gave up over the hot weather and they kept walking towards the lake side by side. They stopped occasionally to admire the top of the trees or hear the birds chirping. Once they got to the edge of the lake, Ariah laid their picnic blanket where they spread their small feast of delicious food and sat opposite each other to savour it.

They chatted as they enjoyed each other's company, sometimes falling onto the blanket as they tried to calm down from laughing at each other's jokes. Alice wanted to cherish this moment forever, she wanted to keep this tucked inside her heart for the rest of her life. Ariah was her only friend, but she would be in Alice's life for a long time, she was sure of that.

"We should do this again next full moon," Alice said as they lay side by side, watching the skies shift to hues of bright orange and purple. "We could bring other snacks or even board games to play while we wait."

It was almost time for the big moment, and Alice had already spotted the round bright sphere in the sky that would keep them company once the sun was down. She closed her eyes and smiled, relaxing as the lingering light bid her goodbye, promising to meet her again the next day.

"That won't happen," Ariah said, her tone final.

"Why not?" Alice couldn't hide the disappointment from her voice. Wasn't Ariah having fun?

Her friend didn't answer. Alice held her breath, waiting for a response, but all she noticed was the coldness growing next to her. Alice opened her eyes and sat on the blanket, searching for Ariah on it. She wasn't there. Behind her, she heard the sharpening of a blade and a cackling that raised the hairs from the back of her neck. She slowly turned.

"Well, well, well," an old man said, his teeth sharp as the claws of a cat, "if it isn't little Alice. Did you get lost in the woods?"

Alice fumbled backwards, her eyes never leaving the man. He held a long blade, the size of her forearm, and wore a red cloak over a black garment.

"Where's Ariah?" Alice mustered the courage to ask. "What did you do to my friend?"

The man raised an eyebrow. "Friend?" He scoffed. "Ariah's not your friend. I guess she did a better job than I anticipated."

The man stepped aside and behind him, a woman with bright fiery-red hair stood with her arm wrapped around a girl with curly golden-brown hair, clutching the pendant of her necklace. Ariah. *The hatred was rooted so deep within her that Alice had to look away.*

"You're a witch,*" Ariah said, her voice carrying so much revulsion that the air was knocked out of Alice's lungs. No, this couldn't be happening. There had to be a misunderstanding.*

"I'm not who you think I am," Alice said, slowly increasing the distance between them. "I'm not a witch."

"She's lying," Ariah said. Alice had never heard her so angry, so mad. "She has the pulse."

"I don't." Alice shook her head. "I don't know what that is!"

She knew, though. And she had it. Every magical being had a different pulse that distinguished them from humans. It was a result of their magicstream. How did Ariah know that?

Alice focused on the space around Ariah, trying to locate her aura. She could barely trace its shape with her eyes for the silver was so light, so weak, it got lost in the darkness that had fallen around them.

Something sharp hit Alice's side, causing her to fall sideways. She hit her head on the muddy ground below her, and her vision spun. Alice briefly closed her eyes, trying to regain her composure.

"Who are you?" she asked with a trembling voice.

"Isn't it obvious by now?" the man spoke again. "You beasts are really dense, aren't you? Finish her."

"Me?" Ariah asked with wide eyes. "I thought you'd be the one doing it."

"Your initiation is only complete once she's gone," the man said. "Get the job done. Leave no trace behind."

"What about her parents?" Ariah continued. "They'll notice she's gone."

"We'll take care of them later, Ariah," the woman said in a light voice. "Now, finish the job. The more we stay here, the worse it is for us. I want to get this done by tonight. And that includes dealing with her family. Why are there so many of them?"

"I'm not a witch," Alice said. Slowly, she stood, shaking her head uncontrollably. "You're wrong."

Alice had read the stories about Magic Hunters, but she always thought they were cautionary tales to keep magical beings in line, to prevent them from using their abilities for nefarious reasons or getting themselves discovered.

They were real. They were on the hunt.

She was the prey.

Alice turned around and started to run.

"Get her!" the man screamed, causing a couple of nearby birds to caw and take flight.

She looked over her shoulder, the picnic blanket and basket becoming smaller in the distance before disappearing into the forest's darkness. When Alice focused ahead, she barely had time to register the woman in front of her, and she only stopped when she bumped into her.

"Going somewhere, are you?" the woman said, clawing at her shoulder. "I don't think so. Ariah? I have her now."

"Grab her hands," Ariah said, appearing in front of Alice. "We don't want her to summon magic."

"Do you think she would be dumb enough to do that?"

"She was dumb enough to befriend me," Ariah said, her eyes going over Alice's face. She looked like a ghost of herself. "I wouldn't put it past her to be dumb enough to summon magic here."

"I'm not—"

Ariah punched Alice's stomach before grabbing her shoulder and pushing her arms behind her back, moving Alice forward towards the picnic blanket and the lake.

"You don't have to do this," Alice said, trying to escape Ariah's grip on her. But Ariah was taller and stronger, and Alice didn't know how to fight. "I won't tell anyone, I promise. Please, Ariah. Please.*"*

"Will you shut up?" Ariah only squeezed her wrists closer together. "I'm tired of hearing you babble over and over. You're so *annoying, you know that."*

Alice wasn't going to cry. She would not give them the satisfaction of seeing her with watery eyes or even begging for their mercy. They would not give it to her. But the level of Ariah's betrayal, the sheer level of deception she had put Alice through, was enough to break her soul, to crush her into a million pieces.

She thought she had found a friend. She thought Ariah understood her. She thought they would be in each other's lives forever.

They stopped at the edge of the lake. Alice glanced at the water's surface, seeing her black hair all over the place, her eyes tinged with panic. She tried to break free again, tried to find a way to escape. Ariah's grip increased again. Something crushed on Alice's wrist and she screamed at the throbbing pain bursting from there.

"Careful, Ariah," the man said, circling them. "We don't want to draw unwanted attention."

"I know!" Ariah glared at him. "I know what I'm doing."

Alice shook her head, her breathing growing frail. Had she been foolish enough to so easily fall into this trap? Had she been so desperate for a sense of validation, for a sense of belonging that she trusted the only person who ever offered her that?

"May you never reincarnate in this realm or any other," Ariah whispered in her ear. "May your lineage die with you, never to be reborn again."

She pushed Alice into the lake. The impact pulsed through her body, a wave of electricity crashing through every part of her. Her body hurt. Her mind went blank. Alice turned around, trying to keep afloat.

"Help!" she screamed as her arms worked tirelessly. "I can't swim."

"Oh." The woman pouted mockingly at Alice. "The poor witch can't swim. That should make for a faster death."

"Please." The water pulled her down and some of it slipped into Alice's mouth. She coughed. "Please! I can't swim."

They laughed and turned around, leaving her alone.

"Make sure she doesn't come back," the man said, patting Ariah's shoulder with a proud smile. "Well done."

"Help me," she said to Ariah when their eyes met. "Please, Ariah. Please."

Nothing. *No matter how much Alice screamed, how much she begged, Ariah didn't move. She stared straight ahead to where Alice was, but her mind was elsewhere.*

"Please," Alice said, her cheeks warm with tears. "Please, Ariah."

Ariah gulped and closed her eyes. The pain in Alice's wrists was too unbearable, but she reached for the nearest tree roots to find something to hold onto, but they were too weak, too slippery.

No matter how hard she tried, Alice was always back in the same place. Under the surface.

She didn't know how long she fought to keep afloat before she allowed the water to envelop her softly, to drown her in its embrace. Alice closed her eyes and pictured what she loved the most. Her parents. Her cat. Her lessons with Aunt Vi. Her book of shadows with diagrams of the moon phases and so many potions and spells she'd have to get a new one for the next ritual.

That wasn't happening anymore, was it? This was it.

You are destined for great things, Alice. *She smiled at the comfort of her mother's voice. Maybe this was the great thing she was destined for.*

She knew the myths of witches who became nymphs. Maybe she was meant to be a forest nymph and ward off the evil that lived within it. That way, she would still be able to see her parents, right?

We'll take care of them, Ariah. *The woman's voice returned to Alice and she opened her eyes, finding the wobbly shape of the bright moon shining beyond the lake's surface.*

No. *No one would hurt her parents. If they were thinking this was the end of Alice, if they thought this was how they could get rid of her family and lineage, they were wrong. They were right about something. Alice was a witch.*

But she wasn't dumb.

Warmth shadowed her, an overwhelming sensation that she couldn't properly contain. She screamed as loud as she could underwater, ignoring the pain in her wrists and the way her lungs begged her for air, and lunged towards the surface.

Before she could stop herself, she was drowning in light.

When she took a deep breath, she regained consciousness. This time, she wasn't swimming back to the shore, unsure of what had happened, only to find blue flames burning the trees all around her. This time, someone held her in their arms, soothing her with a low chant.

"You're okay. It's okay. I've got you. You're safe," Isaac whispered, his breathing brushing against her cheek. "Take a deep breath. Look at me. Alice, look at me."

He tightened his grip around her, and she coughed, turning to face him. Isaac's green eyes glanced gently over her features with concern and worry.

"I've got you," he whispered again, meeting her eyes. "Are you okay?"

Was she okay? She couldn't tell. Her memory was so vivid as if just a few moments ago, she was back in that lake, the warmth and chaos of the flames still lingering on her skin.

"I'm fine," she said, resting her hands on his shoulders. They were sturdier than she expected. "I fell and I can't swim..."

Her head was throbbing with convoluted thoughts as she tried to remember what had happened. Had she fallen into the pool? She had been so careful to keep her distance from its edge—

"Alice," Isaac called her name softly, moving the hair away

from her eyes and forcing her to look at him. "I saw you. As a child. When I grabbed you, I saw you in a lake. But then, you started to glow in my arms, and I was back here. But that's not the weirdest part." At the incredulousness of his expression and confusion of hers, Isaac added, "My tail is gone."

* * *

"It's here," Alice said, her voice foreign to her.

She had barely said a word to Isaac after they left the local pool building, unsure of what was appropriate. *I'm sorry for almost dying in front of you* didn't seem appropriate, but what she despised the most was that Isaac had seen it. He had seen it all.

Alice hated it. Hated that now he knew more about her than she ever intended, that he would probably use this against her, that he probably looked at her as the despicable monster that she was. It wouldn't surprise her if he never spoke to her again. Maybe it was for the best if they ended whatever this was here.

Isaac stopped his car in front of Alice's front gate, turning off the engine. The lights inside the car turned on and she glanced at the familiar building, her heart relaxing in her chest. Nothing would ever feel quite as safe as her home.

"Here." Isaac reached for something in the backseat of his car and extended Alice a grey hoodie. "Wear this."

"I don't need that." She threw the hoodie towards him. "I'm sorry about the car seat. Thanks for driving me home."

"I insist." Isaac grabbed her hand softly and placed the hoodie on it again, offering her a small smile. "I seriously would hate it if you got sick."

Alice stared down at the hoodie, recognising the school's logo on it. She didn't want this. She didn't want his hoodie. This should be it. Once she stepped out of this car, they should go back to being strangers, never to speak to each other again. Alice was sure Isaac would find another solution to his problem. Maybe he would find someone else who was better than her and who could actually summon magic, someone who hadn't burned part of a forest to the ground. Anyone else was better than her to deal with this.

She opened the car door and stepped outside, dropping the

hoodie in the car seat.

"Have a safe drive home," she said. "I'll text you if I find anything."

He nodded, and she avoided his worried gaze. She wouldn't find anything because she wouldn't look for anything. Alice would not text Isaac again, not after what had happened. This was the end, and she didn't regret ending it like this. It was for the better.

Alice closed the door and adjusted her wet hair over her shoulder, the water dripping to her long-sleeve shirt that stuck to her body, making the night breeze ten times colder. She put her backpack over her other shoulder and hugged herself to try and keep warm. As she studied her house's front porch, she decided it would be safer to get inside through her bedroom balcony. She wanted to avoid questions, and considering her appearance right now, if her parents saw her, they would not stop until they got to the bottom of what had happened.

The car door opened and Alice looked over her shoulder, her eyes following Isaac as he walked closer to her, clutching his hoodie in one hand. She rolled her eyes and dropped her backpack in front of her feet, crossing her arms.

"How many times do I have to say that I don't—"

She didn't finish her thought. Isaac stepped closer to her, and carefully placed the hoodie over her head, pulling it down until her head was once again greeted by the cold of the night. He put the hood over her head, his eyes tracing her features carefully, his mouth in a thin line. His hand brushed against her cheek as he moved the hair away from her face, and Alice's heart jumped in her chest.

"You can keep it," he said, gesturing to the hoodie. "I have another one of those at home. And you don't have to act tough."

"I'm not acting tough," she said between gritted teeth. "I'm *fine*."

Except, Alice wasn't fine, but she would never admit it out loud to Isaac. He was the last person she would ever admit it to. She wanted to move her arms to take off his hoodie, but instead, she found herself dressing the hoodie until her hands peeked at the end of the sleeves.

Isaac offered her a crooked smile as Alice shoved her hands

in the front pocket of the hoodie, her feet growing roots where she was standing. Isaac seemed to do the same as he refused to move, refused to look away from her. Even when she glanced at him through narrowed eyes, he didn't seem bothered. His worry towards her was both unexpected and uncomfortable. Alice wasn't used to it.

"Stop staring," she said and grabbed her backpack. "And go home. It's quite late."

"Okay." He nodded. "Text me once you're home?"

She sighed. "I'm home, Isaac. But if it makes you more comfortable, text me once you're home."

"I will." He waved at her. "Goodnight, Alice."

She crossed her front gate and walked to the back of the house, all under the comfort of Isaac's hoodie and the silence of the night. Alice climbed the tree next to her balcony, her heavy clothes making every movement harder. She gripped the tall branches one after the other, and once she was high enough, she jumped to her balcony, landing sloppily on it. Even though this was a routine she was used to, tonight, she was more tired than usual.

As soon as she unlocked her balcony door, she slipped into her bedroom and turned on the lights. She didn't bother to pet Whiskers and instead went straight to her bathroom to take a warm shower and change into her comfortable pyjamas. Once she returned to bed, she grabbed her phone to find a text from Isaac letting her know he was home.

Alice didn't reply. She didn't even open the notification. Alice dropped her phone on her bedside table and closed her eyes, trying to fall asleep, only to dream about flames and forests, and the lynx staring back at her as she heard her younger self crying and screaming for help.

Chapter Thirteen

ISAAC'S HEAD STILL HURT when he woke up in his bed the next morning. He had spent most of the past hours awake, trying to piece together what happened last night. Whenever Isaac attempted to close his eyes, he was back at the pool with Alice. The worry and panic in her features as she slowly sunk to the bottom were hard to forget.

The weirdest part was everything that happened after he grabbed her. For a while, he wasn't in the pool; Isaac was in the middle of the forest witnessing a scene he could not stop, could not interfere. It was as if a movie was playing all around him, the actors set on saying their lines and performing their parts. Even if he screamed, even if he moved, that didn't change the outcome.

It was exhausting to only think about it. Isaac could not even begin to fathom what Alice had gone through. She barely said a word to him after they left the pool, and while he drove her home, Isaac wasn't sure how to bring it up. Should he even bring this up? How could he talk about something he knew nothing about and yet could feel was important to her?

He rubbed his eyes, trying to shake off the dread slowly

consuming him. Isaac would eventually figure it out. There was no other way around it.

As soon as he heard movement outside of his bedroom, Isaac got up and left his room to find his father preparing breakfast in the kitchen. He approached slowly, unsure of what to say to him.

As much as Isaac had promised Alice and Xavier that he wouldn't mention anything to his father, something within him told him that he should. His father was the person who had known his mother the longest, and he might be the only person to have some answers about all of Isaac's predicaments. If Alice's theory was correct, then Isaac's mother had been a merfolk too. It was impossible for his father to not know that about her.

"Good morning," his father said. "Slept well?"

Isaac yawned and collapsed on one of the kitchen stools, lowering his head to the counter. "Not really."

"Stayed up reading?"

Isaac chuckled. "No. I guess I had nightmares."

His father hummed and placed a mug of warm milk in front of Isaac as two slices of bread jumped from the toaster. "Are you sure it was nightmares?" he asked. "Or was it the party you went to last night?"

Isaac didn't lift his eyes. He reached for the mug, its warmth a welcoming sensation against his skin as he held it in his hands.

"I didn't go to a party," Isaac mumbled under his breath. He watched as his father spread butter on his toast unsure of what to say. "I agreed to meet with someone at night, and that's why I came home late. And then, I couldn't sleep."

"Was it worth it, at least?" He couldn't ignore the coldness in his father's voice. "Why didn't you tell me where you were going in the first place? Especially when you only got home at four in the morning. *Four*, Isaac. This isn't like you."

"I know." Isaac rubbed the back of his neck, staring at the inside of his mug. "But I had to—"

"I heard it loud and clear the first time, son." His father lowered the butterknife onto the counter and stared at Isaac. "I'm worried about you, and I can't help you if you don't tell me what's going on. First, you started skipping swimming practice, now you're breaking my rules and not respecting curfew. Not to mention that according to your teachers, your grades aren't getting any better since our last conversation. I don't want to stop you from experiencing the things you should be experiencing at your age, but if you keep hiding things from me, I might as well ground you for as long as necessary."

Isaac knew this day would come. It was only a matter of time. Isaac had never been a bad kid, just a loud and active one. His father always understood that, and Isaac was grateful for it. So many of his friends were deprived of doing cool things because of their parents' strict rules, but not Isaac. That only worked because his father trusted him. Now, Isaac had broken his trust, and he couldn't even explain to him why. Would his father even understand? If so, where would Isaac start?

He hated lying and keeping secrets. It consumed his soul to the point of burning his bones.

"How long am I grounded for?" he asked.

He couldn't tell his father the truth. It was bad enough that he had left the house late at night, but if his father found out he had broken into the local swimming pool to hang out with a girl who almost drowned in his presence, he would freak out. Even if Isaac told him that, he would have to keep out of the conversation that this all was happening because he was a merfolk.

Isaac shouldn't have left his bed this morning.

"If you're not swimming anymore, then you're going to get your grades up. And no more parties until the end of the semester. Whenever you leave at night, you need to tell me where you're going. I won't make any exceptions anymore, not even on weekends. If you break curfew again, I'll take your phone away. Do you understand, Isaac?"

"Yes." He couldn't face his father. It was too much. Isaac's cheeks burned with embarrassment and his throat scrambled to get the truth out. He swallowed it, burying it deep in his stomach. "I'm sorry, Dad."

He wanted to say more. He hated this feeling in his chest, the disappointment looming over him. One day Isaac was everything to everyone, now he was nothing. Everything he loved, everything he cared about, everyone he wanted to keep close, all of it was slipping through his fingers because he couldn't tell the truth. Why did he have to keep his magic hidden from everyone?

Because if they ever saw you with a fishtail instead of legs, you'd become part of a scientific research that would earn a Nobel prize and after that, you'd end up in a museum collection, that's why.

With nothing else to say, they enjoyed their breakfast in silence. Isaac drank his milk slowly and ate his toast with butter while his father sipped on his coffee, skimming through the headlines of the day's newspaper.

"Do you think Mom would be mad at me?"

He regretted those words as soon as they left his mouth. Isaac knew he should never mention his mother. *Never*. She was a forbidden topic of discussion; someone he was only allowed to remember in his head because no one had access to it.

His father lowered his newspaper, scanning Isaac's features. Whenever he looked at his father, he saw an older version of himself, but Isaac knew that his father saw in him what once belonged to his mother.

"I think she'd be upset," his father said, a sad smile greeting his lips. "I'm sure she would be better at getting you to open up about what is bothering you. She had that talent. People trusted her, and she trusted too easily."

"Did she trust the wrong people?"

Isaac shouldn't be asking, but he couldn't help it. If he could get to know more about his mother through his father, then maybe that could help him figure out who he was.

"She did." His father focused on a point in the distance, regret tainting his features, deepening his frown lines. He took a deep breath and blinked away the sorrow in his eyes, taking another sip of his coffee. He tried to discreetly wipe the corners of his eyes, but Isaac didn't miss that.

Isaac bit his lower lip as his heart jumped in his chest. He shouldn't push any further. He should wait for another day, another time when they were both calmer. But he couldn't stop.

"Was that why she died? Because she trusted the wrong people?"

Isaac's father had never told him about his mother's passing. Whenever he asked, he would make up excuses, mentioning how young or immature Isaac was. And yet, with everything else in life, his father treated him exactly the opposite way. He knew it was painful for him to talk about his wife, but she was Isaac's mother too. He was just as entitled to the truth as his father was.

"It's a complicated story," his father said, studying Isaac's features again. "A long one too."

"I have nowhere to be." Isaac shrugged. "You could tell me now."

"I could." His father nodded. "But I don't want to. Not today."

"Then when?"

His father picked up his newspaper again, and Isaac had to fight every inch of his body to not snap it away and force him to answer him. Isaac finished his breakfast as quickly as he could, shoving the dish, mug and cutlery in the washing machine. As he was about to head upstairs, his father spoke again.

"Let's go fishing next week."

Isaac stopped in his tracks and turned around confused. "We haven't gone fishing in forever."

"I know. But you want to know about your mother, and I want to know what is going on with you. It's only fair if we do it in a place she would love."

Isaac crossed his arms, shoving his panic back to where it had emerged from. If he went fishing with his father, then that meant he would be surrounded by water. He could get wet. And if he got wet, then scales would appear. And if that happened— He shook his head. More of a reason to get this matter solved as soon as possible.

"If I don't want to share it, will we still go fishing?" he asked and his father nodded. "And will you still tell me about Mom?" He nodded again. Isaac took a deep breath and pinched the bridge of his nose. "Fine, then. I guess we'll go fishing."

"I'm sure the silence and the stillness of the water will help you reflect," his father yelled as Isaac climbed up the stairs.

Isaac shivered. When he was a kid, he used to go fishing with his father so that his mother could be alone. It was an activity he enjoyed because more often than not, after he had learned how to swim, his father would let him do it for a bit before they packed their stuff and returned home.

Now, that would be different. Isaac didn't remember how to fish. He might find it boring. He might find the silence and stillness too overwhelming. He might say more than he should. It was terrifying.

But the most terrifying part was wanting to jump into the water and swim freely. Allow his father to see him for who he was now, for who he had become. *This is me now.* Everything would be easier if he could do that. And he could. He wanted to. Still, Isaac couldn't deal with the consequences of that.

One thing was him accepting himself. Another was having someone else do it for him.

Isaac was different now, and he could no longer ignore it.

Chapter Fourteen

"ARE YOU READY, ALICE?"

Victoria's voice brought Alice back to reality from the darkness of her mind. They stood at the edge of the forest, both wearing their burgundy cloaks while a grey wolf remained next to Alice, its breaths creating soft clouds of mist. It was cold tonight. Not that Alice was expecting anything else.

She always felt colder during New Moon Rituals.

Without saying anything, she put the hood over her head, concealing her features. Her aunt did the same, and her dark curls squished under it, surrounding her round face with softness. She extended a candle holder towards Alice, and she took it, pursing her lips.

"All you have to do is light it up," Victoria said. "We've gone over it a thousand times."

Alice nodded. This was supposed to be the easiest spell for witches like her to cast. *Summon fire.* After what had happened with Isaac at the pool, Alice wasn't sure she'd ever be as carefree as she was when she was ten or as gifted as she was back then. Summoning fire used to be like breathing to her. It was in her nature. Yet, she wasn't sure she could do it tonight.

The wolf nudged against the back of her knee and she looked down. Xavier kept his golden eyes on her, his tongue sticking out as he breathed. Alice tried to focus on his body pressed against the side of her leg, its weight grounding her, its warmth soothing her.

She gulped and focused her attention on the tip of her fingers and the comforting pulse that flowed through her body. She closed her eyes, imagining the golden current flowing from her chest to her arms, reaching the tip of her index finger. As soon as she felt a soft prickle, she snapped her thumb and index fingers and opened her eyes. A small blue flame, like the one she witnessed at the end of burning matches, lit the tip of her finger. She watched the flame twirl, casting small shadows on Victoria's soft face.

"Light the candle."

Alice did as she was told. She reached her finger to the stem of the candle and waited until it caught fire. The blue flame danced, stretched and retracted until it settled in place. She shook her hand in the air, putting out the flame from her finger. When she glanced back at it, her skin was fine. Only her red nail polish was chipped, but she could scrub the burnt marks off once she was home.

It would take a while before she could think of home.

"Now, we'll follow the flame. Let it guide you."

"Are you sure it's safe?" Alice asked, biting her lip. The blue flame tilted to the right, burning unnaturally.

"Xavier is here with you and so am I. Besides, your parents did the rounds earlier. It's safe. If anyone comes, we'll deal with them. Let's keep moving."

Once Victoria's gloved hand was on her shoulder, Alice sighed and turned right, following the flame's direction. It straightened up after a while, so they kept walking forward. Whenever it tilted or straightened, Alice followed along.

She wasn't sure how deep into the forest she was walking, or how she'd be able to find her way back. She hadn't thought that far ahead. All she wanted right now was to find the spot to perform the ritual. Everything else could wait.

"How much longer do you think we have to walk?" Alice asked, her voice carrying through the trees around her. She glanced up. The dark sky peeked through the top of the trees, its freckles shining brighter tonight. Her heart felt heavy in her chest.

"We walk until the flame extinguishes. Then we'll know we're in the right place."

They kept walking in silence as the leaves crunched under their boots and owls hooted in the distance, their calling a melody Alice wanted to get lost in. Soon enough, the sound of water running reached her ears and she gulped as it grew louder.

Her steps dragged, her focus sharp on the flame. *Extinguish now. Let me stay here.* Instead, she had to keep walking. The sound of insects buzzing replaced the owls and she knew she was close to the only place she never wanted to return to.

"I don't think—"

As Alice stepped forward, the flame flickered and disappeared. The twirl of its smoke climbed up, melting with the air around them, leaving a slight scent of beeswax in the air.

"We're here," Victoria said. "You know what to do now."

"I do." Alice lowered the candle holder and placed it on top of crushed leaves in front of her. "Will you stay?"

"Xavier and I will be nearby. I don't want our presence to affect your sigils or your summoning. Just focus on your task, okay?" Victoria squeezed Alice's shoulder and planted a kiss on her cheek. "You've got this."

"I've got this," Alice repeated, tasting the words in her mouth. "I've got this."

As her aunt and Xavier left her side, Alice lowered her hood and removed her cloak, spreading it next to the candle holder. Tonight wasn't windy, so she didn't have to worry about it flying away. Still, she grabbed the candle holder and placed it over her cloak just in case.

She mentally went over what she had to do next. *Draw the sigils.* From the sheath on her thigh, Alice plucked two sticks, one black, one golden. She used the black one to draw lines over her right palm, a circle split in five. With the golden one, she added different symbols to each of their spots. Small triangles with lines crossing them in the middle, some downturned, others upturned. She left the last empty, the one closer to her wrist, saving the two sticks back in their place. She grabbed a small dagger and pierced the tip of one of her fingers on her left hand. She bit her lower lip to prevent a yelp of pain from escaping. This was one of the worst parts.

Soon enough, a drop of dark blood greeted her pale finger and she smudged it on the empty part of the circle. Alice saved her dagger, staring down at her hand as the blood carved into the lines, burning her skin wherever it touched the gold, never leaving the outer edge of her hand.

She stood still, waiting until all the gold was covered by a dark shade of brown.

Alice stepped over her cloak and sat down, glancing one last time at her hand. The burning sensation was dissipating, leaving in its wake a tingle that spread from her hand to the rest of her body. She watched as the gold lines glowed from under her skin, illuminating her surroundings and revealing its secrets.

A large circle of emptiness surrounded her. The trees were at a walking distance, their branches charred and fallen onto the forest's ground. When Alice looked up, she noticed the semi-circle the treetops made, as if someone had carefully cut them into that shape and continuously worked on keeping it that way. She knew this wasn't the result of anything human.

This was the result of magic fire. *Her* magic fire. The one that almost burned this place down seven years ago. From all the places she had to perform tonight's New Moon Ritual, it had to be here.

She hated it. She hated herself. She hated—

Alice closed her eyes, and pressed her right hand over her heart, shoving these thoughts away. Her anger for what she had done in the past wouldn't help her now. Right now, she had to go on with the ritual. She *had* to get this done.

She focused on the warmth and pulse running through her, ignoring the coldness of her surroundings, the water that dripped far away, the wind flowing through the large branches and dried leaves around her. It was important that her mind became one with her soul, that she stripped off her body entirely while all of this was happening.

It was easier said than done.

Alice took a deep breath, applying all the techniques she had read about to this moment. She imagined a golden line connecting her hand to her heart, wrapping around her body as if she were in a cocoon of light, ready to take flight to another plane. She tried to focus on the warmth her body shed out, thinking of it as a shell she was letting go of before her next step.

Instead, her nose picked up the scent of burnt wood, the thickness of the air too much for her to breathe properly. Alice shook her head, focusing back on her heartbeat, on the gold pulsing through her, on everything that wasn't around her. She pictured herself taking flight, seeing her body from above, feeling herself lightweight while also tethered to something below her.

One step closer to the end, she thought and smiled to herself.

She opened her eyes. She wished she hadn't.

Tall blue flames licked the trees around her, the smoke heavy with a decaying smell. Alice tried to block her nose and mouth, tried to breathe, but that smell was everywhere. She heard voices and turned around, trying to locate the sound.

Nothing.

They were everywhere and nowhere. A man laughing. A young girl screaming, asking for help.

No. She shook her head. *No.*

Alice couldn't breathe. She couldn't even scream. She scanned her surroundings, trying to locate Victoria and Xavier, trying to see someone who could help her.

Help me. That was her voice in the distance, soft and delicate, high-pitched. *I can't swim.*

She looked down through her translucent hands as she floated. Her body remained lifeless below her, shoulders hunched forward, her features covered by the black hair falling over her face. Alice shivered as a cold breeze ran through her, freezing her bones. She hugged herself, gasping at the wet dress stuck to her body. The breeze grew stronger as the flames hissed her name, its sound deafening and all-consuming.

Make it stop! Make it stop!

She flew down to her body, trying to grip it, trying to wake herself up to get out of here. Before she could slow down, she passed through her body towards the flames, halting at the last second. Their warmth greeted her face as leaves and heavy branches collapsed around her as if they were nothing but a house of cards.

You will always be a witch, and you will always be alone.

Not her voice. Someone else's. The anger it carried was familiar.

Who are you? Alice asked in her mind. In a spiritual plane, she had no voice.

Alice tried to cross the flames to find the voice, but her body stopped abruptly at the last minute. When she looked back, she noticed a golden line fully stretched, connecting her to her lifeless body on the ground. If she moved forward, if she broke the line, she would be gone from the physical plane altogether.

Who are you? Alice asked again. She moved in circles around the burning trees, trying to locate what was beyond them. She was unsure of what she would do, unsure of how she could get out of here. She couldn't call for help. It was useless to scream. It was useless to do anything. No one was here. Once she returned to her body, maybe no one would be there, either.

Alice would always end up alone. She would always be a witch, a witch who couldn't summon, a witch who couldn't control her magic, a witch who would forever be lost and scared and afraid, one that would never carry her full power or become who she wanted to because of what she couldn't escape from.

This was Alice. She was destruction, the one you couldn't rebuild from. She was anger, the one you couldn't escape from. She was weakness, the kind you kept hidden only to get it exploited.

Alice wasn't a witch.

She was a lost cause.

As the flames grew taller around her, Alice floated to the ground, watching them twirl around the trees, dancing back and forth, never losing their strength or beauty.

She brought her knees to her chest, resting her head on top of them, trying to keep herself warm. She waited for the flames to burn out, alone in the forest, as *her* magic, as *her* fire, burned the most sacred place a witch could ever have, the most important place a witch should *always* protect.

I did this. I am this.

When she closed her eyes, she hid her face on her knees. Alice waited until her time in this plane was over, until she could return to her body and be connected with it once more.

A warm hand gripped her shoulder before two strong arms wrapped around her and pulled her into a tight embrace, running a hand along her back, trying to soothe her.

"What happened?" her aunt asked, almost out of breath as she joined them. "Did you do it?"

Alice shook her head, burying it deeper into the crook of Xavier's neck. She focused on his fast heartbeat, wiping the tears away from her stained cheeks.

"I couldn't do it." She could barely speak, could barely think straight. "I want to go home."

"Do you need me to carry you?"

She leaned her head away from Xavier's shoulder, her eyes jumping between his worried gaze and flushed cheeks, to the confused expression on her aunt's face.

"Where were you?" her aunt asked, crossing her arms. "I saw your body go numb, Alice. If you weren't performing the ritual, then where were you?"

"I don't know," she said, defeated. "As soon as I ascended, I was surrounded by flames, and I couldn't do anything. Why can't I get this right just once?"

"It's okay, Alice," Victoria said. "It seems like you had trouble ascending, which happens sometimes." Victoria glanced up and shook her head. "Oh, no. I'm so sorry, Alice. We should've skipped it. If I—"

Xavier was the first one to hear it. He let go of Alice and jumped forward, his body shifting into his wolf form in a blink. Alice heard it afterwards. She grabbed the dagger from her thigh and got up in a dragged motion, focusing on the crunching of leaves in the distance. Soon enough, Victoria was also in position, the two of them with their backs to one another, ready to defend themselves or attack whatever was out there.

"Do you think it's an animal?" Victoria whispered. "We weren't followed."

Alice shook her head. The pattern of the crunching of leaves told her otherwise. "It walks. Has two legs. It's walking in this direction."

"How do you know?"

As if on cue, a light in the distance grew stronger as it made its way towards them. Xavier moved to stand in front of Alice while her aunt remained by her side, her hands ready to cast whatever was needed for the situation. Alice kept her dagger in her hand, trying to steady her heartbeat, failing to focus on anything for too long.

Her mind was a whirlwind of thoughts, and she couldn't help but feel responsible for what was about to happen next. If she had given away their location to someone who didn't know about magic, this could end badly.

The crunching of leaves grew louder and Alice changed her stance, pointing the tip of the dagger to the light. If she threw it towards the nearest tree, that could be enough for the person to get distracted and for Xavier to tackle them down while Alice and Victoria ran away.

A wolf in the woods was easier to explain than whatever the three of them had going on right now.

The light cast a human-like shadow on someone with a top hat, their steps slow but certain. Whoever they were, they knew these woods. It was unlikely they were hunters and they weren't drunk either. Whoever it was, they—

"I come in peace!" a delicate, upbeat voice spoke. Alice narrowed her eyes. She knew that voice. "Please don't shoot me or bite me or throw anything in my way."

"Then reveal yourself," her aunt screamed, her voice stern. Nearby, a root from one of the trees travelled to the surface as Victoria glanced its way.

"Please, Victoria. Do you not recognise your sister's voice?"

"Sister…?" The thought died on Victoria's lips as she exchanged a look with Alice. "Gloria?"

"In the flesh!" Aunt Gloria said, opening her arms wide as she walked towards them.

Aunt Gloria was different from what Alice remembered. Her face was more wrinkled along her mouth and eyes, but those didn't diminish the beauty of her hazel eyes or carefree smile. The dark brown hair was different too, now slightly lighter in some places, creating a lovely pattern of unpredictability as it framed her face.

She removed her top hat and the fairy that had lit up her path flew to it, hiding inside. After putting her hat back on, her focus turned to Alice, whom she quickly hugged tightly. "Ah, if it isn't my favourite niece! How are you, sweetheart? You look wonderful. Look at these cheeks. Ah, and your hair is long. The power coursing through you must be immense."

"Thanks…?" Alice blinked away her exhaustion, keeping a polite smile on her lips.

After squishing her cheeks and planting a wet kiss on her forehead, Aunt Gloria let go of Alice and fixed her top hat and the lapels of her deep purple jacket. When she focused on her younger sister, the warmth in her eyes faded and her lips settled in a thin, hard line. Alice could've sworn the forest quieted around them as it braced for impact.

The two sisters stared at each other for a while, frowning at the sight of one another.

"*Victoria.*"

"Gloria."

"I see you still struggle to summon roots. Shouldn't you be past basic spells by now?"

Victoria chuckled, glancing at her sister with disdain. "I see you still have a tendency to struggle with basic greetings."

Aunt Gloria dismissed her sister's comment with a wave of a hand. Her attention shifted to the wolf, and she frowned. "Why is *that* thing with you?" The wolf growled and Aunt Gloria jumped, one of her gloved hands going to her heart. "Not very nice, is it?"

"That's Xavier," Victoria said. "He's Alice's—"

"Friend," Alice interjected, smiling at her aunt. "He's my friend. He's a shapeshifter."

There was no way Alice was going to admit to her aunt she needed a Protector. If Aunt Gloria found out she had put all witches and all other magical creatures at risk of discovery seven years ago, it would only escalate this conversation even more. They could talk about Magic Hunters some other day. Or maybe never.

"Ah," she said, studying Xavier. "What were the three of you doing in the woods? Shouldn't Alice be by herself to perform her New Moon Ritual? And why are the *trees* like this? Did something happen that The Council is unaware of?"

"No." Victoria shook her head, pursing her lips. She tried to meet Gloria's gaze, but when she couldn't, she cleared her throat and smiled. "Why don't we head to Victor's house? I'm sure he and Ingrid would love to know you're here. You probably need to rest too."

"That's quite thoughtful of you, my dear sister." Gloria tapped the tip of Victoria's nose, startling her. "Which is a rarity, coming from you."

Behind Alice, the wind shifted as Xavier returned to his human form. "Is she always this unpleasant?" he asked.

Alice took a deep breath and looked over her shoulder to find him standing right behind her. As soon as their eyes met, he offered her a consoling smile. It was a gesture that relaxed her, but that made her stomach twist in embarrassment too. These smiles were too common now, a reminder of yet another disappointing New Moon Ritual.

"You haven't seen half of it yet," she said, trying to keep the sadness out of her voice. "Wait until you see the three siblings together."

Xavier let out a soft laugh and Alice gathered her cloak and candle holder, her heart sinking in her chest as she stared at the burned wick on the candle. All of this for nothing.

"You'll get it next time," Xavier said as he wrapped an arm around Alice, rubbing her shoulder. "Don't give up, okay?"

"Okay," she whispered.

"I know we can't change the past, but you're safe now, Alice." Xavier smiled at her. He slowed down his steps and stopped in front of Alice, lowering himself so their eyes were at the same level. "I'm here to protect you. I'm here to keep you safe. They can't hurt you anymore."

"I know." She nodded and forced a smile at him. As much as Xavier tried his best to be her friend, Alice knew what they shared wasn't a friendship. It was a mere contractual obligation on his side, one that he fulfilled to the best of his abilities. Once Alice was in Nadalan, this would be over. Xavier would be gone, and like always, she would be alone.

They followed the two sisters as they bickered with one another on the way out of the forest, their conversation boisterous and drowning out all of Alice's thoughts. Xavier tried his best to cheer her up by cracking a joke here and there, but he got no reaction from her. All Alice wanted was to get home so she could drown her misery with a night's sleep.

Chapter Fifteen

ISAAC WAS AS PROTECTED as he could be for the fishing trip with his father. He wore two pairs of socks, the thickest sweatshirt he owned over a T-shirt, not to mention the denim jeans and the heavy boots on his feet. He didn't look like he was going fishing, but it didn't matter. He couldn't risk it. If he touched water, even for the briefest of moments, he would have to do a lot of explaining to his father.

"Is everything in the truck?" his father asked as Isaac put on his bucket hat, now too small for his head. "You know we're going fishing, right?"

"Yes." Isaac nodded and sat on the passenger's seat. "I just thought it would be good to be prepared. In case it's too cold, you know."

His father kept his eyes on Isaac but didn't say much else. He closed the trunk and went to the driver's seat. "Well, let's go, then. We have snacks to last us for more than five hours, so we can stay there for as long as you'd like."

Isaac nodded and kept his eyes on the outside of the car. Half the town was still asleep; the sun wasn't even out yet. He relaxed in his seat as his father drove them to the fishing location where they would be for most of the day. As much as Isaac wanted this to be over soon, he also wanted to get answers to some of his questions about his mother.

All while not having to answer any questions about himself.

"We're going to the lake?" he asked.

"I thought it would be best if we went somewhere else, so we're going to fish at a river."

"A river?" Isaac narrowed his eyes on his father. "The nearest river is one hour away."

"I know." He smiled at Isaac. "Why do you think we woke up this early?"

For the rest of the car ride, Isaac slept. He was too tired to keep awake and the past couple of days had drained most of his energy. What happened with Alice at the public pool was still too much for him to comprehend, and instead of answers, he only had more questions.

Questions he could no longer ignore.

He was still unsure of what had happened, and no matter how many times he turned those moments in his head, he still couldn't explain it. When Alice was in his arms, when he was holding her, his tail was gone. He had his legs underwater and no scales on his body. When he let go of her, his scales and tail returned in the blink of an eye. The worst part was that he didn't know how to bring this up to her again. Alice had said she would message him once she had information, but so far, all his messages had been left on read.

As much as he wanted to give her space, Isaac was desperate for answers. It had been so long since he had shown up to a swimming practice that he was starting to worry he would be removed from the team altogether. He needed to solve this quickly to prevent that from happening. Maybe Isaac should put his ego aside and call her. That way, he could check up on her to make sure she was doing okay and ask for updates on his predicament.

"Isaac," his father called, shaking his shoulder slightly. "We're here. Time to wake up."

Isaac opened his eyes as his father finished parking the car near a beaten-down trail. Through the car lights, he spotted the river not too far away, its surface calm and inviting.

"What do you think of this?" his father asked, taking off his seatbelt. "It's quite peaceful, isn't it?"

Isaac nodded, entranced by the water. He wanted to jump inside at the first chance he got. Unfortunately, he couldn't. "How did you find this place?"

"Some colleagues at work said this was a good spot to fish. I took their word for it, so here we are."

"Are they joining us?" Isaac asked. It was bad enough to be here with his father, but to have to deal with people he didn't know? That would only make it even more awkward.

"They're not." His father squeezed Isaac's shoulder. "It's just the two of us, a cooler with snacks and drinks, and hopefully some good catches."

"And conversation," Isaac added, smiling at his father. "I made a list of questions."

He laughed. "I expected nothing else from you."

They left the car and unloaded it before moving closer to shore where they set up their chairs and fishing gear. It had been so long since Isaac last went fishing that he struggled with his fishing rod, but eventually, he was able to throw the line into the water, taking in the peace of nature around him.

"This is nice," he said as he sat down on his chair, one hand holding the fishing rod. "You can't hear a thing."

Besides the buzzing of insects and the wind blowing through the leaves, Isaac was surrounded by a silence he hadn't experienced before. It was soothing, but it brought forward all the things he wanted to keep hidden. His questions about his mother. His worries about his merfolk abilities. The fact he was keeping all of this a secret from his father.

That was the hardest part. Isaac hated it. He hated secrets and he hated lies.

"Do you think we're going to catch something?" he asked as he traced the tree line in the distance, noticing the sky's blue changing shade. "Is this bait any good?"

"Well," his father sighed and adjusted himself on the chair, "it's store-bought, so I don't know how well it works. I didn't have time to make us bait. Your mother used to help me with that."

His father's gaze got lost in the distance as sadness took over his features. Isaac gulped and focused on his rod, trying his best not to move it. He should have put it on the ground so his hands were free, but part of the fun of fishing was holding the rod. It did make his arm hurt, though.

"I thought she didn't like fishing," Isaac said.

A sad smile crossed his father's face. "She didn't. But she didn't mind helping me with the bait. She was quite good at it."

Isaac nodded. Even though most of the memories he had from his mother were fading, he remembered when he used to go fishing with his father. They always left at dusk, drove to a spot near a deserted beach and stayed there for most of the day. His mother always kissed his forehead before he left, always tugged his bucket hat closer to his ears.

"I don't want you to be cold," she would say.

What Isaac remembered the most from his mother was her smile and her laughter. Sometimes, he could swear he heard it still. He knew it wasn't possible, but here, near the water, he couldn't help but miss her.

"Do I remind you of Mom?" Isaac asked, unable to face his father.

Isaac wanted to know more about his mother, he wanted to know how much of her was left in him. Did they only share the same eyes? Did they have a similar personality? Were they nothing alike?

"In a lot of ways, you're a lot like your mother, yes." His father chuckled, a happy smile tugging at his lips. "You both love to swim. You're great with people like her. She was the most social of the two of us. Always happy to make new friends, always eager to help."

"Mom was great, wasn't she?" Isaac smiled as his vision grew blurry. "I miss her. I wish she was here with us."

"Me too." His father nodded to himself. "Me too."

Isaac shifted in his chair again, resting a leg over its arm while he held onto the fishing rod. After this round, he would stick it on the ground and have a snack. He'd probably have a sandwich or some cookies. He'd save the hot dogs for lunch.

His father cleared his throat and shoved a hand in one of his pockets, shuffling the contents in it. He pulled something out and stared at it for a while before extending it to Isaac without saying a word.

His stern expression did all the talking. Soon enough, Isaac's heart was bursting from his chest as his clothes became too hot for him to wear. On his father's palm lay a fish scale the size of a coin. It was almost opaque, its surface like the one of a pearl.

"Where did you get it?" Isaac asked, trying to keep the panic away from his voice. His hand moved back and forth unsure whether he should take it. He closed his hand into a fist and rested it on his lap, smiling at his father. "It's pretty."

The scale was pretty, but all Isaac wanted to do was throw up.

His father took a deep breath and saved the scale back in the pocket of his jacket, staring at the water. The sky was a light blue now, the river's surface shimmering in delight as the sun climbed up.

"I found it in your clothes," he said, voice deprived of any emotion. "When I was going to put them to wash, this fell from your shirt." He pursed his lips, regret clouding his features before he faced Isaac again. "How long have you been like this?"

Isaac's stomach tightened in a knot. He swallowed louder than he intended, trying to prevent the truth from escaping his lips. He had to come up with something to say and quickly.

"Why do you think that's mine?" Isaac asked, a panicked laugh escaping his lips. This was bad. *Really* bad. One thing was lying to his father in the absence of proof of what he was. But his father had proof, and he was the only culprit, so maybe it was time for Isaac to drop this farce and be honest already.

He hated lying to his father anyway.

"They're just like your mother's, you know. Same shade, same size." He sighed and adjusted his fishing rod. "I thought you wouldn't turn out to be like her."

Isaac blinked as he stared at his father, allowing the words to slowly take shape in his mind. Alice's theory was correct. His mother was a merfolk. "How did you find out about Mom? Are you merfolk too?"

His father chuckled. "I'm not. I knew she was merfolk and there was a small chance you could be one too. How I came to know this information is complicated."

"How complicated?" Isaac raised an eyebrow. "Dad, you understand I'm like Mom, right? Because of this, I can't do what

I've always done. I can't be a part of the swimming team anymore. I can't swim whenever I feel like it. It's awful."

"Your mother and I never wanted this for you. This complicates things."

"What *things*?" Isaac was so close to getting some answers, but every time he seemed to be close enough, he found himself speaking to a wall. "If you're not merfolk, then what are you?"

"Human," his father said.

"Then how do you know about merfolk? Humans shouldn't know about us. That's what—" His father raised an eyebrow. Isaac should keep Alice out of this conversation. Until he knew the full story, at least. "That's what I assumed. No one talks about magic."

"Exactly." His father looked into Isaac's eyes, serious. "And you should keep it that way. No one, and I mean no one, should know about who you are. This is something that should remain between the two of us. No one else."

"No one else?" Isaac asked, gulping. "Not even other people like me? This is just a hypothetical question."

His father held his gaze, studying him curiously. Isaac feared he could see right through him, see that he had asked Alice for help and that she knew about him.

"Your mother didn't tell me much about magic, but she made one thing very clear, Isaac. Your nature should never be known. You cannot trust no one, no matter who they are."

"Do you know why?" He hadn't known Alice for too long, but she didn't seem untrustworthy. If anything, she had gone out of her way to help him.

Besides, he still needed her help. There was so much he didn't know, and she had been the person with most answers. Isaac couldn't cut all ties with her out of nowhere, could he?

His father shook his head, defeated. "I don't. Your mother didn't share with me more than what I needed to know. I wish I had more answers to give to you, but I don't. I'm sure her journals might be of greater use to you, though."

"Her journals?" Isaac's heart picked up pace again.

"Yes. I kept them hidden at her request. She said that if you turned out to be human I should burn them. But since you're not, it's only fair I share them with you."

Isaac nodded. Maybe not all hope was lost. His mother's journals could help him find the answers he needed to figure out how he could conceal his magic. If he had spent all these years without knowing his mother was a merfolk, then maybe she had left him some information on how he could conceal his magic too.

"Do you think I'll be able to join the swimming team again?" As much as Isaac enjoyed the new routine he had, he missed swimming with his friends a lot. "Do you think—"

His father laughed, a rich and deep sound that filled Isaac's chest with happiness. The fishing rod started to bob, but he ignored it, focusing on Isaac instead.

"Once we're home, I'll give them to you. I'm sure they'll have answers to all the questions you have. I wish I could help you more, son. I truly do."

Isaac smiled. "It's alright. Thank you for this."

"Anytime." He reached towards Isaac's arm and squeezed it lightly. "I'm here for you, okay? No more secrets about this between us. I want you to trust me with these things."

"Thanks, Dad."

As much as Isaac wanted to tell his father about Alice and Xavier, he decided against it. He didn't like the lump in his throat and the weight in his chest every time he thought about keeping this from him, but he wasn't sure why he would share about them, either.

His father was human, and humans shouldn't know about magical beings. Until Isaac had more answers, he'd keep all of them in the dark about one another even if that turned out to be a mistake in the long run.

More than trusting others, Isaac had to trust he was making the right call about all of this.

Chapter Sixteen

THE MOOD AROUND THE dinner table couldn't be more awkward. Alice's mother barely acknowledged Aunt Gloria, who kept telling her siblings stories of her time in Otherworld. Considering she hadn't visited them in more than ten years, she had a lot of catching up to do.

Alice remained focused on her dish and the food disappearing from it. Occasionally, she would smile at her aunt or look for reassurance from her father or mother. Victoria didn't hide her unhappiness that Aunt Gloria was around; if it was her sister's head on the plate, she would've mercifully stabbed her by now. Alas, they only had roasted vegetables and meat for dinner.

It was a nice meal, but far from being Alice's favourite.

"So," Aunt Gloria poked one of the peas with her fork and inspected it closely, "how is Alice's magical progress going?"

Silence filled the table. Victoria wiped her mouth and took a sip of her red wine, frowning afterwards.

"It's going well," she said. "Alice is a very diligent student."

Aunt Gloria smiled at Alice and pinched her cheek. "Of course she is. I expected nothing else from my niece. What else?"

"What else do you want to know?" Alice asked, trying not to

flinch at the sharpness of her aunt's fingers on her cheek.

"Oh, you know," Aunt Gloria shoved the pea in her mouth, "how proficient are you? What was the last spell you learned?"

"I know all the spells, Aunt Gloria," Alice said, moving away from her aunt's grasp. "I know how to brew potions, how to cast spells and how to summon my magic."

Lying shouldn't be this easy, but Alice had learned to do it ever since she was young, and she only got better after that infamous day. It was better to lie about what wasn't there than to justify and explain what was. She glanced at everyone around the table before focusing back on her food, shoving some meat in her mouth.

"Well, why don't you do a small performance for me?" Alice almost choked on her meat. "It's been so long since I last saw you summon magic… You've grown so much since then that I fear I missed most of your upbringing."

"You could've visited," Alice's mother said. "The passageway opens once every twenty-nine days. And as a member of the Council, I'm sure you can even cross without having to wait for the right moon phase."

Gloria scoffed. "Likewise, *darling*. You could have taken Alice for a visit to her rightful place, couldn't you?"

"It's not that easy, Gloria," Alice's father said, placing a hand over his wife's and squeezing it. "Alice is not ready to go to Nadalan yet."

"Don't say that, Victor. Alice has been ready ever since she was a child. She was far more peculiar than other children, and you know it. Most of them don't come into power until they are going through puberty, but she was six and already summoning light. At will!" Aunt Gloria turned to Victoria and frowned. "If her magical abilities have strained, then it's because of you. I said from the beginning that Alice should have a qualified tutor to guide her through her magic lessons, not—"

"I have to remind you that I am qualified to teach Alice all her magic lessons," Victoria said through gritted teeth. "If Victor says she's not ready, it's because she's not. *We* are the ones who have spent every day of Alice's life by her side. *We* are the ones who know her better than you do. Just because you want to make her your puppet, it doesn't mean we want to let that happen."

Alice sighed, sipped some juice, chewed some more food, and focused on her dish. With the tip of her fork, she drew lines in the sauce, creating shapes to keep herself entertained.

"We had a deal," Aunt Gloria said, her voice heavy with authority. "I would let you raise Alice in this forsaken place and she would move to Nadalan to pursue her studies after she turned eighteen. You know you can't keep her here forever. Her place is alongside her people, Ingrid. *Your* people."

"They aren't my people anymore." Alice's mother let go of her husband's hand and stood up, grabbing her plate with full force. "Does anyone want dessert? I made your favourite, Alice."

"Thanks," she said, offering her mother a small smile. "I'm still not done with dinner, though."

"Take your time." She turned to Victoria. "Would you like some? The cream is more sour than usual."

"Just how I like it." Victoria winked. "Go work on the desserts and I'll grab the rest of the dinner plates."

Alice's mother nodded and disappeared into the kitchen, dropping her plate with a heavy sound on the sink.

"She's always so difficult to deal with," Aunt Gloria said, shaking her head in disappointment.

"She *is* Alice's mother." Victoria glanced at her brother. "All they want is to keep her safe."

"But don't you believe she would be safer in Nadalan?" Aunt Gloria took a deep breath. "There, she could learn real magic and practise freely. Here, she has to spend all of her life in hiding. I do not want to think what would happen if any Magic Hunters found her."

Alice and Victoria exchanged a knowing look, and her aunt shook her head, warning Alice with a glare. If it depended on Alice, Aunt Gloria would never find out about that infamous day. It was better to keep her in the dark.

"Do you think it would be any different once she was there?" Alice's father asked, fixing his glasses.

"She wants to study in Nadalan, Victor. I *know* she applied. Will you prevent your daughter from following her goals because you're too stubborn to let her go back to her rightful place?"

"We all know the only reason you're so interested in Alice in the first place is because of her abilities." Victoria stood and looked down at her sister. "If Alice had the same abilities as us instead of her mother's, would you be so interested in her well-being? Would you care if she got her education from me or someone else?"

"I care about my niece!"

Alice had to chuckle. She finished her dinner and pushed the plate towards Victoria, who grabbed it and put it on top of the others in front of her. Aunt Gloria glanced around the table, looking for support from her brother. When she didn't receive it, she focused on Alice.

"You know I care about you, don't you, Alice?"

Alice stared intently at her aunt as the words took shape in her mind. "You care about my abilities. I wouldn't say you care about me, though."

"Alice!" Her father yelled while her aunt gasped in shock. "That is no way for you to speak to your aunt. She's a guest."

"An unwanted guest," Alice heard Victoria whisper under her breath, and she smiled briefly at that before a heavy weight took over her chest.

Alice got up from her chair and placed her napkin on the table. She stared at her mother returning with the dessert tray and a grim expression, then at her father's angry eyes, and finally at Aunt Gloria's shock still seeping through her features. Victoria disappeared into the kitchen, probably glad she could get away from this mess for a while.

Alice wanted to get away too.

"Sometimes I wish I wasn't what I am," Alice said. "I know it's not your fault that I'm able to summon fire and light instead of growing vegetables or plants—"

"We can do more than that!" Aunt Gloria said, glaring at Alice.

"It is not your power that defines you, Alice," her mother said in a gentle tone. "It's what you choose to do with it that does."

She chuckled. It was useless. When Alice was six, she was too eager to please, too happy to know she carried something special within herself. Now, she dreaded all of it. More and more she saw herself as a disappointment. She couldn't help but feel that way every time her mother tried to console her over her shortcomings. Alice should be better by now, she should be the most powerful witch her family lineage had ever seen. She was none of that. She would never be that.

"I don't want dessert," Alice said, her voice hoarse. "I'm not hungry anymore."

"Alice—" Victoria tried to hold her arm, but she moved out of her grasp and climbed up the stairs, straight to her bedroom.

Only when she collapsed on her bed and heard the loud bang of the door closing behind her did she allow the tears to spill. She ignored Whiskers as he tried to walk over her back, stopping to rest right next to her face, lying there to block her vision. She ignored the messages on her phone and tried to abstract from the loud conversation downstairs, its tone explosive and demanding.

When her phone rang, she ignored it too. One, two, three times. Whoever was calling her wasn't giving up. She wiped her nose on the back of her hand and grabbed the phone from her nightstand. Her eyebrows furrowed. Why was Isaac calling her?

After what happened at the local pool, she thought he would stay away from her. Now that he knew the rumours were true, he would be dumb if he kept hanging out with her. What she had done— No. She wasn't going to think about that now.

Alice took a deep breath and cleared her throat, getting up from her bed. Only after checking if her window was closed and after locking her bedroom door did she take his call.

"Yes?" she said, her voice coming from her nose. "Why are you calling me?"

"Are you alright?" Isaac asked. "You sound sick. Did you catch a cold?"

Alice wiped her tears and glanced at her reflection in the mirror. Disappointment didn't look very different from when she was sick. Puffiness surrounded her red eyes, her face deprived of her usual rosy cheeks. The only thing that remained was the darkness of her hair framing her face. Not even her eyes looked the same.

"I'm fine," she said, cringing at her voice. She didn't sound fine at all. "Why are you calling me? I thought we agreed this would be a last resort."

"I tried texting you." He took a deep breath. "Are you sure

you're alright? I'm… worried about you, you know."

It was the concern in his voice that almost made her lose the little composure she had gathered for this phone call. Out of all the people who could be worried about her, Isaac wasn't one she would add to that list. She didn't expect that from him. Isaac was only hanging out with her because he needed her help, nothing more.

"You don't need to pretend to care, Isaac."

"Well, but I *do* care. I'm sorry I didn't reach out after what happened at the pool… I should've said something, but I didn't know what. I hope you're not mad at me."

Alice bit her lower lip. *He is just being nice to you. Isaac is not really your friend. You can't trust him. You can't trust anyone.*

"It doesn't matter," she said, looking out the window. Whiskers moved to sit on her lap after Alice sat at the edge of her bed. She ran her hand through its orange fur, following its fluffy tail until the end as her cat tried to hit her face with one of its paws. "Can you get straight to the point? I'm a bit tired."

"Right." On the other side, Isaac ruffled through a couple of pages at a fast pace. "So, you were right. My mom was a merfolk and I have her journals. I've spent the past couple of hours reading them."

"Where did you get them?" Alice asked, rubbing under Whiskers' chin. He leaned towards her touch, purring.

"I'd rather not say how I got them." She sighed and hoped the silence would break Isaac's consciousness to make him speak. "It's better this way."

If they weren't on the phone and if Alice wasn't having such an awful day, she would press him further. "Fine. Are the journals useful in any way?"

"They are. My mom wrote these journals to me, so they have a lot about my lineage and abilities, but that's not why I called." He cleared his throat. "Would you like to meet tomorrow at the cafe near your aunt's flower shop? They have tea if you're not into coffee. I'd like to discuss this with you in person."

"Can't we meet at school?"

"No. Not a chance." He sounded worried. "I need to speak with you and we can't do that at the library. Besides, I don't want people to see us together."

"Of course. I get it." As much as Alice wanted to believe this wouldn't hurt anymore, it did. It was even worse this time around. "I'll go to the cafe, then. After I'm done with classes, I'll go there."

"Good. I'll be there!"

"Was that all?" she asked.

Whiskers got up from her lap and smoothly jumped off her bed, walking to her bedroom door and scratching it to get her attention. Alice rolled her eyes and unlocked the door, allowing him to exit. He sat on the carpet outside and stared at her before licking its paws.

"I will not let you in," she whispered to her cat, pointing an accusatory finger at him. "And don't you dare meow after I close the door. I will *not* let you in. Understood?"

Whiskers didn't care. He resumed his paw-licking activity and Alice returned to her bedroom. She collapsed back on her bed and stared at the ceiling, the static on the phone reminding her that she was on a call with Isaac.

"Are you there?" she asked, switching her phone to the other ear.

"What happened to those people?" His question knocked the air out of Alice's lungs. "Did… Are they alive?"

"I didn't kill them, if that's what you worried about," she said and Isaac sighed. "I don't know where they are now. Magic Hunters don't stay in the same spot for too long."

"Does that worry you? Not knowing where they are."

"They're everywhere, Isaac," she said. "I stopped caring a long time ago."

She stopped caring almost as soon as she stopped summoning. If she couldn't use her abilities, then she wasn't worthy of being hunted down. The thrill, the chase, the victory, all that wasn't there anymore.

She was only a trophy to them when she held her powers. Now, she was insignificant to them.

"I'm sorry you had to go through all that," he said, and he sounded genuine. "When I first heard the rumours, I didn't think they were real, but then—" He stopped himself.

"It's alright. You saw what happened." She pinched the bridge of her nose, those vivid images flashing through her mind.

"It's in the past, though. I don't want to talk about it."

It was a lie, and Alice knew Isaac wasn't dumb enough to believe her. Still, he played along, and she was grateful for that.

"If you ever want to talk about it, I'm here," he said. "You're not alone, Alice. Not anymore."

She chuckled. "And yet, you still don't want to be seen with me at school. I get it, though. I don't blame you. But it would be better if you didn't blatantly lie to me." Before he could say anything else, Alice added, "I'll be at the cafe tomorrow. I'll see you then. And next time, text me. I'll reply to you when I feel like it."

"I'll call," he said before she could hang up. "I like your voice. And I'm not ashamed of you. Or of being seen with you." He cleared his throat. "There are questions I'm not ready to answer yet. Everything is still very new to me, Alice. Only now am I starting to feel comfortable with the idea of being a merfolk. I hope you know I'm not lying when I say this. I *hate* lying. And I'd hate having to lie to you."

"Then if you hate lying to me, you'll tell me how you got your mother's journals tomorrow," she said. He let out a soft laugh and her heart jumped in her chest. She liked his laugh, too. "Do you think we'll ever be friends?"

As soon as the words were out of her mouth, Alice wanted to take them back. It was a stupid question, one that she knew the answer to. "Forget I asked that," she said, mentally slapping herself. "I'll see you at the cafe tomorrow."

Without waiting for his reply, Alice hung up the call and threw her phone across her bed, rubbing her face. She knew she couldn't have friends. The fewer connections she had in this realm, the better it was for when she left for Nadalan. It was easier to make up exceptions for someone everyone knew badly than for someone they knew well.

Except, Isaac wasn't human. He was a merfolk. That should count for something, right? Alice hoped it did.

As much as Alice hated to admit it to herself, spending time with Isaac was something she looked forward to now.

Chapter Seventeen

AS SOON AS ISAAC returned home with his father from their fishing trip, he dove headfirst into his mother's journals. When his father came into his room to call him for dinner, Isaac ignored it. Even as his eyelids grew heavier and his thoughts foggier, he refused to pause the task at hand. Close to midnight, Isaac found some information that warmed his chest with hope. Now that he had a thread to follow, he had an excuse to call Alice and meet up with her. He wasn't sure what made him giddier this afternoon: the clues he had found or seeing Alice again.

Isaac wasn't sure if he was going to bring up to Alice *how* he got his mother's journals. She would probably freak out if she knew his father was also involved in this. Maybe it was best to keep the truth hidden behind some vague answer. *I found them in the garage.* There. That was true. Half of it, at least. Isaac had found them in the garage not by chance, but because his father had told him so. This, he would keep to himself.

For a while, Isaac thought that Alice wasn't going to show up at the cafe. After their phone call the previous evening, he had grown worried about her. Was she sick? She did sound sick on the phone last night. Was she crying? He could have sworn he heard her sniffing and blowing her nose, but he couldn't be sure. He had to believe she would keep her promise even if, despite her usual punctuality, she was late to meet him.

This, however, was not a problem. If she was late, then it meant he had more time to go over his notes and the important pages he wanted to show to her. He had never studied or done so much research in his life, but this had been worth it. Going over some of his mother's journal entries had given him a possible solution to his most pressing problem, and Isaac had a theory that he was eager to share with Alice.

The bell rang as the cafe door slid open and Isaac turned around. His stomach tied into a knot when he spotted Xavier's arm draped over Alice's shoulders, their close proximity a fist that squeezed his heart dry. Xavier's eyes shifted to a golden hue as he scanned the surroundings while Alice whispered something. He pursed his lips at her words, deep in thought, but eventually nodded as his arm dropped from her shoulders. Alice stepped deeper into the cafe, joining Isaac at his table, her entire focus only on him. She smiled, and the squeeze around his heart subsided.

"Sorry, I'm late," she said, gesturing with her head to Xavier who now sat at a table near the entrance. "I had to wait for him before I could come."

"Is he not joining us?" Isaac asked, looking over his shoulder. Xavier's eyes burned against his, and he gulped. Maybe it was good he wasn't here at this table.

"I asked him not to," Alice said, collapsing on her chair. She moved her hair to one of her shoulders, leaning closer to Isaac. He startled at the proximity. "What did you want to show me?"

Isaac blinked, his eyes jumping between Alice's dark eyes filled with anticipation and the shy smile on her lips. He cleared his throat, glancing around the cafe before taking a sip of his iced coffee to try and cool down.

"Aren't you going to order something?" he asked, trying to sound nonchalant. "Their coffee is great."

"I don't like coffee. Besides, I'm not hungry. Or thirsty. Just tell me. I have to go to my aunt's flower shop soon."

"Okay, then." Isaac moved his beverage aside and opened a

leather-bound notebook. He flipped through the pages until he found one with a small drawing and turned it to Alice.

"What is it?" She narrowed her eyes at the pages before picking the notebook up, skimming through the words. "Is this one of your mother's journals?"

"Yes," he said. Then, because he couldn't keep his mouth shut, he added, "I found them in the garage."

"*In* the garage?" Alice looked appalled. "You had what are considered merfolk grimoires in your garage? How did you never stumble upon them? They're in pretty good shape." She scanned his features slowly before training her gaze on him. "You're lying to me, aren't you?"

"I'm *not.*" He wasn't. He had found the journals in the garage. The reason why he didn't stumble onto them earlier was because his father had kept them in a sealed wooden box under some cardboard ones. That's why they were in such good shape. That's why he never stumbled upon them before. "Okay, fine. My dad told me about them."

"So your dad knows you're a merfolk?" Isaac nodded, avoiding Alice's heavy gaze on him. "Does he know about me?"

"Should he?" At Alice's raised eyebrow, Isaac shook his head, defeated. "Look, I didn't tell him anything. He found a scale of mine, said I was like my mom and gave me her journals. That's it. Please, don't ask me more questions about that. I don't want to have to lie to you."

"So there's more…" After staring at him for a while, she shrugged and focused back on the journal. "What am I supposed to be looking at?"

Alice lowered it and Isaac pointed at an illustration. "Do you recognise it?"

She furrowed her brows as she glanced at the image for a while.

"It's a drawing of a merfolk. What about it?"

Isaac's finger moved to the merfolk's neck in the illustration. "What is this he's wearing?"

"A necklace." Alice sounded unsure. "Get to the point, please."

"It's an *amulet.*"

"An amulet?"

"Yes." He opened his bag and pulled another notebook out. His mother's journals, as it turned out, weren't as straightforward as a school book would be. He had to jump around them to find the information that connected illustrations and their meanings. "After I saw that image, I decided to do some more reading about merfolk history. My mother has an entire month's worth of journal entries on the topic. It turns out that since the 15th century, to blend in and not be discovered, they wore a special amulet."

"Amulets are special ways to store magic, yes," Alice said, pursing her lips. "But they are supposed to increase your magical abilities, not the other way around."

He smiled. For the first time, Isaac knew more than she did. How much he had dreamed of this moment. He had always been fascinated by Alice. Isaac hoped that, for a brief instant, she would be fascinated by him as well.

"Turns out," he opened a third notebook and turned it to her, placing it on top of the previous ones, "amulets can also be used to curse, harm or *block* magic. See where I'm going with this?"

She raised her eyes from the notebook to Isaac, smiling at him. "I must say I'm impressed." She grabbed the notebook. "Never took you as the studious type."

"This is more my kind of studying."

Her smile increased. "So is mine."

While he waited for her to read the pages, Isaac enjoyed his beverage and glanced at the street outside the cafe. Since it was late in the afternoon, most people were done with work and were ready to enjoy the few hours of sun left with their friends or family at the local park. If Isaac had swimming practice, he would be at the local pool, probably getting ready to swim for two hours before heading home.

The more time he spent away from practice, however, the less appealing returning to swimming competitions was. Isaac knew he had to return to the swimming team so he could win as many competitions as possible to help him go to a good university. His future relied on that, and he couldn't ignore or throw away the years of hard work behind him. Despite everything, going to a prestigious university was still his main goal.

"According to this entry, amulets can be created, but they need a spell to work properly. It helps if their material is connected to the desirable effect. This means it would have to be made of something that blocks out or absorbs merfolk magic. Did you research that far?"

"Not really. Her journals didn't go further than that," Isaac said. "Do you have any idea what can block or absorb merfolk magic?"

"No." Alice sounded disappointed. She dropped the notebook on the table and sighed, looking out the window. "I'll have to ask my aunt about it. Maybe she knows some information that might be useful. I don't know any spells related to these types of amulets."

He nodded, pleased. After closing the journals, Isaac carefully saved them in his bag, knowing she was keeping an eye on him. Somehow, that made his cheeks warmer.

"Isaac." He lifted his eyes to look at her, smiling. Alice gulped and looked out the window again. "If what is needed is a spell to make the amulet work, I'm not sure I'll be able to help you with that."

"I'd like you to try, at least." Isaac wasn't sure where he was going with this. "I'm sure that you can help me with this too. And if not, then you can still find me someone who can, and for that, I'll be super grateful."

The cafe bell rang again. A group of students entered the establishment talking loudly with each other. Isaac recognised a few of them: they were his teammates from swimming practice. If they were here at this hour, then it meant their coach was still sick.

"Would you like me to leave?" Alice asked, wary.

When Isaac first approached her, that would have been his request. Even last night, when they spoke on the phone, he asked Alice to meet him here because he didn't want to be seen with her. But what if he was seen with her? There was no problem with that. Isaac had been foolish and blinded by his status at school. Now, appearances or popularity weren't as important to him as they used to be.

"Stay." He reached for her hand. "If they're rude towards

you, I'll put them in their place."

Alice glanced at Isaac's hand on top of hers, her expression unreadable. Was it worry that crossed her eyes? Perhaps it was fear, hope. He didn't know. Part of her was still a mystery to him.

"I can handle myself, Isaac." She cleared her throat and pulled her hand from under his, crossing her arms. "Besides, Xavier is here."

"True," he said, feeling bitter about it. "But I could protect you. I'm here. Closer, even."

"Yeah." A small smile pierced through as Alice glanced at the space around him. "I get it. But you don't need to get jealous about it."

"I'm not—"

"Isaac!"

Someone waved at him from the counter and he looked over his shoulder to return the gesture, smiling brightly. His friends quickly turned to spot him, and it didn't take long for them to crowd around Isaac's table and start a conversation. Alice remained close to the window, her focus outside.

"We haven't seen you around the local pool!" Liam said, taking a sip of his drink. "What's up with you? Still sick?"

"Yeah," he said, glancing at Alice. What kind of excuse was he supposed to come up with this time around? "I'm not sure I'm totally recovered, and I don't want to risk it."

Isaac let out a nervous laugh, but his friends didn't seem to catch that. Their focus was on Alice, and soon enough, they started whispering to each other in between shy giggles.

"When Hannah told me she saw you at the library, I thought she was joking, but now…" Liam chuckled. "I guess you're sick, yes. I didn't know you were afraid of not entering university through competitive swimming."

So this was the rumour going around school. Isaac had asked Alice for tutoring lessons to improve his grades. He could live with that. It was better and more believable than the truth.

"I'm not afraid," Isaac reassured him, glancing at Alice. He couldn't help but smile at her. "Alice and I are friends. And what if I'm studying more now? It would do you well once in a while."

"Aish." Liam grimaced. "Me? Studying? As long as I don't fail, I'll never do it. Is *she* any fun, at least?"

Isaac couldn't ignore the look in Liam's eyes. He glanced at Alice with curiosity and wonder, but under all that was a despicable fear and bitterness Isaac couldn't ignore. Alice, however, saw through all his charades.

"I'm *very* fun, Liam," she said, forcing out a poisonous smile. "I'm sure I'm not fun for *your* standards, though."

He crossed his arms. "That's probably right."

"Glad we're on the same page."

Liam chuckled, pointing at Alice with his thumb as he looked at Isaac, baffled. "So you stopped hanging out with us to hang out with her? *Why*?"

"She's fun," Isaac said. "I've found some really cool books thanks to her. She doesn't accept book requests anymore, though. I keep her busy."

"With book requests," Alice emphasised, glaring at Isaac. "*Literally.*"

Isaac was the one flustered after her words. He took another sip of his beverage, disappointed to find that it was mostly over. Why did he say that? Now, he couldn't stop thinking about it.

"I didn't know you had a thing for… *bookworms*. Good for you." Liam took a deep breath and fixed the bag over his shoulder as he grinned at Isaac. "I'm throwing a party next weekend. Location is still undecided. Why don't you come with your friend? Perhaps she can have *our* kind of fun, too."

"Will there be food?" Alice asked.

"And drinks," Liam added. "Music, too."

"I'll see if I can go," Alice said.

"Make sure you bring your swimsuits." Liam patted Isaac's shoulder, offering him a cold smile. "I look forward to seeing you at the party and your new *friend.*"

Alice. Her name's Alice. Why Liam couldn't refer to her by name was beyond Isaac.

He waited until his friends were gone to take a deep breath. He hadn't realised his body had gone stiff during the conversation. Isaac rolled his shoulders back, slowly returning to himself again. When he met Alice's eyes, the last of his worries left him, like a balloon losing its air. Somehow, being in her presence always relaxed him.

Isaac massaged his temples, shaking his head. "Was I like

them?" he asked out loud what should have been a question for only him.

Alice's eyes softened as she glanced at him. She offered him a consoling smile, nodding slightly.

"You're still like them, Isaac. That doesn't make you an awful person, but they are your crowd. You belong with them."

"I wish I belonged with you," he mumbled under his breath. He focused on her, confused. "Why did you accept his invitation? You do realise this is probably going to be a pool party, right?"

She shrugged and stood from her chair, looking down at him.

"I guess we need to work on getting you an amulet and I need to learn how to swim. Besides," she leaned towards him, her eyes lingering on his lips before she met his eyes, "we don't belong together. If we are successful, you'll get your life back. Isn't that the reason why you asked for my help in the first place?"

He didn't answer. Alice sighed and waved him goodbye, letting him know she'd meet him again as soon as she had more information. He watched as she left the cafe, followed by Xavier, who joined her outside, wrapping an arm around her shoulders as he stared back at Isaac with his usual burning gaze.

Isaac collected his belongings and left the cafe soon after, shaking his head as he walked home. Yes, Isaac's initial goal was to get his old life back. However, he was falling in love with this new side of him, with this new life. Was it so bad to want that now?

Chapter Eighteen

ALICE PUSHED THE FLOWER shop door open, a small *ding* announcing her arrival. She expected to find the place without customers, but Victoria was busy behind the counter as she prepared a bouquet of white lilies and blue roses.

The flowers were lush, and Alice spotted the slight glow emanating from them, a result of the fairies' constant work. Most humans would miss it, but there was a reason why her aunt's flower shop was so well-regarded in the community. The flowers were always larger, their smell more intense, and their freshness lasted longer.

Alice waved at her aunt who briefly lifted her eyes in acknowledgement before returning to chat with the customer about the bouquet and his opinion of it. Since it would take a while for the flower shop to close down, Alice stepped to the back room and closed the door, throwing her bag on the couch and collapsing on it, blowing the hair away from her face.

When she went to meet with Isaac at the cafe, she hadn't expected him to ask for her help with amulets. She hadn't expected him to ask for her help with magic at all. After what happened at the pool, Alice had expected him to let it go and ignore her. He hadn't. Worst of all, she couldn't bring herself to admit to him what she struggled to come to terms with: she couldn't properly summon magic.

Besides, when it came to making an amulet, she had no leeway, no skill. Alice said that she would help Isaac, and she would do just that. Her aunt was an experienced witch; she surely could help Alice with Isaac's amulet. She didn't like the idea of someone else knowing about him, so Alice would keep his identity to herself, but she had to ask her aunt for help. It was that or no amulet.

The last thing Alice wanted was to embarrass herself again in front of Isaac. Once had been enough for eternity. She didn't have to go through that again.

The door to the back room opened, and Xavier stepped inside. He carried his usual frown as he ruffled his hair before leaning on the table in front of her, his brown eyes narrowed on her.

"I thought we were going to the library," he said. "It's still early for your witchcraft lesson."

She held his gaze. "You know you can leave, right? You don't need to keep an eye on me here."

"What if I want to be here?" He shrugged. "This is better than being at home."

"And more fun, I'm sure." Alice took a deep breath and pushed her hair to the side, her fingers working as she braided it over her shoulder. "How many spells do you think I'm going to butcher today?"

Xavier pondered for a while, a finger patting his bottom lip. "Probably three," he said, smiling. "But you're going to nail every potion."

"As usual."

Alice let go of her hair, her mind returning to her conversation with Isaac. She should have told him she couldn't summon magic. If she had told him that from the beginning, they wouldn't be here, on the verge of disappointment.

"Did your conversation with Isaac go well? What did his friends want?"

"Nothing you should be worried about. They invited Isaac to a pool party, and by extension, they invited me."

Xavier shook his head and joined her on the couch. As soon as he sat down, she had to move herself in the opposite direction to avoid sinking closer to him.

"That sounds like a recipe for disaster, Alice. You can't swim. And those people are no good," he said, running a finger through his newly bruised knuckles. "Are you going to that party? You know I have to keep an eye on you, right?"

"I know. And you won't need to come with me to the party. Isaac will be there."

"I should be with you at all times, Alice. I know you asked me to give you some space whenever you're with Isaac, but I—" Xavier shook his head. "I don't buy his story."

"There's nothing to buy, Xavi. He's a merfolk who has no one to help him with his magic. According to him, his mother passed away before he moved here. She was a merfolk. He has her journals."

Journals that were provided by his human father, but Alice would keep that out of this conversation. Revealing that would only increase Xavier's worries, and she could live without that.

Xavier's eyes shot to meet Alice's. "Why am I only hearing about this now?"

"He told me last night."

"You were with him last night?"

Alice massages her temples. "Phones exist, you know. He called. I answered. That's why I went to meet him at the cafe."

"And what did he want?"

She pursed her lips, glancing at the shelves on the wall and their display of Otherworld materials and resources.

"He wants me to help him with an amulet. To block his magic."

Saying the words out loud to someone made it even sound more ridiculous. It *was* ridiculous. When Xavier didn't laugh, she turned to look at him, confused. He kept his eyes on her, studying her features carefully.

"You said yes, didn't you?" It was the tone in his voice, so knowing and low, that added a layer of shame to Alice's feelings.

"I can't do it, but I said I'd help."

"And *how* exactly are you planning to do that?" Xavier ran a hand over his face. "One thing is helping him with magic theory, but he's asking you to *use* magic."

"I saved his life once, Xavi," she whispered, afraid her aunt would listen. "I can help him again."

"We don't know if you did it or if it was a mere coincidence." Xavier reached for her hands and held them in between his. "Alice, you *can't* summon magic properly. You should have seen yourself during the ritual. It was scary. How you didn't get stuck in between two planes is beyond me. I get that you want to help him, but you can't do everything." She tried to yank her hands from his, but he kept his grip strong. "I mean it. If this doesn't work, you're putting all of us at risk. *Again.*"

It would never stop stinging no matter how many times she heard it. To Xavier, to Victoria, to her parents, Alice would always be a liability. Maybe Aunt Gloria was right. Maybe she should go to Nadalan with her. At least, there, if bad things happened, she wouldn't be putting people at risk.

She could deal with the shame of not being able to summon magic. She had dealt with it most of her life. It wouldn't be different in Nadalan, but there, she wouldn't feel so much as an outsider.

"I was thinking of asking Victoria for information," she said, and Xavier let go of her hands.

"Your aunt?" Alice nodded. "Will you tell her about Isaac?"

"She doesn't have to know," Alice said.

Xavier chuckled. "That's impossible, Alice. Don't try to fight me on this. You know I'm right."

"Right about what?" Alice and Xavier turned to face Victoria as she stepped inside the back room. "Sorry about not greeting you earlier. I had a client with a very odd request and it took me forever to finish it. I'm free now."

She lowered her headband, shook her head to fix her curls, and put it back on.

"Do you want me to prepare for our lesson?" Alice asked. "What will we be doing today?"

"More basic stuff." Victoria took off her apron and dropped it on the table. "After what happened in the forest, it's important we review all of them. You need to be comfortable with the basics before we advance into harder spells."

"We've been doing that throughout this week, Vi. I know

them all by heart," Alice said, pouting. "Are you sure we can't try other things?"

"No." Her aunt's tone was final. "You may know them by heart but you still take too long to summon magic to perform them. We'll continue to go over each basic spell and potion today, and if you succeed, then next week we might try something different. Now, go grab your grimoire."

Alice couldn't help but roll her eyes as she got up from the couch and opened her backpack. It was the same thing every week. By now, Victoria should know that it was useless for Alice to perform basic magic. Somehow, she never got it right, and because of that, she couldn't try harder spells. What if she ended up succeeding at them? Alice would never know because her aunt never let her try.

"Can I ask you something, Vi?" Xavier adjusted himself on the couch, taking over part of the spot previously occupied by Alice.

"Sure." Victoria nodded. "What do you want to know?"

"How complex is it to create an amulet?"

Alice stared at him, but her gaze wasn't powerful enough to summon a stare back. He remained focused on Victoria as her eyes jumped between Xavier and Alice, her eyebrows furrowed.

"Usually, you need a spell. Oh, and the actual amulet has to be built with specific materials for the desired effect. But before you can even build the amulet, you need to get the Assembly's approval." She crossed her arms. "Why are you asking me this? Do you need an amulet?"

"I don't." Xavier raised his arms in defence. His eyes met Alice as she mouthed a *no* at him. "A friend of Alice needs one."

"A friend?" Victoria looked alarmed. "Alice, what is this about?"

She glared at Xavier, hoping that her eyes conveyed her desire to punch and probably toss him somewhere. This was why she hated having Xavier following her everywhere and knowing all her business. She wasn't allowed to have secrets.

"He's not a friend," Alice said, hugging her thick grimoire as she turned to face her aunt. "He's a merfolk who asked for my help. He needs an amulet to hide his magic so he can continue to live a normal life."

"Okay." Victoria nodded and leaned on the table behind her. She focused on Xavier. "Is this the same boy she did a life potion for?"

Xavier nodded, glancing at his knuckles. Alice's her heart dropped in her chest, making her sick to her stomach. What was her aunt saying? Had Xavier told Victoria about Isaac? They *promised* each other. They promised they wouldn't say *anything* to anyone. Alice couldn't believe it. Before she could stop herself, Alice dropped the grimoire back in her backpack and stomped towards Xavier on the couch.

"You told her?" She shook his shoulders, screaming at him, but he didn't even have the decency to look her in the eyes. "I asked you to keep this between us. You promised you'd keep this between us. Why did you have to tell her? *Why*?"

Xavier got up from the couch and Alice almost lost her balance. He kept his arm around her back, looking down at her. She didn't let go of him. She was too upset for that.

"I wasn't going to be complacent in your murder of someone. Besides, he's not a member of the Assembly. He doesn't exist in the records." He removed her hands from his shoulders, uncurling her fingers one by one. Alice curled them back into a fist as soon as he was done. "I was worried about who he might be. I still worry about what his intentions are towards you."

"I saved his life," Alice said, her voice frail. "I didn't murder him. You *saw*, Xavier. And I can defend myself. So far, Isaac hasn't done anything that makes me suspicious of him. He had many chances to hurt me if he wanted, and he didn't."

"I'm always around when he's near."

"Not always," she said. The confusion that settled in Xavier's lines was enough for her to feel victorious. "Maybe you're not that good at keeping an eye on me when I so easily escape from under your nose."

Before Xavier could say anything else, Victoria stepped in between them, pushing her arms wide to keep them apart. The fire in Xavier's eyes matched Alice's, and she wasn't sorry. Betrayal was painful, and she wanted him to taste it as much as she had. Alice never saw him as a friend, but now, he wasn't even someone she could trust. She would never trust him again.

Alice couldn't wait until she was gone from here and in Nadalan to get rid of him.

"Before the two of you escalate this discussion, I hope you understand that there's a lot at stake here," Victoria said. "That Isaac boy, the merfolk, doesn't exist in the Assembly records. That's a problem. Do you know what lineage he belongs to?"

Alice shook her head. "I saw his scales, but they didn't match any of the active lineages. They're pearlescent white."

"You saw his scales?" Xavier asked, incredulous. "When?"

"When you weren't around." She shrugged. "I met him late at night and saw them in person, and guess what? Nothing bad happened."

She wouldn't mention the fall in the pool or how he saved her from drowning. She wouldn't mention what had happened when he grabbed her. That was a mystery for her to unravel. Alone. Not with Xavier. Not anymore.

"When was it?" Xavier's eyes flashed gold, his voice a low growl. "This wasn't the first time, was it? How many times, Alice?"

"Enough, you two!" Victoria yelled, but that didn't stop Alice and Xavier from glowering at one another. "I'll look in the records of the Assembly about that information. Until then, we'll keep this between us." She focused on Alice and shook her head. "As for the amulet, I can't help you with that. And you can't do it yourself either."

"Why not?"

"Only Assembly registered amulet makers can create or sell an amulet. It's a new rule imposed by the Council a couple of years ago. If your friend wants an amulet, then he has to request it from the Assembly who will pair him with the right amulet maker."

"Don't you know someone who could make him an amulet off the records?" Alice asked. Victoria and Xavier exchanged a knowing look, but neither said anything. "Come on! There must be someone."

Victoria said nothing and Alice collapsed on the couch, defeated. She would never understand half of the rules the Assembly and the Council imposed. They said it was to keep all of them safe, but why did they have to make it so complicated?

It appeared that, when it came to Alice's life, nothing was ever simple.

"I said I would help him, Vi," Alice said, defeated. She shook her head. "If we can't do it, what am I supposed to tell him?"

Victoria sighed and sat down next to her, squeezing Alice's shoulder while offering her a soft smile. She opened her mouth to speak, but the voice didn't come from her.

"You will let that *boy* know he has an audience with the Assembly." The three of them turned to spot Aunt Gloria by the door, her expression serious. Her eyes narrowed on Alice, and she shook her head. "You're a disappointment, you know that? How can you keep something so dangerous all to yourself, Alice? Do you take us all for fools?"

"This is not the time, Gloria," Victoria said, not letting go of Alice's shoulder. "Once we're home, we'll talk about this. Not now."

"You're right." She fixed her jacket and hat, keeping a stern gaze on the three of them. "We'll talk at home. In the meantime, make yourself useful for once, Victoria, and call the Assembly for tonight. You can send our niece and her *shapeshifter* of a friend to get the merfolk. I want everyone in the amphitheatre at eleven sharp. And don't you even *dare* consider skipping it."

Aunt Gloria kept a finger pointed at Alice, her face red with anger. When no words were enough to convey her feelings, Gloria closed the back door with a loud bang and disappeared. Alice's breath caught in her throat. Whatever strength she had was gone from her body. The silence stretched as her thoughts jumbled into an incoherent mess of disappointment, betrayal and doubt.

"There's no lesson today," Victoria eventually said, her eyes jumping between Xavier and Alice. "You should both get ready for the Assembly."

"What should I tell Isaac?" Alice asked, massaging her temples. "That I'm bringing him to his doom?"

"Tell him he's meeting people like him." Victoria pursed her lips and stood up from the couch. "And that he has a lot of explaining to do."

Chapter Nineteen

ISAAC'S EVENING WAS SHAPING out to be the same as every other evening these past couple of days. As he sat on his bed, he kept most of his mother's journals open on the surface and a notebook on his lap where he collected most of his important notes.

This evening, he decided to follow the trail of his mother's magical abilities. She mentioned several times how magical abilities were hereditary, so it was likely that he had similar ones to her. He had made a list of things she referred to throughout the different pages he had analysed so far. They included some that Isaac already knew: he could breathe underwater, see underwater and he could hear better and at longer distances now. However, the one that stuck to him the most was the last one on his list, the one he had circled with a blue marker.

He needed to investigate it further since he had an idea of what it might be, but he couldn't properly explain it in his own words. It had happened multiple times now for him to dismiss it as a coincidence, and the clearer example of it would be when he experienced Alice's memories at the pool. To this day, he still couldn't shake off what had happened. Maybe going down this rabbit hole would help him find some answers.

A knock on Isaac's bedroom door woke him from his thoughts. He placed the journal he was reading on his bed and let his father know that he could step inside. His heart sunk in his chest when his father came into view. Isaac didn't like the concern displayed in his eyes.

"Did something happen?" Isaac asked.

"You have guests," his father said, crossing his arms. "I thought we had agreed to no more parties until you got your grades up."

Isaac furrowed his brows. He had been invited to a party, yes, but that wasn't happening *tonight.* Was there a change of plans?

"Liam came to visit?" Isaac reached for his phone and opened his group chat with his friends. Scrolling through the last couple of messages, no one was talking about a party. They were mostly talking about the next swimming competition happening, a competition that Isaac was still unable to participate in.

He dropped his phone back on his nightstand before getting too disappointed over it. When would this nightmare end?

"It's not Liam." His father shook his head. "It's a boy named Xavier and a girl named Alice. They say they know you, but I've never seen them and you never mentioned them before. Do you know them?"

"I do. We started hanging out a couple of weeks back." Isaac bit his lip, preventing any more information from spilling out. "I'll go meet them."

Isaac got up from his bed and followed his father downstairs, his heart jumping in his chest. He knew for sure Xavier and Alice weren't here to invite him to a party; they avoided them as much as possible. Still, Isaac couldn't help but wonder about the reason for their visit. It had to be something serious and important otherwise Alice would have texted him.

When he reached downstairs, Isaac turned to the entrance hall and stopped. Xavier and Alice stood side by side, both extremely well-dressed for the circumstances. Xavier had his silver hair slicked back, his eyes marked with black on the water line, making the intensity of his stare overwhelming to focus on for too long. He wore a black suit that seemed too tight for him on the shoulders and the buttons of the shirt underneath were holding on to dear life to stay closed.

It wasn't Xavier who got most of Isaac's attention, though. Alice wore a long short-sleeve burgundy dress with matching small gloves. Her hair was braided to the side with small dry blue and pink flowers intertwined throughout, a pop of colour that went against everything else she wore. Even her makeup was dark and heavy, but it wasn't enough to hide the beauty he had grown so accustomed to seeing in her.

"Hi," he said, unsure if she heard it. Isaac was too entranced by her to know how to speak properly.

"Hey," she replied, forcing out a smile his way. "Sorry for appearing like this unannounced."

"It's okay." He smiled at her.

"You can leave us now," Xavier eventually said, waking up Isaac from his trance. His eyes flicked into a golden hue as he stared at Isaac's father. "We'll take it from here."

"Of course." His father cleared his throat, squeezing Isaac's shoulder. "I won't be far. If you need anything, I'll be in the kitchen."

Isaac nodded and waited until his father disappeared into the kitchen to focus back on his visitors.

"Are you here to invite me to a party?" he asked. "What's up with the outfits?"

Alice gulped and took a deep breath, keeping her eyes on her feet. She opened her mouth to speak, but shook her head, giving up.

"You're required to come with us," Xavier said, his voice grave. "It has come to the Assembly's attention that you're a merfolk, and so they require an audience with you."

"What's the Assembly?" he asked. Alice kept fidgeting with her gloves, her shoulders slumped forward. "Did something happen?"

"Alice asked for help with your amulet, and the wrong people found out. None of this would be happening if you had followed my orders to not bother her anymore," Xavier said between gritted teeth. "Now, go to your room and change into your best outfit. You should make a good impression with the Assembly."

Isaac's eyes jumped between Alice and Xavier. "I don't know what the Assembly considers a good outfit. Should I dress as if I am attending an important event like a prom? I think I have a three-piece suit in my wardrobe. I could wear that."

"Do you need help?" Alice asked, meeting his eyes with a look he recognised. "I could see if the suit is appropriate."

"You should stay here, Alice."

"I won't be far," she said to Xavier. "Besides, you know where I'll be. Keep an eye on his father. He can't follow us once we leave." When she met Isaac's eyes, he understood. "Do you want me to come with you?"

"Sure." He gestured to the stairs. "Follow me."

After Alice and Xavier glared at each other for longer than necessary, she followed Isaac up the stairs and he guided her into his bedroom. He gulped as he noticed the pile of dirty clothes in the corner, the mess on his desk and the opened journals on his bed.

"I'm sorry about it," he said, self-conscious. "I don't have many visitors in my bedroom. If I knew you were coming, I would've tried to make it look nicer."

Alice closed the door behind them, leaning against it. She kept her eyes on him, studying him. By now, Isaac should be used to her way of looking at him, but he wasn't. He also couldn't stop staring at her, couldn't stop thinking about the fact that she was in his bedroom. A wave of warmth took over his body and he rubbed the back of his neck.

Maybe he should open a window.

"I'm sorry for what's about to happen," she said after much effort. "It's my fault."

He furrowed his brows, his hand falling slowly to his side. "What's about to happen? You're not going to kill me, are you?"

"No." When she glanced at her feet instead of making a joke about his comment, his heart sank in his chest. "But it might feel like it."

"You're scaring me, Alice. What's happening?" As much as Isaac didn't want to sound panicked, that was exactly how he came across.

Alice stepped closer to him, then stopped. She crumpled her dress in her gloved hands, keeping her distance. The sadness in her eyes was palpable, and Isaac wished he could snatch it away and throw it out the window. Why did she look so defeated?

"I understand if you hate me after what I'm about to tell you, but you should know the truth, and we don't have much time, so please, don't interrupt me." Isaac nodded and Alice took a deep breath, pinching the bridge of her nose. "The Assembly is the governing body of *all* magical creatures in the human realm. They are aware of you, and they'll inquire about you and your life. Since there are no registers of you or your lineage, you are considered a person of interest for reasons I don't understand. This will be a public hearing, Isaac. Everyone will know about your life. And you won't be able to lie."

"I don't like lying," he said, trying to sound relaxed. "Everything will be fine, Alice."

"It won't." She shook her head, pursing her lips. "They don't know about the fire. About what I've done. About the fact that I can't summon magic. You will end up telling them all these things. I don't want you to feel guilty about it." Her eyes traced the walls of his bedroom until they found his closet. "Do you keep your clothes there? Do you have a suit?"

"Yes." He walked to his closet. "I have a suit I wore for a wedding a couple of years ago. It probably still fits me."

"Good. Wear it. The Assembly will put a lot of emphasis on how you present yourself."

"Is that why you're dressed like that?" He gestured to her dress, smiling. "You look really pretty."

"Thank you. It's a requirement for all magical beings to dress up when the Assembly is called. Just show me your suit and I'll leave to let you change."

He nodded and rummaged through his wardrobe, trying to locate his suit. Isaac found a hanger with a cover bag and grabbed it, opening the zipper to look at its contents. "Found it."

Isaac pulled the contents from the inside, laying the three-piece suit on his bed. A dark blue jacket with matching pants and a vest.

"Do you have a shirt? And a tie?"

"I have a shirt somewhere, yes." He opened one of his drawers and pulled a shirt out. "As for ties, I'd have to ask my father."

"That's out of the question," Alice said. After assessing his suit one more time, she pulled a burgundy scarf from the inside of her dress pocket and extended it to Isaac. "Wear it around your neck. Kind of like a scarf."

"Would it be too bad if I didn't take anything?" he asked, taking in the fabric. It was so smooth, it felt like butter in between his fingers. "I don't know how to put this on."

"I'll help you." Alice gestured to the door behind her. "I'll be outside. Once you've changed, let me know. I'll help you with the scarf. And try not to take too long. The later we are, the worse it'll be for you."

Without waiting for his reply, Alice left his bedroom, closing the door behind her. Isaac took a deep breath and dropped the scarf on his bed alongside the dark blue suit, his eyes falling on the open journals scattered around. He'd probably take care of them once he was back home from wherever they were going. Isaac hoped it wouldn't take long.

As quickly as he could, he changed into his outfit. It felt like a new skin he didn't recognise. The shirt was too tight around his torso, its collar scratching at his chin. The vest rested perfectly on top of it, but it was shorter than it should be, like his pants. After choosing a decent pair of socks and some shoes, he called Alice back into his room, holding the scarf in his hand.

"Do you think this is enough?" he asked, looking down at his outfit. He was somewhat uncomfortable. "It's rare I wear suits. I don't know how to walk in these."

"You walk like usual," Alice said, extending a hand to him. "The scarf."

He dropped it on her hand, trying to ignore the warmth in his cheeks when Alice stepped closer to him. Isaac looked at the ceiling as she wrapped the scarf around his neck, careful not to touch him. His eyes travelled back to her and he held his breath, trailing her features until he found her staring at him, her hands resting on his shoulders before she took a step back, admiring her work.

"I'd say you look nice. Have you seen yourself in the mirror?" He shook his head. Alice stepped aside and smiled at him. "You should."

Isaac walked towards his bedroom mirror. It was only a suit but he felt like a completely different person. The burgundy scarf made his green eyes pop and the dark blue suit enveloped him in a serious aura. He didn't look like himself. Isaac didn't know the person staring back at him. When Alice joined him and their eyes met in the mirror, the soft smile on her features faded.

"There's something else I need to tell you," she said.

"What is it?"

"You can require someone to assist you during the trial, similar to a lawyer. I'd like you to call me. If you want."

"I do," he said without breaking eye contact. "You'd be able to help me, right?"

"I'll try." She smiled weakly at him. Isaac focused on their reflection in the mirror, keeping his posture straight. Dressed like this, he couldn't deny how good they looked together and how much he liked it.

Alice lowered her eyes and Isaac turned around, reaching for her hand. It was instinctive to hold her hand in his, to squeeze it lightly as if to let her know he was here. He was the one about to go to a trial he knew nothing about, but here he was, consoling her.

"It'll be fine, Alice," he said. "I don't blame you. I'd never do that."

Isaac wrapped an arm around her shoulders and pulled her closer to him, kissing her temple. As soon as he realised what he had done, his body stiffened, for fear that he had gone too far, that he had done the wrong thing. He stood there, waiting for a comment from her, for her to push him away. Instead, Alice wrapped her arms around his torso, her breathing brushing against his neck as she rested her head on his shoulder.

"Thank you for trusting me," she whispered as his hand ran up and down her back. "Thank you for being a friend."

"Of course." He smiled. "You're one of the coolest people I know. I'd be stupid if I didn't want to be your friend."

Her grip around him tightened and he did the same, unsure if he wanted to let go. Part of Isaac wanted to keep this moment tucked in his heart forever out of fear it would never happen again. Even if it felt natural to hold her in his arms, he wasn't sure Alice felt the same way. The thought of it made his heartbeat increase, and he hoped she wouldn't notice that. He, however, could hear Alice's heartbeat as if it was his own. When he kissed her temple again, her heart's rhythm changed into disarray, becoming quicker and stronger, until it steadied alongside his.

Chapter Twenty

As much as Alice wanted to believe Isaac's words, she knew she should prepare for the worst. She didn't remember many of the Assembly meetings, but she did remember the panic of those on the stand, their questioning a source of mockery and disdain for those watching the trial. It was ruthless.

She didn't want Isaac to have to go through that on his own, not when she could help him. She *would* help him. Alice just hadn't completely figured out how that would be.

Isaac tightened his grip around her, resting his head on top of hers. She didn't care if her makeup got smudged, if her dried flowers fell from her braid. Here, in his arms, Alice felt a sense of safety she had longed for in a while. It was as if his embrace created a barrier between her and the outside world. Despite the intensity of his heartbeat, she didn't feel as anxious. Maybe he was right. Maybe everything would be okay in the end.

Someone knocked on Isaac's bedroom door. Alice and Isaac looked at one another, startled.

"We're getting late," Xavier said in a stern voice. "You should hurry. Let's not make the Assembly wait. Everyone's already in a bad mood."

"We'll leave in a second," Alice replied as she stepped away from Isaac. "We'll meet you downstairs."

"I'll stay here for two minutes. If you don't step out, I'll step in. Even if I have to barge through the door."

"That won't be necessary." Isaac grabbed the jacket from his bed and after staring at his reflection for a bit longer to regain his composure, he smiled at Alice. "Let's go."

She stepped in front of him. "Promise you'll call me. When you're on the stand. I don't want you to be alone in there. I want to be able to help you, and I can't do that from the crowd."

"I will." Isaac reached for her hand. His thumb traced circles around her gloved palm, and Alice's heart fluttered. "I'll call your name. I'm getting nervous now."

"You'll be fine." She squeezed his hand in what she hoped was a reassuring gesture. "I won't let them be too tough on you."

He laughed and Alice smiled. Behind them, the bedroom door opened and Xavier stepped inside, stopping when he spotted Alice and Isaac. His focus jumped from them to their hands together, a frown growing on his face.

"Are you done with whatever you've got going on?" he asked.

"Yes," she said. "We're ready to go."

They left Isaac's house and started to walk towards their destination. Instead of letting go of Isaac's hand, Alice kept holding it, relaxing in his presence beside her. She could tell Xavier wasn't pleased about it, but she didn't care anymore. After he broke her trust, his opinions were worthless to her now.

"Is that yours?" Xavier asked Alice as he pointed to the scarf around Isaac's neck. "Couldn't he find a tie?"

"He'd have to ask his father for one," she said. "I thought it'd be best not to risk it."

"You did well," Xavier said, his eyes darting to Alice and Isaac's hands together. "The less people that know about this, the better."

Alice rolled her eyes. "Right. Because you would know a lot about that."

"This wouldn't have happened if you hadn't accepted his request," Xavier said. "I instructed him to stay away from you. We don't know who he is!"

"I'm *right* here!" Isaac took a deep breath and glanced at

Xavier. “Look, all I wanted was for Alice to help me figure out how I could go back to my normal life. I never intended to get involved in these messes. All of this is unknown to me. I’m just a guy who happened to become a merfolk at the wrong time. Nothing more. So quit acting like that.”

“I can’t," Xavier said between gritted teeth, stepping closer to Isaac. “I was assigned to protect Alice and identify all possible threats to her. I’m *here* to keep her safe. And right now, you’re a threat, and I don’t trust you. I’m not going to quit acting like this.”

“Is this because of what happened with those Magic Hunters when she was younger?” Isaac blurted out.

Alice closed her eyes and pinched the bridge of her nose, letting go of Isaac’s hand. “Can we not talk about that right now?” she asked. “Let’s just keep quiet until we reach the Assembly.”

As they continued their walk towards Alice’s house, Xavier stepped in between Alice and Isaac, separating them. She took a deep breath and hugged herself, rubbing her arms to keep the cold of the night away. After a while, she felt the weight of Xavier’s jacket on her shoulders and she fought the urge to take it off and stomp on it. That was what he deserved. He wasn’t this controlling or suspicious before. What changed?

Xavier quickly extended both of his arms, preventing Alice and Isaac from moving forward. His eyes flashed golden as he scanned their surroundings, his features growing sombre.

“Do you think someone is following us?” Alice whispered, glancing over her shoulder.

The cold breeze shook the tree leaves and the lack of functioning streetlights only made it harder for Alice to view her surroundings and locate any potential threats. She focused on the empty darkness ahead of her, holding her breath in anticipation.

“Oh, it’s a lynx!” Isaac said, pointing to somewhere in the distance behind them. Alice could barely see anything there, but Xavier nodded in acknowledgement. “Are lynxes native to this area?”

“Apparently they are,” Xavier said, relaxing slightly. “Let’s keep moving and avoid the main streets.”

Xavier and Isaac kept walking, but Alice stood there, waiting for the lynx to reveal itself. As expected, the animal stepped into the light, its eyes fixed on her, and she took the opportunity to inspect its aura. It was a very faint shimmering silver, one that was too weak to be of a healthy animal.

"Are you alright?" she asked, taking a tentative step towards the lynx. When it didn't move away, she took another. "Are you hurt?"

She knew animals didn't understand her—there was a spell for that, but Alice couldn't properly summon magic to use it right now—so she hoped her relaxed nature and slow approach would do the trick. Lynxes weren't harmful, but they liked to be left to their own devices. Alice would let it be, but first, she wanted to make sure it was alright.

The lynx sat down on the concrete road, its attention on Alice. She removed one of her gloves and extended her hand towards its nose, allowing it to sniff her.

"Come on," she said, smiling at its bright hazel eyes, "I'm your friend. I only want to make sure you're okay."

The lynx sniffed her hand and she smiled at the cute black tufts on its ears and the white fur on its chin, the long tips on its side giving it the shape of a bowtie. Lynxes were such beautiful animals, but this was the first time Alice was up close to one. It was gorgeous. A giant cat, some would call it. So far, it had a better temperament than Whiskers.

Xavier grabbed her hand midair, earning a glare from her. He was fuming right back at her. "Leave it. It's probably going out for food, and we're late."

"But—" She turned to where the lynx was, finding the spot empty. Alice glanced around. "Where did it go?"

"It doesn't matter," he said, pulling her sloppily to where Isaac was a few steps ahead. Alice obliged but got rid of his hand around her wrist, rubbing it to try and soften the pulsing pain.

Alice kept her distance from Xavier as they avoided the main streets and stuck to secondary roads on their way to her house, always following the shadow path. She enjoyed walking at night, the quiet the darkness brought. It was comforting, an invitation to stay a while and enjoy the view. Instead, she had to keep going, keep moving. That didn't stop her from slowing down occasionally to look over her shoulder or at the cloudy sky above them. It was sad that she couldn't see the stars tonight. She always enjoyed their reassuring company.

"Where are we going?" Isaac asked.

"To Alice's house," Xavier said, narrowing his eyes on Isaac. "We'll access the Assembly through there."

Alice chuckled. "That's one way to put it."

"It doesn't stop it from being true," Xavier said. "But get ready to walk a lot. And see very little."

"What is *that* supposed to mean?" Isaac glanced at Alice. "Is the Assembly at your house?"

She shook her head. "You'll see it when we get there."

They walked in silence until they reached the familiar building of Alice's home. She took the lead and opened the squeaky gate, allowing Xavier and Isaac to step inside, and then climbed the stairs that led to the entrance door as quietly as possible. Instead of ringing the bell, she knocked, and her heart jumped in her chest with anticipation.

As soon as the door opened, Victoria stared at the three of them expectantly. "What took you so long?"

"Isaac had to find something to wear," Alice said, gesturing to him. "We're here now. Where's my mom and dad?"

"Already in the tunnels." Victoria closed the door behind them. "They went with Gloria. I stayed to go with you since it's been a while, and I was afraid you didn't remember the path."

Victoria's heels clicked on the wooden floor as she stepped deeper into the house, turning back to look at them. Her cheeks had an unnatural rosy tone that matched her lips, and her curls were pinned back in an array that made her appear much older than she was. Her pantsuit, however, brought back all the playfulness Alice knew from her aunt.

"Follow me," Alice said as she joined her aunt.

Isaac scanned his surroundings, focusing on the wall shelves with small trinkets, the large colourful stones that decorated the fireplace. Several paintings greeted the walls, and when thought he could move closer to one of them, he bumped his leg on the coffee table.

"Careful," Xavier said. "Watch where you're going."

"Sorry," he mumbled, extending an apologetic look to Alice. "I'll pay more attention now."

She nodded and opened the door to her right, turning the lights on. Inside, a small study with walls covered in bookshelves invited them in. She stepped inside, followed by Victoria, a reluctant Isaac, and an annoyed Xavier, who closed the door behind him.

"There are a lot of books here," Isaac said, nodding to himself. "Family heirlooms?"

Alice didn't answer. She went to the desk on her right. Behind it was a portrait of three people on the wall, something that didn't go unnoticed by Isaac. She had seen it so many times, she had forgotten it existed.

"That's a family heirloom," she said, smiling at Isaac. "And a family tradition too."

"Whenever a witch comes into power, it's common for them to get a portrait taken with their parents or guardians," Victoria added. "Alice looks rather cute, doesn't she?"

"She was a cute kid, yes." Isaac nodded, a smile growing on his features. "How old was she?"

"Five or six, I can't remember." Victoria smiled at Alice. "Have you found the drawer?"

"On it!"

Alice abstracted from the conversation around the room and focused on opening the third drawer on the desk and patting the top of it inside. It didn't take long for her fingers to find a small button. She lifted her eyes to the small crowd near one of the bookshelves where Isaac had leaned on to hear Victoria's stories about Alice's childhood. Xavier kept his attention on her, meeting her gaze before she looked away.

"If I were you, I'd lean away from that," Alice said to Isaac, clicking the button.

"Why should—"

The bookshelf behind Isaac slid to the side, and he didn't move away in time. He lost his balance and tripped backwards, almost falling down the stairs. Thankfully, Xavier grabbed his arm and pulled him upwards, preventing Isaac from falling.

"Are you okay?" Xavier asked as he kept his hand wrapped around Isaac's upper arm.

"Yeah." Isaac nodded with wide eyes. "I'm okay. I was just surprised, that's all."

"Sorry," Alice said, moving away from the desk. "I thought the trigger took longer to activate."

Xavier let go of Isaac and stepped back, allowing Alice to join them in the semi-circle around the secret passage the bookshelf had revealed. Isaac turned around and gasped, and if it wasn't for Alice's hand on his shoulder, he would have tripped back again.

"Where does it lead to?" he whispered to her. "It's very dark."

"Not for long." Victoria gestured to Alice. "Would you mind doing the honours?"

Alice removed one of her gloves and after snapping her thumb and index fingers, a small blue flame appeared on the tip of her index finger. She walked closer to the opening and placed her finger on top of one of the candles hanging from the wall inside, watching the flame twirl and twist until it became two. In a few seconds, the rest of the candles mimicked its behaviour, coming to life in a downward zig-zag pattern without Alice's assistance. As she stared at the stairs made of stone, Alice couldn't spot where they ended in the distance.

"How deep is this passage?" Xavier asked, looking over Alice's shoulder. "Where does it end?"

"I don't know." Alice looked at everyone, taking in their bewilderment. She focused on Victoria. "Should we get going?"

"They should go first," she said, glancing at Xavier. "Are you sure you can handle this matter?"

"Yes. I know what I'm doing." Xavier put a hand on Isaac's shoulder, forcing him to look at him preventing him from moving any further. "There are rules you must follow once we step inside. For starters, you can't address anyone. You should always keep your head down and only speak when asked to. Is that clear?"

"Yes." Isaac nodded. "Can't speak with anyone. I can do that."

"Good." Xavier patted his shoulder with more strength than necessary. "We're ready to go, then. Fix your suit."

Alice removed Xavier's jacket from her shoulders and extended it to him, watching as he put it on in one swift motion. Isaac patted down his vest and fixed his cuffs before glancing at Alice for approval. She stepped closer and rearranged the scarf around his neck, her cheeks heating up as she realised how close she was to him.

"I think you're good now." She smiled at him. "Xavier will keep an eye on you, okay? And once you're on the stand, you know what to do."

"I know." His fingers brushed against Alice's cheek, lingering there for a while. "We'll see each other in a bit."

Xavier stepped forward, starting to climb down the stairs slowly, before turning around to look at Isaac expectantly. Reluctantly, he joined Xavier, and they descended a few more steps together before waving at Victoria and Alice.

"I'll come to meet you once I deliver Isaac," Xavier said, his features softening as he stared at Alice. "This shouldn't take long."

"It'll take a while," Victoria said, gesturing to them to keep going. "We'll follow right after you."

They didn't follow right after. Victoria and Alice stood at the top of the stairs, staring at a strange never-ending flight of stairs, waiting for Isaac and Xavier to disappear from their view. Once they were out of sight, Victoria walked to the top of the stairs and pressed her palm against the wall. The flames flickered as a small landing slid from the wall a few steps below, seemingly stretching into a long corridor. Alice blinked.

"What did you do?"

Victoria shrugged. "I decided it would be best to send them through deeper tunnels. You know, so they don't cross paths with familiar faces. But you better be ready to hear people complain about your lack of punctuality."

"It's fine." Alice put her glove back on. "I'm used to that."

Victoria nodded and helped Alice fix her sleeves and shoulder line, smiling at her. "Isaac seems nice."

"He is." Alice pursed her lips together, avoiding her aunt's gaze on her. "I hope it all goes well for him at the Assembly."

Without waiting for her aunt to move into the passage first, Alice fixed her posture and started the slow descent to the Assembly, unsure of how this ludicrous plan would play out. Soon after her aunt joined, she heard the dry *thump* sound of the bookshelf falling back into place, and she knew there was no getting out of this now.

Chapter Twenty-One

ISAAC COULD NO LONGER tell where he was going. After losing sight of Alice as soon as he started to climb down the stairs, Xavier guided him through a series of never-ending corridors. Turn right, then left. Climb a flight of stairs. Turn left again.

It was common for Isaac to trip forward; he couldn't make out anything around him. Despite the sturdy stone pavement below his feet, the walls around him were rough. The atmosphere was cool, the air stale as Isaac tried to breathe. Behind him, Xavier seemed unbothered by his surroundings.

"Are you sure we're going the right way?" Isaac asked, his voice muffled. He expected it to echo.

"We're almost there," Xavier said, tightening his grip on Isaac's shoulder. "And keep your voice down. You shouldn't talk with anyone."

"Does that include you?"

"Yes. We aren't supposed to know each other. You're not supposed to know anyone around here."

Isaac sighed. He got that message loud and clear the first time, he didn't need to be reminded of it every time they turned a corner. Whatever this was, Isaac just wanted to get this over with. He wanted to go home, continue to read his mother's journals and sleep. He wasn't sure how late in the night it was, but his mind wasn't as focused as usual.

Isaac almost tripped again as his feet bumped against a small step, marking the change in his surroundings. Ahead of him, the new corridor was much more inviting, with lights placed at equal distances, a soft earthy scent in the air as they kept walking. The walls were a smooth beige, whereas below his feet the stones were of multiple colours now, creating patterns under his feet. Far away, a bright source of light caught Isaac's attention.

"Where are we?" he asked, glancing over his shoulder at Xavier. "What is this place?"

"Keep your mouth shut and your eyes down. I won't warn you again."

A few more steps ahead, the corridor opened to reveal doors on each side, all made of a dark wood, with details at the centre of its frame. They were carvings of animals, flowers and other mythical creatures that Isaac knew from fairy tales. A sea serpent, with its tail forming the shape of the number eight. A phoenix, with its wings opened to the side, its beak pointing upwards to the surface, as flames burned under it. There were others that he couldn't name, countless he didn't recognise.

Before he could comment on it, they climbed down a long flight of stairs on their left, instead of continuing forward to the bright light. They landed on a similar corridor where everything was less detailed and stripped of the beauty Isaac had spotted upstairs.

Xavier gripped his shoulder and opened a wooden door to his right. He gestured with his head to Isaac. "Step inside. Don't make me drag you."

"I won't." He raised his arms and stepped into the room, followed by Xavier, who closed the door behind them.

The room wasn't what Isaac expected to find down here. The walls were covered with several lamps, all illuminating his lush surroundings. On the wall opposite Isaac, large windows gave view to an inner garden where small fireflies flew from one bush to the other, occasionally spinning with one another. Maybe they weren't fireflies. Maybe they were fairies, like the ones at the flower shop. He wasn't sure how plants could flourish like this underground, but it was probably the result of a spell of some sort. Around the room, several cushions and a large couch took centre stage as well as a cart with food and other refreshments, including tea.

"Are you sure we should be here?" Isaac asked, glancing at the golden seashell detail on the wallpaper. "This seems a lot for someone they don't like."

"We're not monsters," Xavier said, crossing his arms as he leaned against the door. "Besides, most rooms in the caves look like this."

"Why?" Isaac asked.

"Some magical beings can't live on the surface, so they spend most of their time here. Besides, sometimes while travelling across realms, it's safer to stay underground. It also helps that you can access most portals through the vast web of caves and galleries."

"So this is kind of an airport and hotel combined into one?"

Xavier shrugged. "Something like that, yes. But that's not all."

Isaac sat on the couch, relaxing. Under Xavier's stern gaze, he grabbed a slice of lemon cake from the cart. "Are you sure I can eat this? Do you want some?"

"I'm fine. Besides, I don't eat when I'm working."

Isaac nodded and took a bite of his cake, humming in delight. He poured himself some tea and took a sip as well, satisfied with this small meal. After devouring his cake and tea, Isaac wiped his mouth and leaned back on the couch, keeping his gaze on Xavier. He remained near the door with his back against it, eyes focused on something in the distance. As much as he knew Xavier wanted him to remain quiet, Isaac had never been one to keep his mouth shut for long.

"So… *Alice*," he started. "She's upset with you, isn't she? Is it because of me?"

Xavier glared at him as his jaw tensed. Isaac chuckled. So Alice *was* angry with him. It didn't please Isaac that it might be because of him, though.

"If I were you, I wouldn't go down that line of thought," Xavier said. "Alice is not staying in this realm for much longer, and when she leaves, I doubt she'll remember you." At the confusion breaking into Isaac's features, Xavier smiled. "Oh, so she didn't tell you that she was leaving..."

Isaac narrowed his eyes on Xavier, unable to ignore his smug expression that made Isaac's skin crawl. Alice and Isaac weren't *that* close, but the idea of her leaving brought an unexpected pain to his chest that he couldn't get past. She didn't have to keep Isaac informed of what she did with her life, but he wanted to be a part of it. Realising that knocked the air out of Isaac's lungs, and he wasn't sure what to do about it.

A knock on the door brought Xavier to his senses. The smile disappeared from his features and he opened the door, glancing at whoever was on the outside. After exchanging a couple of words with the person, he turned to Isaac.

"Time for you to go. This man will take you to the next location. We'll meet back here once this is over. Remember what I said." Xavier held his gaze and Isaac nodded. "Good. I'll see you from the gallery."

Xavier slipped out of the room, leaving Isaac alone with his nerves flourishing deep within him.

"You must be the lost merfolk." A man stepped inside wearing a shirt with so many ruffles Isaac wondered if he was from a different century. "Many people are curious about you."

Isaac bit the inside of his cheek until he tasted blood. He gulped and focused on his feet, waiting for orders to move to his next location. *How many locations are there?* Isaac wasn't easily terrified, but he found himself looking for a sense of familiarity in his surroundings. This was so different from what he was used to, so out of his comfort zone.

"Follow me, boy," the man said, offering him a smile. Isaac didn't miss the sharpness of his teeth, which made him flinch.

He got up from the couch and exited the room to the dark hallway, listening to the murmurs of conversations nearby. The man started to walk and Isaac followed him, trying to remember where he was going. Two flights of stairs down, a long hallway, a left before climbing some stairs again.

Even though he couldn't make out conversations, Isaac could see light at the end of this corridor and make out shapes of people in the distance. The closer he got, the louder the chatter became with people laughing and using big gestures to express themselves.

It was only when he crossed the door that reality sank in.

"Council," the man said, bowing to a woman with a top hat nearby. "The boy is here."

She smiled at him. "Thank you for your service."

The man guided Isaac to the only chair in the centre of the stand and disappeared into the dark corridor, closing the door behind him with a loud bang. The sound carried through the space, causing some of the voices to turn into murmurs.

"So you're the boy my poor niece is infatuated with," the woman said, narrowing her eyes at him. "What's your name?"

"Isaac," he said in a whisper. "Isaac Kallan."

"Kallan, you said?" She raised an eyebrow, and Isaac nodded. "That's quite a peculiar surname."

"I think it's normal," he said. What this woman might find peculiar was that instead of taking his father's last name, his parents had given him his mother's.

She scrutinised him with such despair that Isaac had to look towards the crowd.

His mouth opened in surprise. He had never seen anything like this, never been in a place like this. He had seen pictures of amphitheatres, but he had never been in one, especially not one underground. How were they able to build such a large structure inside? If he looked up, he could almost swear he could make out the stars in the night sky from here, but he didn't feel any cold. *Magic,* he concluded. He was surrounded by magic.

Isaac scanned the crowd as he looked for Alice. Everywhere, people wore elegant clothes, all bothered by their conversations and importance. The few that glanced at Isaac whispered with one another behind feathered fans or other concealing objects. He had never felt so exposed as he did here.

Above the main crowd, he spotted a row of galleries where even more people stood. They had carvings on their front, similar to the ones he had seen in the doorframes on his way here, but the one that caught Isaac's attention was the one at the centre with a large phoenix embedded with several different crystals around its wings. Alice stood at its edge, her eyes sinking into him. He attempted to smile at her, but he was too stiff to move, too scared to even think. Next to her, he spotted Xavier, who promptly placed a hand on her shoulder to pull her away from the front of the balcony. She brushed his hand off, glaring at him with such intensity that he feared Xavier might combust on the spot.

Alice fixed her gloves and stepped away from the edge of the gallery, walking in the opposite direction of Xavier, camouflaging in the shadows. Now that Isaac knew where she was, he took a deep breath, relaxing slightly.

"Silence, everyone," the woman spoke to the crowd and a small hammer hit the wood podium on its own. "I'd like you all to take a seat. We're already running behind schedule, and I would not like to keep you here for longer than necessary.

"As you may know," she continued with an authoritative voice, "it has come to *my* attention that there is an unregistered merfolk in town, which poses several problems to *all* of us. We were able to capture him, and we brought him in for questioning. We ask that if you have questions, pass them to your order representative so they can ask them when it's time. Shall we proceed?"

"Yes," the crowd chanted as people sat down on their chairs in a wave.

In the galleries, a few people remained standing, including Xavier who, from the corner of Alice's gallery, kept his eyes on her.

"Well, I, Gloria Beaumount, as a high member of the Council, will conduct this questioning," the woman said and the wooden hammer hit the podium again, the sound echoing in the large space.

Isaac slowly raised his arm. After a wave of gasps, the woman turned to face him. At her expectant expression, Isaac said, "I was informed that I could ask for a representative while I go through with my questioning. Can I ask for it now?"

"Who told you that?" she asked, her voice angrier than he expected. "You are under trial. There is no way—"

"The boy has every right to ask for a representative, Council," the man with sharp teeth spoke as he sat on his chair in the front row. "He may be unregistered, but the same rights apply to him. Whether you like it or not, we're all equal here." He leaned forward, smiling at Isaac. "Tell me, boy, would you like me to represent you?"

Isaac's heart jumped in his chest as he shook his head, a wave of laughter spreading through the crowd. Everything was too much. He was too hot, too cold, voices were too loud, he could barely hear what people were saying. His vision grew blurry, so he shut his eyes, trying to recompose himself.

"It is unlikely he knows anyone in here, anyway," Gloria said, followed by a snarky chuckle that hid something that Isaac didn't miss. *Fear.* "But tell me, Isaac Kallan, who do you wish to have representing you?"

He pursed his lips. He could ignore Alice's suggestion, could go through all of this by himself. He could keep her out of this, which was the best option for her, considering he wasn't supposed to know who anyone around here was. He should do that. It would probably be safer for her that way, too.

He shouldn't ask for her help again. He shouldn't even consider getting her help. And yet, when he opened his eyes, the words that rolled out of his tongue were the exact opposite.

"I ask for Alice Barlow to represent me during this questioning."

If Isaac had expected these people to keep quiet after his request, all of that came crashing down as soon as the pointy-teeth man started to laugh at Gloria's wide eyes on Isaac, her jaw clenched with anger. In the crowd, people yelled and shouted words at him in languages he couldn't understand, but he made out a few words from the ones he did. *Traitor. Spy. Who does he think he is?*

He glanced at the gallery where he last saw Alice. His heart thumped in his ears as he hoped to glimpse her, even if it was just to see her shake her head and deny his request. This was bad for her too. Maybe even worse for her than it was for him.

"Silence!" Alice's voice echoed through the amphitheatre, a sound that Isaac associated with comfort now. She stepped closer to the edge of her balcony and glanced down at who looked up at her. "I accept Isaac Kallan's request. From here on out, I am representing him. So judge him fairly. Even on the stand, he is one of us."

"He is *not* one of us." Isaac heard Gloria snarl to herself. Her hands turned into fists. "None of them are."

Alice disappeared again, followed by Xavier a few steps behind. Isaac's heart jumped in his chest with anticipation, his eyes glued to the door on the side of the stand. Whatever would happen next, he would be okay. With Alice by his side, Isaac knew he could do this.

He didn't know what awaited him, but he would survive it nonetheless.

Chapter Twenty-Two

ALICE'S HEARTBEAT PULSED THROUGH her body as she disappeared from her family's gallery in the Assembly amphitheatre. She quickly scanned her surroundings and ran down the stairs, trying her best not to trip on her shoes. Despite the complicated maze that the caves were, if she kept climbing down, she would eventually find the entrance to the stand.

Behind her, Xavier tried to keep up with her, but she was more agile at cutting corners and he kept falling behind.

"You shouldn't be doing this," he said, leaning on a wall to catch his breath. "Remember that you know nothing about him, Alice. Nothing."

She stopped and turned back, finding his piercing eyes staring at her. "And you do? Have you been spying on him? Collecting information and keeping it from me?" She chuckled. "That seems to be your speciality, right? To keep things from me."

"I was *trying* to keep you safe."

"Well, look at where that brought us." She gestured to their surroundings, the wall light greeting Xavier's features, his eyes shifting from dark brown to golden.

She felt it then, that intense pull of his stare, the vacancy of her thoughts.

"Alice, listen to me. This is a mistake. We will return to the gallery, okay? You'll tell people you made a mistake. They'll understand." Xavier extended a hand towards her. "Come on. I'll take you there."

Alice's feet remained glued to the ground, her focus on Xavier's golden eyes. *I should go back,* she thought. *I should join him.* Her mind was clear of all confusion, and she only had one focus in mind. Holding Xavier's hand and joining her family at the gallery. Where was she, anyway? She glanced around, trying to locate herself. Had she gotten lost in the corridors again?

She took one step forward, then another. Xavier nodded at her, a soft smile on his lips as she got closer to him, his hand reaching out towards her. She glanced at his eyes—now brown again—and at his hand. Alice slowly raised her hand, unsure if she should take his. Despite every part of her body demanding her to do so, something else within her pushed back, screamed at her not to do this.

"Why was I here?" she asked, meeting his gaze again. His eyes shifted to their golden shade and when Alice felt the same lightness as before, she shook her head at him. "Don't you *dare* use your commands on me. You did it just now, didn't you? Answer me!"

Xavier said nothing. He kept leaning against the wall, hand stretched towards her. She slapped it away.

"Go away," she said. "I don't want you near me."

"Alice—"

"Stop it, Xavier! Just stop!" she yelled, her cheeks burning.

Whenever she thought he couldn't stoop any lower, Xavier found a way to surprise her. She hated him. Hated him more than she hated herself. She hated him to the point of never wanting to see his face again, of never wanting to cross paths with him again. He said he was *trying* to protect her! Who tries to protect while doing this? Alice's heart sunk to her stomach as a hole took shape in her chest. She should have never believed any of the words that came out of his mouth.

"They'll see you as a traitor," he said, his voice low. "You're a witch, Alice. He's a merfolk. You know how this usually goes."

"Let me be their traitor, then," she said with open arms, stepping backwards. "At least I'm not a coward like you."

Xavier shook his head. He ran a hand through his hair as he paced around the corridor, his jaw clenched in anger. When his stare burned into Alice, she recoiled, watching him tower over her as he got closer. Xavier merely stood there, the warmth of his body something familiar she wanted to forget. Everything about him used to be comforting, but now it only brought her pain and disappointment.

"Let me be a coward to you, then. At least, I'm *something*."

"You're *nothing* to me," Alice said between gritted teeth. "You never trusted me, and I was stupid for ever thinking I could trust you. We're not equals. We're not friends. We're *nothing* to each other. Don't forget that, Xavier." She met his eyes and pushed him away, but he remained solid as a rock. "If anyone is a traitor, it's you."

Alice turned her back on him and kept walking, her steps echoing through the corridor.

"Do you think he'll care? After you're done helping him. Do you think he will stand by your side? He is using you, Alice."

"I don't need him to care," she said. "I don't need *anyone* to stand by my side. I'll be alone, and there's that."

Alone without magic. Alone without friends. Alice's future was shaping out to be one of solitude. She should be content, relieved, even. If she was alone, there was no one to disappoint. If she was alone, there was no one to count on, no one to trust, no one to rely on. That would save her from this pain and misery. The fact she was hurting because of Xavier made her mad at herself. This shouldn't be it.

"I'll stay here," he said, keeping his distance from her. "I'll be nearby."

Alice sighed and opened the heavy door and stepped onto the platform, earning a few stares and whispers from the crowd. As soon as she spotted Isaac, she smiled at him, a gesture he reciprocated. She stayed next to him, hand on his shoulder, gripping him slightly. Despite everything, she was happy to see him. Happy to be here on the stand with him so she could help him.

Aunt Gloria scanned her with precise judgement, going over

her flushed cheeks and flying hairs, to the rumpled dress around her knees and waist, to her sneakers that shouldn't have been her shoe choice for the evening.

"You're picking the wrong battles, Alice," Aunt Gloria said, before turning to the crowd with a smile. To her, this was a performance, one where she was the hero and Isaac was the villain. "Now that Alice Barlow is here on the stand to represent Isaac Kallan, we shall proceed with the questioning. First, the boy will have a truth potion. Then, we'll move to the first section of this trial."

"Is a truth potion really necessary?" Alice asked as her aunt walked to the podium and grabbed a flask with a fluorescent blue liquid inside.

Aunt Gloria ignored her and extended the flask to Isaac. He drank it swiftly, frowning afterwards. The truth potion was supposed to keep people from lying. Alice had learned how to do it, but she never considered an occasion where she would need such a potion. Now, she saw more than one.

She shook her head at the thought of Xavier. He wasn't important anymore.

The questioning started soon after the minor spell. Alice felt a warm tingling sensation around her, and gripped Isaac's shoulder, earning a worried glance from him. She reassured him with a nod.

The first section of the trial was simple. Aunt Gloria asked Isaac a couple of questions such as: what was his name, where was he from, what kind of magical order was he a part of, when did his abilities manifest. Isaac answered all the questions diligently, comfortable despite the amount of people staring intently at him.

Alice would never get used to it. As much as she liked to dress up for these events, being in the spotlight always made her question all her choices.

"Are you an orphan?" Aunt Gloria asked, leaning on the podium next to her. On it, a feather moved, occasionally dipping its tip on a jar of golden ink, writing down everything that was said in this room onto a piece of paper.

"No." Isaac shook his head. "I live with my dad. My mom died when I was young."

"Is your father the one with merfolk lineage?"

Isaac shook his head. "It was my mom."

"And what is your merfolk lineage, then?"

"We weren't able to identify it," Alice chimed in, giving Isaac some time to breathe. This resulted in whispers from the crowd and an eyebrow raise from her aunt.

"So you were unable to identify his lineage… How long have you known about him?"

"I'm not the one being questioned, Council," Alice said. "But I believe it is in Isaac's best interest to know what his lineage is."

Her aunt held her gaze for a while, waiting for Alice to break and let out more information than she should. She wouldn't. Alice would steer this questioning to their task at hand, which was to get Isaac his permission to acquire an amulet.

"Well, I guess it is important for us to identify his lineage, so we can add it to the records and solve this pressing issue. Can you show us your scales at will, boy?"

Isaac lowered his eyes and shook his head.

"Fine, then." Aunt Gloria rolled up the sleeves of her burgundy button-up shirt. "We'll do this the old-fashioned way. It might be better if you took off your jacket."

"What for?" Alice asked as Isaac removed his jacket, extending it to her. She took it and folded it on her arms, her heart jumping in her chest.

"You'll see," her aunt said. "Your arm, boy. Roll your sleeve up until your elbow."

Isaac did as he was told and extended his arm to Aunt Gloria. She removed her gloves, exposing calloused hands with deep scars on the back of them, and grabbed Isaac's arm, pressing one of her palms on his forearm.

"Now, this will hurt," she said. "There is no shame in crying or screaming. Are you ready?"

Isaac shook his head. "No."

"Well, too bad. We have to get this done."

The air shifted around the three of them, becoming warmer. Alice noticed the change in Isaac's skin as it turned into a bluish brown, the golden veins shining across his body, their brightness stronger in his arm. Aunt Gloria pressed her hand more into his skin and Isaac yelped, biting his lower lip as sweat beads formed on his forehead, slipping down his face.

"What are you doing?" Alice asked, sounding more worried than she'd like.

"I am doing what has to be done. Until I see scales on his skin, I will continue to increase the magic flowing in his body."

Isaac screamed again, leaning his head backwards as he stared at the ceiling, his breathing shallow as he tried to get rid of Aunt Gloria's grip, tried to get rid of the pain. His eyes became erratic, jumping onto everything until he closed them, letting out one last yelp of pain.

"I'm thirsty," he said before his head fell to the side, almost knocking Isaac out of his chair.

"Keep him in place," Aunt Gloria demanded. "I need to see his scales."

From the crowd, people leaned one way or the other to get a better look at what was happening. Alice positioned herself as best as she could to protect Isaac from the prying eyes all around. This wasn't a show. It looked more like a punishment than anything else.

When Isaac's ears started to change shape, Alice's eyes jumped to his hand, where small pearlescent scales started to grow on its surface.

"Those are the scales," Alice said, pointing at them. "Do you recognise the lineage?"

Alice knew if anyone would have the answer it would be her aunt. As a member of the Council, the governing body of all magical creatures in both the Human Realm and Otherworld, Aunt Gloria would know what lineage Isaac belonged to.

"It can't be," Aunt Gloria whispered, her wide eyes jumping from Isaac's scales to his features. "It can't... How is it possible?"

"What are you talking about?" Alice asked. "Council?"

Her aunt was petrified, glued to the ground as she stared at Isaac, unable to let go. Alice noticed the scales spreading up his chest into his collarbone, and she knew this wasn't natural. If Aunt Gloria kept pushing Isaac's magic like this, he would enter another blackout. Having seen him go through this once, Alice wasn't looking forward to seeing it happening again.

"Council, I believe you already know the lineage, so please, let go of his arm." Her aunt didn't listen. Alice stepped closer and tried to remove her aunt's hand, to no avail. "Aunt Gloria, please, let go of him. We already saw his scales, no need to keep this going!"

"It can't be." Her aunt shook her head. "She's gone. I made sure it all got taken care of. She's—"

Alice removed her glove and grabbed Isaac's hand in hers. She wasn't sure what she intended with it, but she expected the result to be similar to the one she had witnessed at the local pool, when he held her in his arms. Maybe the same would happen here and her aunt would return to her senses when she saw his scales disappearing.

The scales on his neck and jaw were the first ones to fade, followed by the ones across his arm and hand. His elbows and knuckles were last, the scales sinking back into the skin as if they had never been there.

Aunt Gloria shook her head and pulled out one of the scales on Isaac's arm at the last moment. She stepped back, almost tripping as she regained her composure. She focused on Isaac briefly, then on Alice, then on their hands together. She fixed her top hat before rolling down the sleeve of her shirt, slowly regaining her composure.

"Lineage is identified," she said to the audience, who had remained silent for the last few moments. "The boy will not answer any further questions regarding it since we have more pressing matters to deal with. Let's allow him to recover from the shock while we enjoy ourselves. Then, we'll proceed with the rest of this trial."

Chapter Twenty-Three

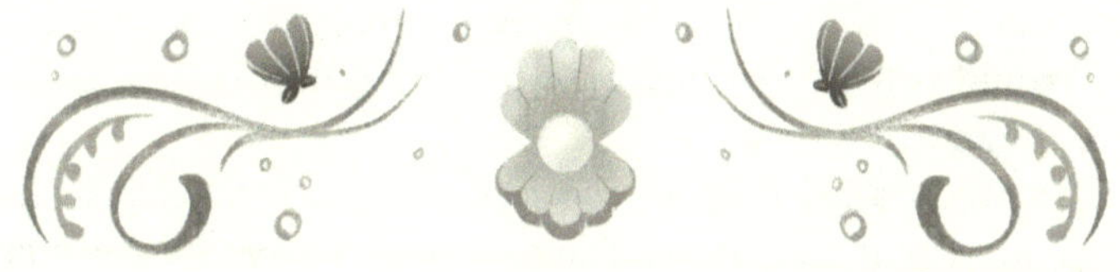

ISAAC'S ARM STILL THROBBED in pain as he opened his eyes, staring ahead at the curious crowd in front of him. People were slowly returning to their places, some enjoying colourful beverages in crystal glasses, others grabbing miniature food from floating trays. Near the front of the stage, a row of people kept their arms pointing towards the crowd, lowering and raising them to control the silver trays that moved across the room. In the galleries, people sat on cushioned chairs, enjoying food and drinks as well, completely unaware of what was happening below. He stared at the gallery above the main entrance in the centre, trying to locate Xavier, but the three people there merely stared at whoever was next to him, their features drowning in concern.

He gulped, slowly turning his head to the side, frowning at the throbbing sensation in his arm. His muscles were sore, a machine that required oil to not shriek. Every movement felt mechanical, brutally slow. Isaac could barely keep his eyes opened. It seemed like he had been hit by a truck.

"How are you feeling?" Alice said, her eyes carefully studying him.

He felt the press of her warm hand on his, a sensation he had grown used to. Even with his eyes closed, Isaac could make out sounds around him, but what got most of his attention was this simple touch. He knew Alice was a witch, but her touch was always different from any other. Her hands were always hot, but they never burned him. Her touch was always overwhelming, but something within him soothed, slowed down. Whenever he held her hand, the world around him relaxed and everything unimportant faded from view. Nothing was fighting for his attention anymore.

"Tired," he said. "Everything hurts."

Alice nodded, her eyes trailing to his forearm. She opened her mouth to speak, closed it and shook her head. "I'm sorry about that. I'll make you some healing ointment to help with the scar. Would you like to continue with the trial or do you need to rest some more?"

His eyes trailed back to the oblivious crowd, who laughed and chatted as if they weren't here. It was surreal how so many of them paid little attention to Alice and Isaac, how they remained in their little world. Not too long ago, they were calling him a traitor. Now, they didn't seem bothered by his presence.

"Is this always like this?" he couldn't help but ask.

"Yes." She pursed her lips, scanning the crowd as well. "To them, this is a party. Always has been. Even if someone is being convicted, they find a reason to celebrate. They say it is to keep us safe, but I'm not sure what they're keeping us safe from."

"What happens after someone is convicted?" he whispered, trying not to draw too much attention. "Do you think I'll get convicted?"

"You won't," she reassured him. "There's nothing to convict you for. But if you were, you'd be exiled to Otherworld, barred from crossing to the Human Realm ever again. What happens after that, I don't know. Once you stop existing here, you stop existing altogether. That's what my aunt always told me, anyway."

The hammer hit the podium once again and the lights flickered with it. The trays in the middle of the crowd floated to the people in front of the stage and after grabbing them, they exited to the opposite side from where Isaac had stepped in.

After a sharp hit from the hammer again, the room grew quiet and most conversations ceased to exist.

"We shall proceed with the rest of this trial," Gloria said, fixing her hat. She turned to Isaac, her eyes sharp as she stared at him. "How did you meet Alice Barlow?"

Isaac cleared his throat, glancing briefly at Alice. She squeezed his hand tighter. "At school. We're in the same class."

"Did you regularly speak with her before your abilities manifested?"

"No." He shook his head. "I had no reason to."

"Then, what changed?"

"I grew a tail?" he said as if the reasoning wasn't obvious. "And I thought Alice could help me. So I asked her about it."

Gloria narrowed her eyes on him. "Why did you think that?"

Isaac's heart jumped in his chest and he tightened his grip around Alice's hand. This was it. The moment Alice had warned him about. The moment where he would expose her in front of all these people for something that had happened in her past. He would have to mention the rumour, how he came to know it, and how it was true.

He scanned the crowd, noticing how people leaned forward to hear him better, their eyes dissecting every part of him.

"I—" He inhaled sharply. After offering Alice one apologetic look, he said, "I heard a rumour about her."

"And what was that rumour?" Gloria pressed. "You must tell me the truth, boy."

Isaac nodded. He had taken a truth potion earlier, but he felt different than when he started this questioning. For once, he had time to ponder his words. His tongue wasn't demanding him to say the first thing that crossed his mind. His thoughts weren't as focused either, and he could keep the majority of them to himself. What if he could lie again? It was worth giving it a shot if that meant he could keep Alice away from these prying eyes. He knew how much she hated attention, and he was starting to understand why.

"The rumour was that Alice dabbled in witchcraft. It wasn't hard to consider that since, well, Alice was always alone at school and she's a bit… *mysterious*. Besides, I was desperate. It was that or nothing. I figured if the rumour wasn't true, she wouldn't tell anyone about me. If she did, no one would believe her."

"But if the rumour was true..." Gloria raised an eyebrow at him, expecting the rest of his answer.

"Isaac assumed that if the rumour was true, I would help him with an amulet. Which I denied," Alice said, looking down at him. She was trying very hard not to smile. When she focused back on the crowd, she fixed her posture, her voice carrying with authority throughout the space. "Isaac Kallan asked for an amulet so he could hide his merfolk origins from humans. Prior to all this, Isaac was part of our school's swimming team, something he wishes to keep doing while keeping *all* of us safe. He is one of the best students in it, having won several medals in multiple competitions. I believe it is in the Assembly's best interest to give him permission to acquire an amulet. It would raise less suspicion than having him quit altogether."

From the crowd, a few people nodded in agreement with Alice's statement, murmuring between each other. Gloria crossed her arms as she stared at Alice, shaking her head slightly.

"You're just like your mother," Gloria said to Alice as if that was an insult. She turned to the crowd. "We will discuss this amongst ourselves. Does anyone have any more questions to ask Isaac Kallan?" Gloria scanned the people in the front row, who shook their heads. "Okay, then." The hammer hit the podium again. "We'll consider this questioning over. Now, it's time for its deliberation. Alice, will you please escort that boy out? But do not leave. Your insight will help us tremendously."

"Of course, Council."

Isaac glanced one last time at the crowd before following Alice towards the door, picking up the pace so he could walk alongside her.

"Thank you," he whispered.

"It's not over yet," she opened the door for him and smiled, "but I'll fight for you."

Isaac's lips parted, unsure of what he should say. Those words replayed in his mind until they became a silent chant he tucked deep into his heart. Alice would fight for him. Those words shouldn't leave his heart in such disarray, but they did.

A realisation dawned on Isaac as he crossed the door. This was it. The moment he had been waiting for. The end of all this mess. He was so close to reclaiming his life back, so close to going back to the swimming team, to doing what he always loved to do. He should be overjoyed. The idea of it, however, turned his stomach into a knot.

"I'll come and find you," she said. "Hopefully, I'll bring good news."

"Yes." He nodded and accepted his jacket back from her. "I hope it's good news."

Alice smiled one last time at him and closed the door with a loud thud, drowning Isaac in darkness. He blinked to adjust to his new surroundings, spotting Xavier leaning against the wall, his eyes deprived of any emotion.

"How did it go?" he asked, arms crossed over his chest.

"They're going to discuss whether or not I'm allowed to get an amulet."

Isaac removed the scarf around his neck, folded it neatly and saved it in the pocket of his pants. After undoing the top buttons of his shirt, he felt more like himself again. Isaac started to mindlessly walk forward and Xavier joined him, keeping his arms behind his back.

"Was it tough?" he asked. "I heard you scream."

"I think that woman pulled out one of my scales." Isaac lifted his arm and held it to the light, inspecting the wound. It appeared like a deep cut, the blood drying around the open flesh. When Isaac tried to touch it, he frowned at the pain. "I passed out and then woke up again."

"Sounds about right." Xavier sighed.

Isaac mindlessly rolled his sleeve down, covering his wound with the fabric. Around the cut, the white fabric tinged with blood, but he didn't think too much of it.

They reached the room from before and slipped inside, with Xavier closing the door behind him. The cart with tea and cake had been moved out, and Isaac's stomach growled. He was thirsty and hungry and tired. He couldn't wait to get home and drift off to sleep.

"If they give you permission to get an amulet, will you stop talking to Alice?" Xavier asked, earning a confused look from Isaac. He raised his arms in defeat. "I'm just asking. Will you?"

"I hope not," Isaac said, collapsing on the couch and lying

on it. "I like Alice."

Beautiful sea motifs decorated the ceiling; tall waves and large ships and four different merfolk, each with a different tail and scales. Isaac narrowed his eyes on one of the drawings, focusing on the scales on its tail. They were a shimmering white, almost like a pearl, and under Isaac's gaze, they appeared to come to life.

"What are these drawings on the ceiling?" Isaac asked, pointing at it.

"These?" Xavier stepped closer to the centre of the room. "Merfolk, I guess? They probably chose this room for you because of that. Why do you ask?"

"Are the merfolk supposed to represent something?"

"If you want them to. Maybe they're connected to the legend of the Four Seas."

"Four Seas?"

Xavier nodded, stepping closer to the couch. "It's an origin myth for merfolk. The four sacred merfolk lineages. Your mother's journals didn't say anything about it?"

"No." He shook his head. He had read about something similar elsewhere, though. "What's a sacred lineage?"

The door behind them opened and Isaac sat on the couch. Alice stepped inside, her cheeks flushed from exercise as she smiled at him. She walked until she collapsed on the couch next to him.

"I have good news," she said. "They have agreed to give you permission to get an amulet. My aunt is writing the decree as we speak and Victoria will give it to me tomorrow because she'll decide who your amulet maker will be. But you'll get your amulet!"

"That's great," Isaac said, although he didn't feel particularly excited. "Do you know when we'll get it done?"

"Tomorrow afternoon, maybe?" She shrugged. "But I'll let you know as soon as I have the decree with me. I'll text you."

He nodded. "Thank you, again."

Alice glanced to the side, and upon finding Xavier, the smile on her features disappeared. The softness of her eyes was replaced by something sharp and poignant—something mirrored in Xavier's eyes. Despite his tense jaw, he appeared devastated.

The more he looked at her, the more sadness sunk into his frown lines, the more he appeared less like himself. His tough shell—the one he carried everywhere—was gone. He was nothing more than someone scared.

"Do you two need a minute?" Isaac asked, feeling like he was interrupting something. "I could step outside for a bit while you talk this tension out."

"There's nothing to talk about," Alice said, standing from the couch. She fixed her dress and put her gloves back on. "Xavier will take you home. I'll head back to mine with my family. Goodnight, Isaac."

Alice offered him a small smile before disappearing from the room, leaving them alone again. Xavier took a deep breath as he ran a hand through his hair, pacing around the room while he muttered to himself.

"What happened between you two?" Isaac asked. "Are you sure you can't sit down and talk things out?"

"No." Xavier shook his head. "Words won't fix this."

"Then what will?"

"Time. Space. I don't know." He rubbed his face, letting out a frustrated sigh. "I hate what I did, but I had to do it."

"Does she know why you did it?" Isaac asked.

"I can't tell her," he said. "And even if I did, I doubt she would understand. There are many things I don't tell her. She doesn't need to know them."

"Why aren't you honest with her, then?" At that, Xavier glared at Isaac, and he raised his arms. "I'm just saying. Maybe she would understand where you're coming from. Keeping all of this to yourself is clearly not the way to go. She's clearly mad at you."

"And how would you know that?" Xavier chuckled. "You know nothing about my relationship with Alice. You know nothing about what she or I have been through. I can't depend on Alice. My burdens are not hers to carry."

"I never said they were." Isaac stood from the couch, grimacing at the pain in his body. He closed his eyes to regain his balance and then faced Xavier again. "But shouldn't you allow her to make that choice? Why are you making that choice for her?"

"Because it's the right choice!" Xavier yelled. "When you want to keep someone safe, you keep things from them. You act as their shield. You become their arrow. You don't tell them where they can find those things. You're there to be those things for them."

"Yes, but you also trust them," Isaac said. "You can't be those things if there's no trust to begin with. How will you be their arrow or shield if they don't trust you?"

"That's the difference, Isaac," Xavier said, his face flushed with emotion. "It's not about trust. It's about duty. And to do your duty right, you lie. You hide. You deceive. But if it means *I* get to keep Alice safe, I will do all of that. Over and over. Trust is not a shield or an arrow. Trust is like a mirror. And mirrors break." Xavier lowered his head, his voice failing him. "The one I shared with Alice is broken. I don't think it was ever whole to begin with."

Chapter Twenty-Four

ALICE STARED AT THE address on the crumpled piece of paper in her hand. "Are you sure we have to go here?" she asked. "Can't we go anywhere else to get his amulet?"

Victoria paced around the flower shop, moving some of the vases around. She stopped in front of one, pulled out a couple of dying flowers and put them in a bucket she carried under her arm, before walking to the front of the shop and dropping it on the counter, staring at Alice.

"Gus is the best amulet maker I know. I went there this morning and he agreed to do it for Isaac. It's the best I could do on such short notice. Accept it and get the amulet done for your friend."

"Fine." Alice grabbed her phone and texted Isaac the address. "I'll get going before he closes. See you tomorrow for another lesson."

"Don't forget the decree." Victoria leaned on the counter and grabbed a small red envelope from under it. "Show him that and tell him you're my niece."

After a tight hug from her aunt, Alice grabbed her jacket and backpack and exited the flower shop, finding the town centre already drowned in darkness. She preferred the warmer weather when the days were longer and she could leave the flower shop and find this place at its golden hour. People tended to stay out until later during those months, and she appreciated the muffled sounds in the background that their quiet existence provided.

As she walked towards the antiques store, Alice knew she was being followed. Despite leaving her house earlier in the morning and almost escaping school without his notice, Xavier had been with her everywhere she went while keeping his distance. It was upsetting and infuriating, but turning around and confronting him was not something she wanted to do. If she ignored him long enough, he'd probably get bored and would go away on his own. Telling him the opposite didn't seem to cause any effect, anyway.

Alice slowed down her steps as she approached the antiques store show window. It was more cluttered than she remembered. Besides chandeliers hanging from the ceiling, each corner had a different lamplight, and two upholstered chairs took centre stage on opposite sides of a wooden table, one of the few enchanted objects on display. On the table, besides a couple of piled books that Alice wasn't sure anyone would ever buy, was a vintage music box, its aura different from anything she had ever seen. It was a purplish blue, almost dark enough to be considered black, and it brought a chill down Alice's spine.

"It's cursed," she heard Xavier say behind her.

As much as she wanted to know how he knew that, she only briefly glanced at his reflection on the window before stepping inside the antiques store, a soft bell announcing her arrival.

Alice tentatively crossed the cluttered space, trying to ignore how much some of the objects around her drained her energy. Their auras weren't just golden or silver. Some objects had purple and red auras; she could find almost all the colours of the rainbow around her. The bell rang again and she didn't look over her shoulder, pretending she hadn't noticed Xavier's entrance.

She walked to the very back of the room, finding a small hidden section with crystals and handmade jewellery. If these had been made by Gus, then Victoria was right, he was a fine artist. The attention to detail on the materials used and the highlight of the crystals and their imperfections warmed Alice's heart. She grabbed one of the necklaces with a green jade wrapped in gold wire, dangling from a simple golden chain.

"It is rather a special crystal, isn't it?" a mellow voice spoke.

"I guess," Alice said, putting it back in its place. "I was never one to learn a lot about crystals."

She turned to the side and smiled at who had spoken. The man in front of her was probably in his late twenties, the same age as her aunt. He carried a red patch over his right eye that partially covered a deep scar that went from his temple to the corner of his mouth. Alice knew it was rude to stare, but she had never seen such a deep scar. When she found his grey eye staring intently at her, she took a step back. From the corner of her eye, she spotted Xavier walking closer to them.

"I am Augustus," he said, extending a gloved hand to her, "but everyone calls me Gus."

Alice gulped and shook his hand, surprised at how tight his grip was. "I'm Alice. Victoria's niece."

"Oh. So you're the rebellious witch." Gus offered her a crooked smile. "She spoke very highly of you."

"Did she mention an amulet?"

"She did, yes." He let go of her hand and looked over her shoulder. "Is he the one that needs an amulet?"

"No. The one that needs it is on his way." Alice opened her backpack, pulled out the small envelope and extended it to Gus. "Here's the decree."

He remained focused on Xavier for a while before snatching the envelope away from Alice's grasp. Gus went to the counter at the front of the store and Alice followed him, not wanting to lose the envelope out of her sight.

She noticed that the red on Gus's eye patch matched his gloves and the overcoat he was wearing. Its texture reminded Alice of a snake's skin, but she could very well be wrong about that.

"What does he need the amulet for?" Gus asked as he read the decree.

The bell rang as Isaac stepped inside, taking a deep breath as soon as he spotted Alice. A few moments later, he waved at Xavier, who nodded in acknowledgement but remained in his spot at a safe distance from Alice. She wanted to roll her eyes at that.

"This is Isaac," Alice said as soon as he approached her. "He's the one that needs the amulet."

"Well, I am Augustus, but you can call me Gus." He shook Isaac's hand. "I was asking Alice what you need your amulet for."

"I need it to block my magic," he said, "so that when I swim, I don't turn into a merfolk."

Gus nodded, pursing his lips. "So you want to hide your magic from humans?"

"That's it, yes." Isaac smiled.

"Well, follow me, then," Gus said. As Alice was about to join them, he stopped her. "Not you, though. Or him. Just Isaac. I'll return him to you in one piece."

"I hope so," Alice muttered under her breath, which earned her a small shoulder squeeze from Isaac. "Scream if you have to, okay?"

"It won't come to that," Isaac reassured her. "This shouldn't take long, right?"

She shrugged. "I don't know. It will take as long it has to."

Isaac followed Gus to the back of the shop and they stopped near the crystals Alice had spotted earlier. Gus opened a door, revealing a small room with a long working table that reminded Alice of the one in her aunt's flower shop. After Isaac stepped inside, Gus closed the door before she could make out anything else. Alice took a deep breath, swallowing down her concerns. She didn't like being here. It was disconcerting.

While Alice stayed as close as possible to the door, Xavier paced around the store, occasionally picking objects up and turning them in his hands before putting them down and moving to the next one. She tried to entertain herself with the rest of the jewellery in the back of the store, trying to imagine herself wearing some of it. Alice picked up a ring, this one with a blue stone shaped like a half-moon. It had matching earrings and a necklace, both of which she found later in higher shelves.

When Xavier walked closer, he picked the moon necklace up from one of the top shelves. Alice dropped the ring and increased her distance from him, crossing her arms as she leaned on the wall, waiting for the door to open so she could leave this place with Isaac and his amulet.

"He was hunted," Xavier said, putting the necklace back. At the confusion in Alice's expression, he added, "That's the origin of Augustus' scar."

She nodded, her throat dry. Alice didn't know of many people who had been hunted by Magic Hunters, and the topic always made her skin crawl. It was never easy to talk about it.

"How do you know?"

"I asked him about it," he said. "When I first came here from Otherworld, he and Victoria were the ones who welcomed me. He probably doesn't remember me, but I didn't forget him. He was living proof of what could happen if I didn't protect you properly."

"They're not hunting me anymore," she said. "I can't summon magic, so I lost all my value to them."

Xavier picked another necklace up, the one with the green jade. His fingers traced the stone on it, a soft smile on his lips before he put it back, his expression growing sombre. He went over each piece of jewellery, picking it up, studying it, putting it back.

"In exchange for a better life for my family, my parents were offered a job for me in the Human Realm," he said, picking up some vintage picture frames from a shelf in the middle of the store. "All I had to do was protect some witch I knew nothing about, around people I had never met, but it sounded easy enough for a shapeshifter like me. My parents accepted it that same day. Told me I was honouring my family lineage by doing this. I didn't want to come. I liked home." He wiped his eyes, blinking the tears away.

A sad smile greeted his face then, and Alice's heart broke in her chest. There was so much about Xavier she didn't know, so much he kept hidden. She didn't understand why he was telling her all this now. Was it the remorse for lying and deceiving her? Or was he manipulating her with all these words to get her to forget what he did? Alice wouldn't so easily move past that.

"You deserve a better life than one protecting me," she said. "One where you're free to do what you want, away from here, away from me. Then, you can go back home to see your family again."

"I don't think I want to go back," Xavier whispered, not

looking at her. "Life back home… it's different. I like it here. I have a good life here, Alice."

She snarled at him. "You think this is a good life?" She didn't expect to sound so bitter, and yet, she couldn't keep the poison from her words. "This isn't a good life, Xavier. You're just as tired of following me around as I am of seeing you everywhere I go. I'm not allowed to have secrets from you. I'm not allowed to have friends you don't judge. I'm not allowed to live a life that is not tainted by your *stupid* sense of duty or morality. Do you think that's a good life? Do you, Xavier? Because I don't. I hate it."

Fire burned in Alice's cheeks and chest. Xavier blinked as if what she said had never crossed his mind. It probably hadn't. In his desire to pursue his duty, he forgot that her life was involved in that too. He thought of her as someone only meant to protect, not as someone who had hopes and dreams, who had a life to live. A life that, with each passing day, included him less and less.

"Will you ever trust me again?" he asked, worried eyes scanning her features. "I'm sorry, Alice."

She didn't reply. Alice cleared her throat and leaned away from the wall as the door opened. Gus was the first one to step out, wiping his gloved hands on a piece of white cloth. Isaac followed after a while, clutching in his hand what was his newest most prized possession.

"Well, your friend is back in one piece," Gus said, scanning his surroundings. "And I'm glad that despite the loud conversation, you did not break anything. Next time take it outside, please. Amulet making is an art that requires deep levels of concentration."

"I apologise," Alice said to Gus, then focused on Isaac. "Did it work?"

"I still need to test it." He opened his hand to reveal a necklace with small black gems interwoven on the golden chain.

"There are several precautions to have with it," Gus said as he walked to the front of the store, and the three followed him a few steps behind. "The amulet is attuned to Isaac and his abilities, which means it only works on him. If he loses it, he will need to get another one done, which he will have to pay for. I only do the first amulet for free. It's also important to take the amulet out every once in a while. Once a month is enough if you are actively swimming. Perhaps during a Full Moon. You can use it to recharge your amulet. I believe that's about it. Anything else?"

Gus glanced at them, and Alice shook her head, alongside Isaac who saved his necklace in his wallet. Xavier pointed to the back of the room. "I'd like to buy something," he said. "Can I do that now or should I come back another day?"

"I never refuse business." Gus laughed and patted Xavier on the shoulder, pushing him towards the back. "What is it you want to buy?"

Once they were at a safe distance, Alice turned to Isaac and smiled.

"How do you feel about us testing your amulet tonight?" she said. "We could have a swimming lesson too."

"Well, I'm available," he said. "Should we meet at the entrance of the local pool?"

"Sure. I'll see you there."

"Will Xavier join us?" Isaac glanced at the back of the store. "We could invite him."

"For what? I'd rather not have him there." Alice sighed and checked her watch. "I have to get going. I'll see you later, right?"

"I'll meet you at the pool building." Isaac shoved his hands in the pockets of his pants, eyes narrowed on Xavier in the distance. "I'm going to join them. I want to see what Xavier is buying."

As Isaac joined them in the back of the store, Alice exited the establishment and went home, enjoying the solace of her company and the lack of footsteps following behind her.

Chapter Twenty-Five

IT WAS COLD TONIGHT, but Isaac's excitement kept him warm. He climbed the stairs to the local pool building, finding the place empty and devoid of life as he waited for Alice. Behind him, Xavier kept glancing over his shoulder as he joined him at the top of the stairs. Xavier sat on one of the steps and stared mindlessly ahead before focusing back on his scarred knuckles.

"What's the story behind that?" Isaac asked as he sat next to him. "Did you hit something or someone?"

"Both," he said, but didn't elaborate further. "I'll stay here until Alice arrives. Then, I'll leave. Don't tell her I was here, though."

Isaac nodded. It was strange to see both Alice and Xavier behaving like this. Earlier in the antiques shop, Isaac wasn't sure what they were fighting about, but it seemed serious. Not to mention the glares that Alice gave Xavier. Whereas before he had been terrified of Xavier, now he didn't want to get on Alice's bad side. Xavier still terrified him, but Isaac was growing used to him.

"She's still pretty pissed at you, you know."

Xavier chuckled. "You don't think I know that? I tried to

apologise, but I think I just made everything worse. She won't even talk to me." His eyes flashed gold and he nodded with his head towards the right side of the street. "She's coming. I'll be nearby if you need me. Alice is terrified of water. She almost drowned once, so *please* be careful with her. Don't make me regret this."

"You can trust me with her," Isaac stood, followed by Xavier. "What made you change your mind?"

Xavier shrugged and looked longingly towards where Alice was coming from. "She needs to be with someone she trusts, and I can't be that person for her. You can. With you, Alice feels limitless." He narrowed his eyes on Isaac. "So you better not mess this up, Fishboy. Without you, Alice has no one."

Isaac nodded, giving Xavier a small smile that he hoped was reassuring enough. He didn't want to mess things up with Alice, didn't want to break Xavier's trust over this either. After everything they had done for him, this was the least he could do.

The two exchanged a quick handshake before Xavier disappeared in the opposite direction, fading from Isaac's view as Alice's steps became louder. He turned to greet her with a wave, and Alice returned his gesture with a smile. Without saying much else, she unlocked the door and they stepped inside, going to the changing rooms to get ready. When they met by the pool, Alice was wearing a black training swimsuit, her eyebrows furrowed as she stared at the swimming cap in her hands.

"How am I supposed to put this on?" She dropped her gym bag on the bench next to her.

"Usually, with hair as long as yours, you'd do a bun and then put the cap on. Let me help you."

Isaac grabbed the swimming cap from Alice's hands and watched as she grabbed her hair in a ponytail and twisted it into a loose bun. "What now?" she asked, fixing the swimsuit around her armpits and frowning. "This fabric is itchy."

He laughed. "You'll get used to it. Now, I'll put this on you."

Under Alice's attentive gaze, Isaac stepped closer to her, stretching the swimming cap with both of his hands. He started towards the back of her head and then stretched it to the front, pushing it down to cover all of her hair. When he finished, he smiled at her.

"How ridiculous do I look?" she asked, fixing her hair on the side of her ears, covering it properly. "I feel weird."

"You look okay." He clapped his hands, the sound echoing in the large space. "Now, are you ready for a swimming lesson? We'll go at your pace."

"If you're worried I'll drown again, I have no plans for that," she said. "What will we start with first?"

"First, we're going to warm up."

Alice nodded and Isaac guided her on his warm-up routine. They rolled their shoulders back and forth, stretched their arms and legs and ran in place. Once they were done with that, Isaac walked to the edge of the pool and jumped inside, the water splashing around him, hitting Alice's face and legs slightly.

This time, he wasn't terrified to embrace his tail. He swam around the pool, testing his limits, laughing at himself. This was nice. He loved the freedom of being himself and not being scared of what would come to him. With the amulet on, Isaac would get to keep being a merfolk whilst he remained on the swimming team. He didn't have to choose one over the other. He could have both.

When he returned to the surface, Alice was sitting at the edge of the pool, swaying her legs in the water. She kept staring at the water's surface, taking slow but deep breaths.

Isaac swam towards her and stopped when he was close enough to feel the movement of the water against his scales. She lifted her eyes to meet him, trying her best to smile. That wasn't enough for him to ignore the fear in her eyes.

"It's cold," she said. "Aren't you cold?"

"I'm used to it. Being underwater helps, you know." He placed his hands on each side of her legs, looking up at her. Being this close to her made his heart jump wildly in his chest. This close, he noticed the freckles on her shoulders, and he wondered what it would be like to kiss every single one of them. To kiss her. "Your body becomes one with the water."

She rolled her eyes, splashing his face.

"Says the merfolk to the witch." She chuckled. "Of course your body becomes one with the water. Mine just…" Alice shook her head. "Never mind."

"Swimming is a skill, Alice. I was a swimmer before I was a

merfolk. I learned how to swim. I'm good because I trained day and night to be the best. Yes, maybe being a merfolk helped me, but that's not all." He offered her a hand. "I can help you. Take my hand. I won't let go of you."

She glanced between his hand and his eyes, pursing her lips. He waited until she eventually nodded and grabbed his hand.

"Fine," Alice said, holding his gaze. She placed her other hand on his shoulder, not shying away from applying all her strength to him. "Hold me, okay?"

In between many curses and complaints, she stepped into the pool, wrapping an arm around Isaac's neck, while gripping his hand. Alice kept her eyes closed as Isaac held her by the waist, not letting go. Although this would not lead her to learn how to swim, he would not be mad if this was all they did this evening.

"You can open your eyes," he whispered. "You're safe. I'm here with you. I'm not letting go. Can you put your feet on the ground?"

She shook her head, not opening her eyes. Her muscles were tense, and she kept her grip strong around Isaac. He knew telling her to relax would be useless under these circumstances. Isaac moved towards the end of the pool with Alice in his arms, until she could put her feet at the bottom of the pool and stand on her own.

"You can open your eyes, Alice," he said, letting go of her waist, the water height around her shoulder level.

Alice blinked, looking down at her feet at the bottom of the pool, then at his legs, then at his smile. "Where's your tail?" she asked. "Are you wearing your amulet?"

"No." He shook his head. "But I'm holding your hand."

Isaac intertwined their fingers, planting a soft kiss on her palm to reassure her. Her cheeks blotted with a crimson shade, almost matching the swimming cap she was wearing, but she didn't let go of him.

"Stop staring." She splashed him again, but her shy smile told him she wasn't upset.

"I can't help it." He shrugged. "I like to stare at you."

Alice cleared her throat, trying to seem unbothered by his comment. The colour on her cheeks betrayed her. "What will we do now?"

"First, I'm going to teach you how to float," he said. "Try to lay horizontally on the water's surface."

"Is that possible?"

"Yes. Try it. I'll be holding you. We'll stop if you want. Just say it."

Isaac placed a hand between Alice's shoulder blades and helped her lay back on the water's surface. She kept her eyes on him, panic seeping through her features. Her body tensed up under his touch, and the grip around his hand increased.

"Alice," he whispered softly, "I need you to let go of my hand so I can grab your legs. I'm not letting go, okay? I'm just holding you differently. Can you do that?"

She gulped and nodded. Alice closed her eyes and he waited, watching as she chanted to herself in a low voice to try and gather her courage. As soon as she let go of his hand, Isaac grabbed the back of her knees and his tail returned.

"Stretch your legs," he said, and she did so. "That's it. Now try to relax. Focus on where my arms are holding you. I'm not letting go. I'm here."

"Is your tail back?" she asked.

"Yes."

Alice took a deep breath and opened her eyes, focusing on the ceiling. "Good. That's good. I still don't know why it happens, though."

"You seem to have the same effect on me that my amulet will have," he said. She narrowed her eyes on him, and Isaac shrugged. "It's just an observation, nothing more."

Isaac took advantage of Alice's deep thoughts to increase the distance between his hands and her body. He was careful not to move too abruptly so he wouldn't break the illusion. After some time, however, Alice was floating on her own.

"How much longer do I have to stay like this?" she asked. "This is quite nice actually."

"I don't know." Isaac smirked and crossed his arms over his chest. "Do you want me to join you?"

When Alice noticed his crossed arms, she panicked. She lost her balance and yelped as she turned to her side, face down, moving her arms to try and press the water away as if it was a solid material and not a liquid. Isaac quickly pulled her out of the water, pressing her back against his chest, feeling her erratic heart pulse against him.

"You said you wouldn't let go!" she said in between coughs.

"I wanted you to try and do it on your own," he said. "You were doing it. Do you want to try again?"

"No." She shook her head. "I think I've had enough swimming for the day. I don't like this."

"You're scared. That's normal. How about I show you how I do it?"

"How about we test your amulet instead?" she suggested. "I'll just keep away from the pool at Liam's party. I can do that."

"Okay." He rested his head on her shoulder, keeping her back pressed against him. "If you fall into the pool for whatever reason, I will come to the rescue."

"You'll be a hero," she said, then shook her head. "Or a fool. But I hope it won't come to that."

"It won't." He planted a soft kiss on her cheek, his chest burning right afterwards. "I'm sorry I did that. I should've asked first."

Alice chuckled and turned around to face him, smiling. "It's okay," she said. "I don't mind it."

"Okay," he whispered, wrapping an arm around her waist. Alice stared at him, and he couldn't help but focus on her lips. He decreased the distance between them, cupping her cheek as he leaned closer to her, his heart jumping in his chest. She took one step closer to him, pressing her body against his, her eyes finding his. He smiled back at her, brushing his nose against hers, closing his eyes as her breathing brushed against his cheek.

Isaac forgot how to breathe as her hands climbed his chest slowly, leaving a tingling sensation behind until they found his shoulders, the warmth from them overwhelming. He waited for Alice to close the distance between them, for her lips to touch his.

"We should… We should go test your amulet," she whispered, not moving away. "To make sure it's working properly."

"Okay." Isaac bit his lower lip, leaning his forehead against hers, disappointed. He tried to calm down his heart, to stretch this moment for longer, but it was impossible. "Do you want help getting out of the pool?"

Alice let go of Isaac and moved away from him. He immediately felt colder. "I can leave on my own."

He watched as she walked to the pool stairs and climbed them, leaving the pool. Isaac splashed his face, shaking his head as he tried to cool himself. He and Alice almost kissed. It almost happened. But it didn't, and he couldn't help but wonder why. The wave of disappointment that enveloped him was hard to ignore. It was clear that Isaac wasn't vaguely interested in Alice. What he felt for her was not that, but he wasn't sure how to define it. Maybe he shouldn't define it. It was probably something only he felt, otherwise, she would have kissed him. Right?

"I'll go grab the amulet," she said. "Can you tell me where it is?"

Isaac sat at the edge of the pool and moved his tail out of the water, waiting a few minutes before it disappeared. He stood up once his legs were back and walked to the bench to grab a towel and used it to dry his body. He sat for a while, wiping the rest of his body.

"It's in my wallet," Isaac said to her. "You can grab it."

Alice took a deep breath and grabbed the amulet from inside of Isaac's wallet, putting it back inside his gym bag. She stared at it for a while before joining Isaac on the bench, a slight pout on her lips as her fingers traced the chain and interwoven crystals.

"This is it," she said, forcing a smile at him as she extended him the necklace. "The moment you've been waiting for."

"Yes." He accepted the necklace, pursing his lips. "It's been a long time coming."

"You'll get your old life back. Finally." She cleared her throat, and removed her swimming cap, dropping it on her side of the bench. Alice undid her bun, her black hair cascading down, creating a layer between them. "I'll be here."

Isaac nodded and put his necklace on, making sure it was properly closed. He expected something within him would shift or the atmosphere around them would change. Everything remained the same.

He walked to the edge of the pool, staring at his reflection on the surface. *This* was it. The moment Isaac would get his life back. The moment he would return to the swimming team and continue to work towards a good future. His old life would be his again. Shouldn't he be happy about it?

Isaac jumped into the pool, keeping his eyes closed. He allowed the water to surround him, to become an extension of him. Lately, he was capable of staying underwater for a long time, but right now, he couldn't breathe. When Isaac returned to the surface, he glanced down and let out a small laugh.

"Alice? You *have* to see this."

"What?"

Alice glanced at the pool with her arms crossed and a disappointed expression. Isaac moved his legs upwards and allowed one of his feet to be out of the water and used it to try and wave at her.

"It worked!" he said. "I have my legs back. I can swim normally again."

"That's great." She forced a smile his way. "I'm happy for you." Why didn't she sound happy for him, then?

Isaac swam some more, practising some of the strokes he knew best, remembering how it used to feel. He laughed, the sound echoing through the space around him. This was great. *I can finally go back!* He went to the edge of the pool and sat on it, before standing up and walking towards Alice on the bench. She had dried most of her body and put a shirt on, avoiding looking at him.

"Thank you, Alice," he said. "For helping me. I seriously couldn't have done this without you."

"Yes." She nodded. "I'm glad everything is solved now."

She stood from the bench and opened her gym bag, extending a folded grey hoodie towards him. "I thought you should have this," she said, not meeting his eyes, "since it's yours."

"I said you could keep it."

"I don't want to keep it." She glanced at the ceiling, blinking.

"Why not?" Isaac removed his cap and threw it on top of his gym bag. "I'm not taking it back."

"For starters, I don't wear hoodies. Secondly, it makes no sense for me to keep it. We're probably not going to hang out after this, and having it would remind me of you, and I'd rather not have that happen."

Isaac stood there as Alice placed his hoodie on the bench between their bags and shoved the rest of her belongings inside her gym bag, walking towards the exit afterwards. He hated this. This wasn't how this entire thing was supposed to go.

"We're friends, Alice," Isaac said, going after her. "Friends help each other out. And if you think I'm going to ignore you at school or stop talking to you, you're wrong. Unless *you* want that to happen. Because if you don't, then I'll continue to bother you with magic questions and whatever else you allow me to bother you with. I like having you around, you know."

Isaac grabbed her wrist and she turned around, facing him with a grim expression. He brushed the hair away from her face, putting it behind her ear before running his thumb across her cheek, his eyes tracing the small scar on her brow.

"Have you ever considered that there might be people who like you for who you are? Who genuinely care for you?" he asked, meeting her dark eyes. They were still as beautiful as the first time he saw her. But they weren't as angry anymore. They were hopeful now. "I'm one of those people, Alice. And as one of those people, I'd like you to keep my hoodie. It should feel like a warm hug from me, and it should remind you that you're not alone. Not anymore, at least."

Alice gulped and placed her hand over his, her eyes tracing his features one by one. Then, she dropped his hand and fixed the bag on her shoulder. "I guess we still have Liam's party to go to, right?"

"Right." He nodded. "And we could hang out at the cafe after school. And at school. Or here."

She laughed and his heart relaxed. "I don't think I want any more swimming lessons," Alice admitted. "But everything else sounds good. If you'd like. You can say no."

"I won't say no." He walked closer to her and opened his arms.

"No." She stepped back. "Don't you dare. You're still wet and I just put my warm clothes on."

"Good thing you have an extra hoodie, then."

Alice rolled her eyes. "You're not going to quit on that hoodie, are you?"

"Nope. Not a chance."

He enveloped Alice in his arms and pulled her closer, planting a soft kiss on the top of her head. She wrapped her arms around his torso, her warm hands causing goosebumps to spread on his back and shoulders. Isaac smiled to himself, resting his head on top of hers.

This was the life Isaac wanted now. One where Alice was a part of it, one where he could swim again and accept his true origins. There was still so much about himself and his abilities that he didn't know, but he would figure it out with time. He didn't have to rush coming to terms with who he was. Now, he had time on his side, and he'd enjoy each and every moment it provided, starting with this one.

Chapter Twenty-Six

ALICE FELT LIGHTER AS she stepped inside her home, dropping the gym bag near the entrance. The lights were dimmed in the living room and a warm scent of herbs and baked goods permeated the air. Her stomach growled. She hadn't eaten anything before going to meet with Isaac, afraid the food would not stay in her stomach for too long. Now, she felt like she could eat this world and the next.

She took off her shoes and hung her coat, keeping Isaac's hoodie on. Alice followed the scent and the muffled whispers to the kitchen where Victoria sat at the table with Alice's parents.

"Took you long enough," her father said, inspecting her hoodie with concern. "What happened?"

"The amulet worked," Alice said, trying her best to keep a straight face. Her mother pulled out a nearby chair, and Alice sat down, taking a deep breath. "And Isaac tried to teach me how to swim. It didn't work."

"So he gave you a hoodie as a consolation prize?" Victoria asked, smirking at Alice. "That's sweet of him. What else did he give you? A goodnight kiss?"

"No," Alice said, but couldn't stop her cheeks from warming

up at the thought of what almost happened at the pool. "But he drove me home."

"Where did you test the amulet?" her mother asked, looking at her over the rim of her mug. "Did you go to the lake?"

"We went somewhere else," Alice said and cleared her throat. "Are you having tea? Did you bake something?"

"I made some blueberry muffins to take to tonight's Coven meeting. I saved you some, don't worry. Do you want to eat one now?"

"Could you make it two?" Alice pouted. "And some tea as well. I'm hungrier than usual. Where's Aunt Gloria?"

The three of them exchanged a worrisome look, but none of them met Alice's gaze. Her mother stood to get tea and muffins ready for Alice, while her father sipped his drink, finding some new interest in the fridge magnets. Victoria sighed and lowered her eyes to her almost empty plate.

"She already left," she said, collecting the crumbs outside of her plate by squashing them with her finger. "Said she had somewhere else to be and did not want to wait until you got home to go there. You know how she is. Obnoxious."

"She's your sister," her father said, fixing his glasses.

"She can be my sister and be obnoxious. One thing doesn't invalidate the other, Victor. But I'm glad she's gone. I can finally have a sense of normalcy in my life. Speaking of normalcy, where's Xavier?"

Alice ignored her aunt's question. The last thing she wanted was to talk about Xavier. The more she tried not to think about him, the more everyone around her seemed to remember he existed.

"Did she say anything before she left?" Alice asked, hoping to deflect her aunt's questions. "Was she upset with me?"

"She's pissed off," Victoria said and her brother warned her with a stare. "But not at you. It's mostly at us because we let you live your life instead of treating you like a prisoner."

"Well," her mother said as she placed a mug with steaming tea and a plate with three muffins in front of Alice, "she appeared particularly upset this time around. She probably didn't like the result of the Assembly trial considering what happened. Did she ever tell you about Isaac's lineage, Victoria?"

"No." She shook her head. "She only asked me how long Alice knew him for, which I obviously refused to answer. Did she tell any of you?"

Her parents shook their heads, and Victoria pursed her lips, deep in thought. Alice sighed and took a sip of her tea, wondering whether she should bring up what had been bothering her ever since she exited the pool building.

"Do you think it's possible for someone to lose their magic?" she blurted out. "Or maybe be able to block other people's magic when they touch them?"

Everyone shifted their focus to Victoria, who was the most knowledgeable of the three adults in the room. She finished her tea and wiped her mouth on a napkin.

"You can't lose your magic, but it can fluctuate over time. Although, it used to be a form of punishment a while ago in Otherworld. It doesn't happen anymore, but there are reports of it. As for blocking someone's magic when you touch them, there's an old academic theory about that."

"What does that theory say?" Alice asked, leaning forward to hear her aunt better. Her father did the same, pushing his glasses back.

"Well, it says that magic can't be created nor destroyed. It can simply be transformed, which leads us to conclude that magic is a form of energy. And since energy is everywhere and magic is energy, then magic is everywhere too. The theory states that in order for magical beings to exist, the opposite must be true."

"Beings without magic?" Alice asked. "But aren't those humans?"

"That's what they thought." Victoria nodded, satisfied. Alice felt like she was back in the flower shop having another witchcraft lesson. "The problem with the theory is that it completely ignores the core issue of the question. *Balance.* If magical beings exist and they can summon magic, the opposite is not human beings, because humans don't have access to magic. They're not part of this. The opposite of those who can summon magic are those who can absorb it."

"The Universal Balance," her father said, leaning back in his chair. "Isn't that what you did your dissertation on?"

"Kind of." Victoria shook her head. "I wanted to dive further into the topic but they said my hypothesis was stupid so I gave up."

"What was your hypothesis?" Alice's mother asked.

Victoria took a deep breath, getting all conspiratorial as she smiled at them. "My hypothesis was that besides a universal balance, there's also an inner balance. We all absorb and summon magic to a certain degree. Because magic is energy. And magic *is* everywhere."

"It sounds plausible," Alice's father said.

"In theory, yes, but no one wanted to fund my study, so I could never prove it. Annoying, but it's the reality of Academics." Victoria shrugged and then focused on Alice's parents. "Shouldn't we get going? As much as I'm enjoying this conversation, we have to meet with the Coven."

"Of course." Her father smiled and got up from his chair. "Let me just go grab my coat. I'll be back."

"I'll go grab mine as well," Alice's mother said. "Are you sure you don't want to join us, Alice?"

"Nope." She shook her head. "I'm quite fine enjoying my muffins and tea."

Her mother smiled and kissed her cheek, leaving the kitchen while Alice enjoyed her second muffin slowly, mulling over her aunt's words.

"What was the colour of Isaac's scales again?" she asked, bringing Alice back to reality. "When you had that big fight with Xavier at the flower shop, you mentioned you had seen his scales, but I forgot what you said. What colour were they?"

"I'd describe them as pearlescent white," Alice said. "They weren't an exact match for milky white or the translucent one in the current active lineages book. Why do you ask?"

Victoria shrugged and stood up, offering Alice a small smile. "I was just curious, that's all." She pursed her lips as she studied Alice, narrowing her eyes. "Who knows about this?"

"Besides me and Isaac?" Her aunt nodded. "Just you and Aunt Gloria, I guess."

"Xavier doesn't know?"

"Maybe. And can you stop mentioning him?"

Alice swallowed a big chunk of her muffin and had to drink

some tea to help it go down.

"Are you still upset with him?" Victoria sighed and shook her head, sitting back on her chair. Alice stared at her, waiting for her to continue. "I know it may not seem like it, but you're very lucky to have someone like Xavier by your side. He was concerned about your safety, and rightfully so. He sees the world differently. He sees it in a way that keeps you safe."

"That doesn't give him the right to do what he did, though," Alice said. "He shouldn't have gone behind my back to tell you about Isaac when we *promised* each other we would keep it between one another."

Victoria sighed and shook her head slightly. "I'm glad Isaac didn't turn out to be someone dangerous. But if he had, we wouldn't be having this conversation. Even if it doesn't seem like it, Xavier always had your best interests in mind, nothing else. All he did, all he ever does, it's never out of malice. He always does it out of concern for you."

"It's hard to believe that when he never tells me anything," Alice said, glancing at the crumbs on her plate, scattered around like stars in a sky. "He keeps so much from me, Vi. I don't know who he truly is. It's frustrating."

"I know it is, but it's for the best." Victoria looked over to the entrance and stood, squeezing Alice's shoulder as she walked by. "And you should stop wandering at night by yourself, okay? We don't know who's out there."

"What do you think I should do?" she asked her aunt before she exited the kitchen. "I don't trust him anymore. I don't want to forgive him. Does he even deserve my forgiveness? After everything he has done, he still keeps following me around like nothing happened."

Victoria offered a consoling smile at Alice. "Why don't you call him? He could keep you company so you're not alone. Maybe you could chat about those things. Now is not the time to make enemies, Alice. If anything, you should keep the ones you care about close. That includes Isaac."

"Why do you say that?"

Alice didn't like the tone in her aunt's voice. The cheerfulness was gone, replaced by something eerie that made her uncomfortable. Victoria shrugged and exited the kitchen, not bothering to give her answer. She joined her parents in the living room as they finished getting ready to leave.

"We'll lock the door," her mother announced as she opened the front door, waving at Alice. "We're not expecting any visitors, so don't open it to anyone."

"I won't." Alice stood from the table and grabbed her plate and mug, dropping them in the sink to wash later.

When the front door closed, she sighed and left the kitchen, ready to go change into some more comfortable clothes. She stopped when she spotted Xavier standing near the entrance, hands in his pockets, looking slightly lost.

"They let me in," he said, biting his lower lip. "I thought I'd use the front door for once."

Alice nodded and returned to the kitchen to do the dishes. From the living room, she heard Whiskers hiss at Xavier, and he muttered some sort of response back at her cat, but that only made him hiss even more.

As she wiped her mug with a kitchen towel, she peeked into the living room, finding Xavier sitting on the couch, arms stretched across the back of it while he stared at an unbothered Whiskers on the coffee table as he licked the fur from his belly.

"You may hiss a lot, but I get it," he said to her cat. "You want to keep her away from danger. If you think about it, you and I have a lot more in common than you'd think. Do you think we should call it a truce?" Xavier shook his head and massaged his temples. "Why am I talking to a cat? It's not like it's going to solve anything."

Xavier was right about that. After storing the mug and plate in their respective cabinets, Alice joined him in the living room, sitting on the opposite end of the couch. Whiskers jumped out of the coffee table and sashayed towards his scratching box, all while wagging its tail.

"There are blueberry muffins in the kitchen," Alice said, grabbing the TV remote and skipping through the different channels. "You can make yourself some tea too."

Xavier nodded but didn't move from the couch. They stayed there, side by side, not glancing at each other as the movie Alice had selected played, filling the awkward silence between them.

Whiskers returned to the coffee table after a while, and Alice leaned closer to him, trying to butt her nose against his. "Have I told you how adorable you are?" she whispered and he meowed, hitting its paw gently on her nose. "Yes, you are. The most adorable."

From the corner of her eye, she spotted Xavier smiling fondly at the exchange, looking towards the TV as soon as she leaned back on the couch. When her eyelids became too heavy for her to keep her eyes open, she closed them, the muffled sound of the TV drifting away. As much as she tried, Alice couldn't prevent her head from leaning on Xavier's shoulder, and she was too exhausted to move in the opposite direction. Instead of pushing her away, he adjusted himself on the couch so she could doze off comfortably against him while they waited for her parents to return home.

Chapter Twenty-Seven

ISAAC HAD MISSED THIS. Swimming with his friends, the freedom to move without dreading if a tail would suddenly replace his legs and expose him in front of all these people. It was nice. It was invigorating. He would even dare to say he had never been in better shape, and his Coach seemed to agree.

"I think you're ready to return to the competitions," he said to Isaac once practice was over. "It's nice to see you've made a quick recovery. It was as if no time had passed in between the practices you skipped."

He laughed at that, his hand clutching the thin necklace around his neck. It was one of his most prized possessions now, alongside his mother's journals. He was far from being done with reading them all, but with each entry, he got to know her better, which helped him understand the extent of his abilities too.

Despite being back on the swimming team, he wasn't hanging out with his friends as much. Whenever he wasn't at school, he either went home to study or read his mother's journals, or he would meet Alice at the cafe. At school, they still kept their distance. Isaac wanted to avoid awkward questions and Alice wanted to avoid unwanted attention. It was the best for both of them.

"You're bringing your girlfriend to the party?" Liam asked Isaac when they entered the locker room to get changed. "Seriously, out of all the girls you could have, you chose that one?"

"Alice is not my girlfriend." Isaac opened his locker and pulled out his gym bag, dropping it on the nearby bench. "We're just friends. And for the record, she's great."

"She might not be your girlfriend *yet*, but the way you look at her tells a different story," Liam said, throwing his swimming towel at Isaac who caught it midair. "I mean, I don't judge who you choose to date, but you have to admit she's something else. And not in a good way."

People giggled around the locker room and when Isaac glanced at his teammates, he was disappointed to find that all of them shared the same sentiments about Alice. "Do you really think she's that bad?" When no one replied, Isaac got his answer. "I appreciate your vote of confidence."

"We're just looking out for you," Liam said. "We're all wondering if she tricked you into falling in love with her. You know, with a spell or something. Has she shown you her crystal ball yet? I'm sure every witch has one."

Everyone laughed, a sound that echoed through the walls of the locker room, seeping into Isaac's bones. His jaw remained clenched as he put on his hoodie, not bothering to take a shower before heading to the cafe. No. He wouldn't stay here longer than necessary.

"Well, if you're going to bring her to the party," Liam continued, squeezing Isaac's shoulder, "remember we're doing it in the forest. Same place as the bonfire from last year."

Isaac nodded but didn't say anything else. After he finished getting dressed, he grabbed his gym bag and exited the locker room, making sure the door banged as loudly as possible on his way out. The muffled voices behind him offered him no comfort, no sense of belonging anymore.

This was what Alice had dealt with all her life, and Isaac had contributed to the problem. Not once had he stood up for her. He used to think like them. That she was weird and scary, that the rumours were true. The thought left a sour taste in Isaac's mouth.

People like Liam didn't deserve someone like Alice in their lives. Alice was one of the greatest people Isaac had ever met. She had stood by his side, guided him through all this mess and never once had she asked for anything in return. She was confident and brilliant and beautiful and so much more. Isaac's heart was always full whenever he thought of her. She was the best, no doubt about it.

Isaac sighed. Maybe Liam was right in some of this. Isaac was starting to think of Alice as more than a friend, and he wasn't sure if he should. Their friendship was something recent, and if Xavier was right, Alice was leaving soon, so did it make sense for him to try and pursue a relationship with her? What if instead of getting closer to her, he only pushed her away? He didn't want that. Not when some sense of normalcy had returned to his life.

After fixing the gym bag strap over his shoulder, Isaac left the public pool building and drove to the cafe. Inside, the scent of black coffee, steamed milk and baked goods took over his senses, and he relaxed.

In the far back, someone waved at him, a gesture he reciprocated. He crossed the room until he reached Alice's table.

"How did practice go?" she asked, pushing a plate with a glazed doughnut towards Isaac. "That's for you."

"Thank you," he said, adjusting himself on the chair across from her. "Practice went as expected. Coach said I'm in good shape and he thinks I can return to competitions soon. I think that's good."

"I think it's great." Alice smiled at him.

From the corner of his eye, Isaac spotted Xavier studying him from a nearby table. When Isaac looked at him, he averted his gaze. This was better than yesterday. When Isaac met Alice here, Xavier had been a couple more tables away. He'd be sitting with them in no time.

"So," Isaac said after taking a large bite from his doughnut, "how is your preparation going for the New Moon Ritual?"

"As well as it can go with my limitations." She flipped through a couple of pages of her notebook, pursing her lips together. "I still take too long to summon, but I'm hoping it'll be better this time around. What about you, have you found anything new in your mother's journals?"

Isaac shook his head. "Not in her journals, but I think I've figured out my lineage."

Alice lowered her notebook and focused her attention on him. "How?"

"Well," Isaac said, "when Xavier and I were waiting for you in the Assembly, I happened to notice a painting on the ceiling of the room we were in, and he mentioned the legend of the Four Seas as well as the sacred lineages. So, I went back to the library to get the mythology book you recommended—because I was almost dying the first time I read it—and it turns out that they do talk about sacred lineages there."

"And?"

"And," Isaac glanced at Xavier, finding him concentrated in their conversation, "they describe a merfolk with a similar tail to mine. It might be a coincidence, but aren't all these myths based on something real?"

"What did it say?" Xavier asked Isaac, earning a glare from Alice. He ignored her. "Did it mention a name, a location, something?"

"The merfolk is called Helmi throughout the story."

At that, Alice and Xavier looked at one another, their expressions unreadable. Xavier took the opportunity to join the two of them at her table.

"Do you think he could be right?" Xavier asked her. "You've seen his scales."

"I don't know." Alice shook her head. "Most sacred lineages are extinct, though. Do you think that's why my aunt freaked out? Why she didn't say anything about his lineage at the Assembly?"

"Probably," Xavier said.

Isaac gulped, his eyes jumping between Alice and Xavier. When none of them added anything else, he asked, "Am I supposed to be overjoyed or deeply worried?"

No answer.

"I'll look some more into it," Isaac said, rubbing his chin. "I might have misinterpreted the story."

"Are we still going to Liam's party?" Alice asked after a while, changing the topic of the conversation again. "I'm assuming the ritual would take me two hours—maybe less if it goes bad—but after that, I could meet you there."

Isaac swallowed a large piece of his doughnut, coughing afterwards. His heart sank in his chest when he thought of what had happened in the locker room earlier. He knew how much Alice was looking forward to this party, mostly because it was the first time she had been invited to something of this sort. However, Isaac could not, in good conscience, let her go.

"I think we should skip it," he said, his eyes meeting his half-eaten doughnut.

"Why?" she asked, an edge to her voice.

"Liam is not a good guy," Isaac said. "I'm afraid he might make fun of you, that he might make you uncomfortable. Besides, the party is happening in the forest. He's having a sort of bonfire."

"Wouldn't you stand up for me?" she asked, her voice a mere whisper. The pain in her eyes was too much for Isaac to comprehend. He shook his head and looked away again. "I get it. I have no problem with Liam or the party being in the forest. We should go. After everything we've been through, we deserve a little celebration. Besides, we don't have to talk to him. We can just be there, enjoying each other's company."

"I have to side with Isaac here," Xavier said, pointing his thumb at Isaac. "Liam is the scummiest guy this town has to offer, Alice. Skipping this party sounds like the best decision."

"I didn't ask for your opinion," she said, glaring at him.

"He's right, though," Isaac said, chiming in. "I think skipping the party would be for the best. We'll have other opportunities to celebrate."

"Besides, you don't know how drained you'll be from the ritual," Xavier added and Alice rolled her eyes. "I might have to carry you home."

"I'm glad the two of you are getting along," Alice said, skimming through a couple more pages in her notebook. "But we're going to that party. And if you don't want to go, then I'll go alone."

"Nope." Isaac shook his head.

"Not a chance," Xavier added. "We're going with you. I'll

stay with you during the ritual, and then we'll meet Isaac at the party."

They remained in silence while Alice buried her nose in her notes, Isaac enjoyed his doughnut and Xavier sipped on his chamomile tea. It was such an odd combination to see a guy like him enjoying something as soft and relaxing as tea, but that was who Xavier was, Isaac had come to realise.

For the sake of the three of them, Isaac hoped that whatever mountain had risen between Xavier and Alice would come down and allow them to be friends once again. This cold atmosphere was not it. Isaac didn't want to take sides, he wanted to enjoy his time with his two new friends.

He wasn't sure if Xavier considered him a friend yet or just an acquaintance he respected more now. Isaac knew it would take them a while to fully trust one another, but they would get there eventually. After all, the most fulfilling friendships were always the ones that bloomed unexpectedly. Maybe this was one of them.

Chapter Twenty-Eight

"ARE YOU SURE YOU don't want me to go with you? We could do it like last time. You don't have to go alone."

Victoria sat next to Alice on the living room couch, her concerned eyes studying her niece. They had spent most of the afternoon reviewing the spells and the ritual's order so that Alice could be better prepared for what was about to happen. She knew it wouldn't be easy, but she didn't feel as frightened as she did last time.

This time, Alice embraced the darkness.

"I'm not going alone," Alice said, gesturing with her head to the person standing near the door. "Xavier is going with me. My parents' orders."

Xavier smiled at Victoria. "I'll keep my distance."

Her aunt nodded in defeat and extended to Alice the candle holder and a dark blue candle. "Remember to light the candle at the forest's edge and follow it until it extinguishes. You know that—"

"I know, Vi." Alice wrapped her hands around her aunt's. "I'll succeed this time. You don't need to worry about it."

After gathering the rest of her belongings for the ritual, Alice carefully shoved them in her backpack and offered it to Xavier to carry for her. She hugged her aunt tight and went to say goodbye to her parents in the kitchen, who sat by the breakfast table while looking over some old grimoires.

"Are you already going to perform the ritual?" her mother asked, shifting her attention to Alice.

"Yes. Xavier is coming too," she said, not hiding her displeasure. "I'll text you once that's over and I'll be back from the party before you know it."

"Remember to take deep breaths," her father added, smiling at her. "And it's not magic that controls you, Alice. It's you that controls it."

"I know."

"Good." Her mother offered her a thumbs-up. "We'll be rooting for you. Would you like some tea and a slice of cake once you're back?"

"I'd love that."

Alice hugged her parents and dropped a kiss on their cheeks before heading back to the entrance where Xavier was already putting his shoes on. Alice did the same, and once they were done, he grabbed the backpack from the floor and put it over his shoulder and they left Alice's home in silence.

The weather was colder than she had expected as they walked to the forest's edge. Alice glanced at Xavier every once in a while, her lips parting for her to speak, but no words came out. As much as she should continue to ignore him, the growing worry in her chest demanded her to fill the silence with something other than her thoughts. So conversation would have to be.

"Do you think I'm going to make it this time?" she asked, keeping her eyes focused on the tall trees in the distance.

"You've practised, haven't you?" He shrugged. "I don't see why you wouldn't make it. You're better prepared this time around."

Alice nodded and put the hood over her head to keep her ears warm. She shivered. "Why is it so cold tonight?"

Xavier raised an eyebrow at her. "You feel cold?"

He slowed down his steps and took a deep breath, keeping his eyes on the sky. Eventually, he cleared his throat and shook his head, joining Alice a few steps ahead. "Do you need my jacket?"

"No." She shook her head. "I just need to keep walking."

They continued to walk at a steady pace while Xavier kept his attention on their surroundings. Occasionally, Alice caught a glimpse of his eyes flashing their golden shade, his brows furrowed as he stared at the dark alleys and streets they passed by.

As much as Alice loved the nighttime, something was different tonight. It was colder and quieter. Even the town centre appeared like a ghost version of itself. The majority of the streetlights flickered and stayed off for longer than usual. The closer they got to the forest's edge, the more it became a prevalent issue. On one of the streets, all streetlights were off.

"Do you think it's magic?" Alice whispered to Xavier, whose focus remained on the turned-off streetlights. "It's a New Moon and sometimes—"

"Magic doesn't mess with electricity," he said. "Not this kind, at least. It's *humming*."

"What do you mean it's humming?" Alice asked as Xavier stopped in his tracks.

He walked closer to the lamp post, his eyebrows furrowed as he looked up. Alice joined his side, following his line of sight, but if he was seeing something, she couldn't spot it.

"Usually, if a lamp is not working for whatever reason, it stops humming. You can't hear it, but I can. If this was broken, it wouldn't be making this sound." His eyes flashed golden again and he grimaced but didn't move his hand away from the post.

Alice followed his gesture, placing the hand on the lamp post, feeling its cold surface against her skin. She closed her eyes briefly to focus, and the cold melted away, replaced by a golden current that reached for the tip of her fingers. When she opened her eyes and looked up, the light was on.

"You felt it too, right?" She glanced at Xavier. He nodded, and his expression only grew sombre by the second. "Why would someone block light with a spell?"

As soon as Alice removed her hand, the light flickered again and shut down, drowning them in darkness.

"They either are stupid," Xavier said, adjusting the bag over his shoulder, "or they don't want people moving this way."

"We have to get to the forest, though," Alice said, glancing around the empty street. She didn't like any of this. As much as she wanted to, she couldn't ignore the knot in her stomach for much longer. "The faster we get there, the faster we get to do the ritual and the faster we can go to the party."

"You're really set on going to that party, aren't you?"

"I texted Isaac saying *I'd* be going. You can skip it if you'd like. Can you pass me my phone?"

Xavier sighed and removed her phone from the front pocket of the backpack and extended it to her. Alice pressed the home button and, after a while, her phone turned on. She pursed her lips.

"What is it?" he asked. She extended the phone to Xavier, who looked at her, confused.

"Just hold it. And try to use it."

As soon as the phone left her hand, the screen went black. Xavier pressed several of the buttons and Alice gulped, her heart catching up in her throat.

"I don't think the spell is working only on the post lamps," she said. "I think it's everything that uses electricity or some sort of battery."

Xavier shifted the phone in his hands before returning it to Alice, who held it with both hands and watched it come to life as she pressed the side button. She checked her messages, but Isaac hadn't texted her yet. She pouted and saved her phone back in her bag, closing the zipper of the front pocket as Xavier studied his surroundings once more.

"Leave no trace behind," he mumbled under his breath, pursing his lips. "Whoever did this is trying to hide something."

"Do you think more witches are performing rituals tonight?" Alice asked, earning an eye roll from Xavier.

"Why would they need to use a spell to block everything here, Alice? They could use a ring of protection to keep danger away. I don't think this is a witch's doing." He took a deep breath and shook his head, repulsed. "There's a strange scent in the air too."

"We should keep going," Alice said, moving away from the lamp post and walking towards their destination a few streets ahead. "Maybe we're seeing things where they don't exist."

She didn't believe any of those words. Xavier was right; something about this *was* strange. Every magical being knew they were forbidden from using spells and other magic tricks to intervene with how humans lived their lives. This might be a small, harmless spell, but what if it wasn't the only one? What if Xavier was right and someone was trying to leave no trace behind? She shook her head, focusing on the tall trees ahead of her. This didn't matter. What mattered was that she was going to perform her New Moon Ritual tonight and she would succeed.

She had to. There was no other option.

Once they got to the edge of the forest, Xavier opened the backpack and pulled out the candle holder and the candle Alice had to burn. She quickly got it all ready, snapping her fingers together until a small blue flame appeared on the tip of her index finger.

"You're getting better at this," Xavier said, putting the bag behind his back.

Once the flame stabilised, Alice nodded and they entered the forest, following it into the woods. Crushing leaves under hers and Xavier's boots was the only sound keeping them company for a while until music reached their ears, a loud, electric boom coming from up ahead. They kept moving until the flame extinguished, not close enough to where the sound was coming from. That was good. Hopefully, no one would find them here.

Alice set down the candle holder and removed her cloak from her shoulders, setting it on the ground before stepping onto it.

"You can move back now," she said to Xavier behind her. "I'll be fine."

"Are you sure?" he asked, his eyes still focused on the top of the trees. They shifted to gold until he blinked again. His hand reached towards Alice's shoulder, but instead of squeezing it, he stopped midair and ran it through his hair instead. "I won't be too far. You've got this."

Alice watched him disappear into the darkness behind her and she cleared her throat, grabbing the golden and black stick for her thigh holster and drawing the circle in black and the different triangle shapes in their sections. Her skin tingled under the lines, but she ignored the sensation by grabbing her small knife and pressing it on the tip of her finger.

As soon as her blood entered the golden and black lines, she'd have to keep going and perform the ritual all the way through. This time, no matter what happened, she would keep going. No flames, no darkness, and no past incident would stop her from reaching her goal.

Except for the explosion up ahead, followed by a high-pitched scream coming from deep in the forest, close to the lake ahead. Alice's eyes shot in its direction, the tip of her knife pressing her skin ever so slightly as she tried to make out any shapes that could reveal the origin of the sound. Behind her, the sound of crushing leaves grew louder until Xavier grabbed her wrist, moving the knife's tip away from her finger.

"We have to go," he said. "Someone's here."

She looked at him, confused. "What do you mean someone's here?"

A second scream. This one was louder, deeper, guttural. They all came from the same direction. Alice saved her knife and stood up, almost tripping against Xavier. He kept his hand on her shoulder, his eyes a golden shade as he scanned their surroundings. He gulped as his grip increased on Alice's shoulder.

"Did Isaac tell you where the party would take place?" he asked.

"Not the exact location. Why?"

"I'll go investigate," he said, gripping her shoulders with his hands, forcing her to look at him. "Stay here, okay? Don't move. You're protected where you are. I'll be back."

Another scream. Xavier was gone as the first flames broke out ahead.

Then it clicked. The strange atmosphere. The silence. The coldness. It was the lack of magic in the air. Someone knew. Someone knew and *they* were back. But they weren't here for Alice. No, whoever they were here for was ahead. Whoever they were after was at that place, near the lake.

Isaac.

Alice's heart jumped furiously in her chest as she tried to control the wave of panic surging from within her. They were after him, right? It had to be. He was the only magical being in the area they could be targeting. Isaac didn't know much about this world, and Alice had put a huge target on his back. By bringing him to the Assembly, she had exposed him to all the other magical beings, and they all knew who he was now.

She had to do something. If she stayed here, it was only a matter of time before the flames got to her. Besides, without the ritual, she could not guarantee she was protected as Xavier had claimed.

After pacing around while she pondered her options, the flames only got taller in the distance, the smell of smoke more intense. Up ahead, the screams of the crowd mixed with the screeching of burning wood.

I'm not staying here without doing anything.

Alice ran as fast as she could towards the sounds, hearing the muffled voices in the distance, some shouting orders, others simply crying for help.

The air caught in her lungs as she tried to take a deep breath, unable to shake her worries away. She knew she should slow down, that she should come up with a better plan in case what she found ahead was as dangerous as she suspected it was. Alice couldn't do any of that. She could only think about the fire, and the people trying to escape it. She could only think about whether or not Isaac was okay.

She was so blinded by her desire to find him that she missed the shadow catching up to her. It lunged at her and knocked her to the ground, wrapping her in a veil of darkness as the burning trees slipped from her view.

Chapter Twenty-Nine

ISAAC FOLLOWED THE TRAIL laid down by Liam towards the lake in plain darkness. He had tried to use his phone flashlight to light up the path, but it wasn't working. The worst part was that he didn't have any service here, which meant that if he wanted to text Alice about his location, he'd have to leave the party, walk back to the edge of the forest and then try to message her. Doing so wouldn't guarantee his success, but he wasn't pleased about being here by himself.

He wasn't pleased to be here at all.

Still, this was an effort he was willing to make. If Alice wanted to come to this party after performing her New Moon Ritual, the least he could do was support her once she arrived. *If* she arrived. He had no guarantees she'd end up showing up.

As soon as Isaac spotted a bonfire burning in the distance, he knew he was walking in the right direction. He picked up his pace, held his jacket closer to his chest and emerged from the tall trees to a small opening where most of his classmates and friends were already enjoying some beverages, snacks and good conversation. Somewhere in the surroundings, someone played dance music, causing a few people to move to the rhythm with happy smiles.

"There he is!" Liam yelled as he pointed at Isaac.

"Here I am!" Isaac yelled back. He walked closer to his friend, scanning the table in front of him. "What do you have?"

"Booze. And some water and juice too." Liam sipped his drink, then looked over Isaac's shoulder. "Your girlfriend's not coming?"

"She's not my girlfriend," he said. "And she'll meet me here later."

Liam scoffed. "You can forget about her, you know. Look around, Isaac. There are so many beautiful girls around and you chose the most boring and pathetic one to spend your time with. It's never too late to change your mind. Unless you're afraid she might hex you or something."

"I'm not afraid of anything when it comes to Alice," Isaac said. "And could you please stop trying to pester me about her? If she was any other girl—"

"That's the problem, Isaac. Alice is not every other girl. She's a *witch*."

"How can you be so sure of that?" Isaac crossed his arms, challenging Liam with a look. "Have you spent more than five minutes with her to know if what you're saying is true?"

"I don't have to spend more than five minutes with her to know what she is. You know what she did, Isaac. Everyone in this town does. Why are you turning a blind eye to the truth?"

Because it isn't the truth, you idiot. Isaac grabbed a plastic cup and filled it with some red juice. After taking a sip, he grimaced. Someone had tempered the drink with alcohol. Why wasn't Isaac surprised?

"I'll go say hi to some people," Isaac said. "And you better stay away from Alice if you're not planning to be nice to her."

He patted Liam's shoulder with more impact than necessary and then moved away from the table towards a small crowd near the burning flames of the bonfire to meet with the rest of the swimming team. Most of his colleagues were happy to see him, but as soon as someone asked about Alice, the mood shifted. Isaac tried not to let this get to him, but after a while, it became tiresome. How could they continuously hold a rumour against her that wasn't even true? No one had ever bothered to get to know Alice. They all believed in a made-up story that didn't match the true events in the slightest. The worst part was that Isaac used to be like them. He used to believe the rumours and he wasn't ever curious or bothered to find out the truth. The worst part was that he couldn't even tell them they were wrong without exposing Alice.

As much as he wanted his friends to get to know the amazing person she was and treat her like the rest of them, he didn't need them to accept her. Alice didn't need them to be valued and appreciated. She had Isaac and Xavier. She had her family. She had herself too. Alice already had everything she needed. Why did he want her to have more than that?

After a short lap around the bonfire, Isaac decided to step away from the crowd and find someplace to sit and wait for Alice. He leaned against one of the thick trees nearby and slid down until he hit the ground. Isaac grabbed his phone, finding his screen black. *Strange*. He could've sworn he had left his house with most of his phone charged. No matter how many buttons he pressed, his phone didn't turn on. This meant he couldn't text Alice or read her reply. If his phone wasn't working, then going back to the edge of the forest wouldn't solve his problem.

Isaac sipped on his beverage as he glanced at the people around the bonfire, trying to locate if any of the new arrivals looked like Alice. She wasn't here yet. Nor was Xavier. His heart shrunk in his chest with worry and anticipation. Had her ritual started already? Isaac hoped it was going well. If not, he still hoped she showed up here. He'd try to cheer her up then.

He took a sip of his drink only for someone to cover his eyes with cold hands. Isaac chuckled, trying to move away from their grasp, but whoever it was didn't budge.

"Come on now," a sweet, delicate voice spoke. "You have to guess."

"I have no idea," Isaac said. He pulled the hands from his eyes and looked over his shoulder, finding Alice smiling at him. "Hey. I was just thinking about you. How did it go?"

She sighed and sat down next to him. Alice grabbed the cup from his hand and chugged the rest of the drink down before wiping her mouth with the sleeve of her shirt. As his eyes went over her clothes, Isaac couldn't help but wonder if she had gone home to change. They were too casual for what she usually wore. Alice always dressed up for these kinds of events.

"The usual." She shrugged and gestured with her chin to the small crowd around the bonfire. "So this *is* the party?"

"Yes…" Isaac focused on Alice, studying the way the light from the fire played with her eyes. He was so used to their darkness that he was surprised by the warmth they carried. "Where's Xavier?"

Alice turned to look at him and blinked. Then, she got up and extended a hand to him, smiling. "Xavier went home. He said it wasn't worth it to come here. Besides, he knew I was meeting with you, so he didn't bother to come with me. Should we get more drinks?"

"I'm good," he said, unable to ignore the harshness of his heartbeat. Alice narrowed her eyes on him, and he couldn't quite understand her expression. "But do you want something to drink?"

Isaac pursed his lips. There was no way Xavier would let her come to this party alone even while knowing Isaac would be here. That wasn't like him. Even if she was mad at him, he would never leave her side. Something else was off about her, too. Her hands. Alice's hands were always warm, a side effect of the fire magic pulsing through her.

Isaac slowly stood and smiled at the girl in front of him. A girl that looked so much like Alice, but he was almost sure it wasn't. He stepped closer, his hand finding her chin as he moved the hair away from her face, focusing on the middle of her eyebrows. The skin was smooth and perfect, with no scars. Alice had a scar on her eyebrow. He knew she had.

This girl wasn't Alice.

He took a step back, dropping his hand to his side. The girl in front of him stood there as her smile lines deepened with worry.

"We could go get drinks," he said. "Let's go." Isaac gestured to the table and waited until the impostor turned around to scan his surroundings. He had to get out of here. He wasn't sure who this person was, but he had a small suspicion which would be hard to kill. Instead of following her, Isaac turned around and started to run, but his escape was short-lived when someone grabbed his arm and pushed him against a tree with a knife against his neck.

"If I were you, I wouldn't do that," the impostor said, pressing the blade against his skin as she moved closer, her breath brushing against his cheek. "Here's what's going to happen. You're going to follow me out of this party and you're going to keep quiet."

"And if I don't?" Isaac said between greeted teeth. He couldn't breathe properly. "What do you want?"

She smiled and laughed. When Isaac blinked, the person pressing a knife against his neck wasn't Alice. It was another girl, this one with lighter hair, the colour of honey. Her eyes appeared to be a light brown in the darkness, but he couldn't be sure. However, it was the angry nature of her stare that helped him put a name to her face. It was the same one he had seen in the girl from Alice's memory, the same one that had tried to drown her.

"I know you." He narrowed his eyes on her.

The pressure of the knife against his neck loosened briefly as she processed his words. Isaac took this moment and reached his hands towards her, trying to grab her shoulders to butt his head against hers, but all he could do was pull her necklace free, leaving a slight mark that made her flinch. The girl studied him with wide eyes before pressing the knife to his neck again, a sharp pain building there. Isaac yelped, but she didn't budge. He clutched her necklace tighter against his palm.

"Noah?" she called.

From the corner of his eye, a large figure approached the two of them, standing behind Ariah. His forehead glistened with sweat as his harsh dark eyes studied Isaac before he broke into a toothy smile.

"Is he the one she wants? I thought he'd be bigger."

"You'll have time to train him and bulk him up before he has to meet her." She patted Isaac's cheek aggressively before removing the blade from his neck and kicking him in the stomach. "He will need it if he wants to make it. And who knows? He might even make us some good money if we play our cards right."

Isaac grunted as he fell forward, trying to breathe. Noah

grabbed him like a sack of potatoes and put him over his shoulder before shoving something into his mouth, preventing him from screaming. That didn't stop him from trying.

"Is everyone in position?" Ariah asked and Noah grunted in agreement. "Good. Send the signal. Then burn everything to the ground. Leave no trace behind."

No. No. Isaac tried to get rid of Noah's grip around his torso, but he only clutched him tighter and used his free hand to whistle.

The girl fell a couple of steps behind, placing herself in Isaac's line of sight and keeping her focus on him. Behind her, the flames on the bonfire grew out of control. The first sparks touched the tall branches, kissing them with warmth and light, a kiss that travelled through the rest of the leaves and branches until it hugged the trunk of the tree, burning it from the inside.

Then, the screams began. Isaac was too far away to spot the chaos in the distance, but in between the lower greenery, he spotted two golden eyes staring back intently at him.

"Move faster." Ariah pushed Noah, causing him to almost trip. "I don't want to be here when the worst part starts."

As Noah adjusted Isaac on his shoulder, the necklace slipped from his fingers, falling onto the forest's ground, probably lost forever. He wasn't sure if the wolf nodded at him, but Isaac nodded back, making a silent promise with it. The wolf lowered his head and disappeared, joining the chaos deeper into the forest, as the flames grew taller and more ravenous than ever.

Chapter Thirty

ALICE HAD A HARD time breathing. She coughed, leaning on her side to try and sit down, grimacing at the pain in her torso. It didn't help. Everything in her body appeared to be heavier and warmer too.

As she lifted her eyes to look at her surroundings, the air was knocked out of her lungs. With all the strength she could muster, Alice stood, watching the bright orange and red flames paint the trees, their sparks flying uncontrollably.

She couldn't see anything other than the brightness and intensity of the flames. She couldn't hear anything beyond the falling of branches and the low scream of leaves being burned to death. Glancing around, Alice didn't know which direction to go, she wasn't even sure where she was heading to. What had happened?

The previous moments flashed through her mind. The first burst of fire. The screams. The running. The impact on her stomach. Her brief encounter with consciousness and Xavier's face before all faded away again.

Alice coughed again, leaning over her stomach to try and catch her breath. She had to get out of here. The point wasn't to find a way back home, the point was to escape the fire and get to safety.

With weak legs, Alice moved away from the ring of fire, her feet too heavy for her to run. She wasn't sure how long she wandered for. She wasn't even bothered if the flames burned her clothes or reached for her skin; none of that mattered. She was a fire witch, a Forger. The uncontrollable nature of the flames was part of her identity. Part of who she was. It was also part of why she didn't give up.

She wasn't sure how long she wandered until she spotted a grey wolf lying on its side, its chest rising and falling as a low whine left his body. Alice approached slowly, coughing into the charred sleeve of her dress, earning a curious glance from the wolf. Its golden eyes blinked, but before Alice could take a deep breath in relief, she noticed the dark red stain on his fur near one of its back legs.

"Xavi? What happened?"

The wolf closed his eyes briefly, attempting to move, but the growl of pain that left him froze Alice's heart. Without thinking twice, she tore a strip of fabric from her dress and wrapped it around the wound in the wolf's leg, making sure to tie it as hard as she could.

"I'll get you home, okay?" She petted his head, earning a small nudge from him. "Can you walk? Even if it's slowly?"

With Alice's help, the wolf got back on all its paws, except for the injured one that he kept from touching the ground. He kept his tongue sticking out, the heavy pants reminding Alice that not everyone could deal with this heat or air. Fire might be a part of Alice, but it wasn't a part of Xavier.

"I'll lead the way," she said.

Xavier didn't listen to what she said. With his teeth, he grabbed what was left of the bottom of Alice's dress and pulled her to follow him. Side by side, and moving slower than any of them would like, they walked towards uncertainty and away from most of the flames, the cold of the night slowly settling against Alice's skin. She shivered, rubbing her hands up and down her arms, keeping them close to her chest to stay warm.

Far away, she heard sirens, and if she abstracted from her heavy breathing and Xavier's panting, the hiss of the fire was louder than ever. She briefly closed her eyes, the scent of burnt wood bringing tears to them. *Not again.* The only solace in this situation was that she was sure she hadn't been the one to cause this fire. That meant that nature would grow with time instead of being gone forever. She was grateful for that, at least.

The wolf tugged at her dress again before letting go and moving forward on its own, stopping ahead with its nose down on the ground and then looking up at Alice expectantly. She sighed and approached him, following his line of sight. In all the dirt around, she spotted something shiny and reached for it, grabbing it with one of her hands.

"What's this?"

It had to be something magical, she concluded. With all their burnt surroundings, if this was a normal necklace, it would've melted because of the high temperatures. It didn't. Its condition was pristine. The silver of the chain was clean and the centrepiece wasn't damaged. Alice narrowed her eyes on it. She had seen this necklace before. Although she couldn't pinpoint where, she was sure of it. The purple gemstones, the big translucent crystal in the centre…

"It's Ariah," Xavier said, his human form lying on the ground as he struggled to breathe. "He dropped it."

Alice's eyes widened and she almost dropped the necklace in shock. Her heart picked up the pace in her chest and it was hard to breathe again. Her legs were too weak for her to keep standing, and she collapsed on the ground, her fingers tracing the sharp lines of the crystal, the pattern of the gemstones around it. Her hands warmed with the magic emanating from it, only adding to her wave of confusion that turned her stomach upside down.

Ariah wasn't a magical being; she didn't deal with magic. She was a Magic Hunter.

Magic Hunter.

Her eyes jumped to Xavier who looked at her with anticipation.

"She has him?" she said, her voice higher in pitch than she anticipated. "She took Isaac?"

Xavier nodded before closing his eyes, laying his head down on the burnt leaves. The fabric Alice had tied around his thigh wasn't enough to stop the bleeding, but that wasn't the only wound he had. His shirt was ripped, his pants shredded. She spotted lines of red across his chest, dark bruises on his face and arms.

Alice gulped, clutching the centrepiece of the necklace in her palm. The crystal tugged at her skin, but it didn't matter if she bled or not. None of that mattered. Her pain was secondary to the bigger problem at hand.

Ariah was back. She was alive. She had Isaac. Alice didn't know for how long, didn't know how long she had to get him back.

Alice opened her palm, glancing at the bloody gemstones and crystal, the smudged black and golden lines in her hand.

She would not stop until she found Isaac. She would not stop until Ariah was gone.

If that meant having Ariah give her last breath against Alice's blade, then so be it.

Acknowledgements

Writing has always been a part of my life, but self-publish a book was a completely new experience for me. I've written many stories over the years, but this is the first one I share with you, the first one I took from a small draft to a polished manuscript and into your hands. I loved everything about this experience and I couldn't be more grateful to the people who guided me along the way, either with their expertise or words of encouragement, so a few thank yous are in order.

To my wonderful cover designer, Catarina, thank you for creating me the book cover of my dreams and the greatest chapter banners I could've asked for. It was incredible to work with you, and I appreciate your patience and care through every stage of the process.

To Gabby, my copy editor, I'm so grateful for your feedback and for pushing me to become a better writer and to make this book the best it could be. This story is much better thanks to your guidance and excitement.

Marley, thank you for your help on this book's blurb and for always motivating me to keep going. It's incredible to share this writing journey with you. Missy, it's always great when we brainstorm, share ideas or joke around. Thank you for everything.

To Rita, my best friend and the person who has read most of my drafts, thank you for sharing your reactions and thoughts and showing endless excitement about what happens next (even when I don't know yet). I'm so lucky to have you in my life.

Mom, thank you for your patience and understanding. I

know you were worried when I said I wanted to self-publish a book but I appreciate you giving me the space to try and do it. To my sister, your support doesn't go unnoticed. Thank you for making me laugh and being the greatest sister of all time. Dad, it took me a while to tell you I was writing a book, but when you found out, you wanted to get a copy as soon as possible. Thank you for asking for updates and being excited about this whole thing.

To Marta, thank you for our lunches and your support too. You were the first person to whom I said I was writing a book. Your reaction made me comfortable to share this with more people, so thank you for being so cool about it.

To my early readers, thank you for believing in this story and sticking around to see it grow. To all ARC readers, reviewers and bloggers, I appreciate your kindness and excitement around this story. Thank you for spreading the word and encouraging others to pick this book up.

Finally, to you who's reading this, the biggest thank you goes to you. Thank you for giving this book a chance. Thank you for giving *me* a chance. With so many great books and authors out there, I'm forever grateful you've chosen this one to spend time with and get lost in. I hope you enjoyed it. I also hope you can forgive me for this book's ending. Rest assured, this is only the beginning.

Dear Reader

Thank you so much for reading *A Spark of Magic.* I hope you enjoyed reading it as much as I loved writing it. I can't wait to share the rest of Alice and Isaac's adventures with you.

If you'd like to keep up with my writing adventures, you can sign up for my newsletter or follow me on social media (check the next page for more information).

Also, if you loved this story, consider reviewing it or recommending it to a friend (or two). That helps indie authors like me a lot.

I'm so grateful you have given this story a chance. I hope you stick around for the rest of the series.

Cheers,

Tari

About The Author

Tari Riley is a YA and NA fantasy and romance author. When she's not writing as if her life depends on it, you'll probably find her reading, listening to music, solving jigsaw puzzles, watching shows (she loves a good K-Drama) or creating mood boards and playlists for her stories. That's right; everything is an excuse for Tari to daydream about her stories.

A Spark of Magic is her YA debut novel.

Connect with Tari

Threads: @authortaririley

Instagram: @authortaririley

TikTok: @authortaririley

Website: www.authortaririley.com

If you'd like to read exclusive stories, sign up for her newsletter or find Tari elsewhere on the internet, check out her Linktree in the QR code below!

www.ingramcontent.com/pod-product-compliance
Lightning Source LLC
LaVergne TN
LVHW091152150826
845672LV00005B/1127

* 9 7 8 9 8 9 3 5 6 4 5 1 6 *